continued . . .

"A passionate tale . . . [Fletcher] is one of those gifted writers who makes the unbelievable believable."   —*Rendezvous*

"A heartwarming story."   —*The Romance Reader*

"Ms. Fletcher's world . . . is a fascinating and enriching place to visit."   —*Romantic Times*

The Irish Devil

"A richly textured medieval romance."
                    —*Historical Romance Reviews* (4 stars)

"[Ms. Fletcher's] talents are unfathomable, and I expect nothing but the best from her."   —*Rendezvous*

Magical Moments

"A refreshing romance with classic elements, sure to cast a spell on a wide and appreciative audience."
                    —*The Romance Reader*

Wedding Spell

"Light, bright, and entertaining . . . I flew through the pages."
—*Rendezvous*

The Buccaneer

"The witty characterizations, unique situations and swash-buckling action combine to make a terrific fast-paced romance that is thrilling to the very last word. This sensuous romance is a delight—right down to the very last sigh."
—*Affaire de Coeur*

"*The Buccaneer* is a grand adventure and a . . . romp on the high seas. Fast-paced and well-written, it sizzles!"
—*The Paperback Forum*

Whispers on the Wind

"[This] ghostly romance is a treat. Lively, passionate . . . a fine adventure."
—*Affaire de Coeur*

"An exquisite mixture of suspense, fantasy and blazing passion. The plot is fresh and the characters are remarkable. This is a magnificent book that is worth another read."
—*Rendezvous*

Remember the Magic

DONNA FLETCHER

B

BERKLEY SENSATION, NEW YORK

This is a work of fiction. Names, characters, places, and incidents either
are the product of the author's imagination or are used fictitiously,
and any resemblance to actual persons, living or dead, business
establishments, events, or locales is entirely coincidental.

REMEMBER THE MAGIC

A Berkley Sensation Book / published by arrangement with
the author

PRINTING HISTORY
Berkley Sensation edition / January 2004

ISBN: 0-425-19327-6

A BERKLEY SENSATION™ BOOK
Berkley Sensation Books are published by The Berkley Publishing Group,
a division of Penguin Group (USA) Inc.,
375 Hudson Street, New York, New York 10014.
BERKLEY SENSATION and the "B" design
are trademarks belonging to Penguin Group (USA) Inc.

PRINTED IN THE UNITED STATES OF AMERICA

10 9 8 7 6 5 4 3 2 1

For my patient *nephew Richard F.X. Pizzuta*
and his new bride, Lisa.

May you be blessed from the heavens above
with a lifetime of magical love.
May you experience all the joys and pleasures of life
with few tears and minus the strife.
And when your final days here are done
Know that the magic of love has truly begun!

One

Silence surrounded Sydney. A strange buzzing sound reso-nated in her foggy mind and she was unable to focus on her surroundings. A whisper of a breeze stroked her face and she breathed deeply of the strong scent of pine, birch and berries.

She was home.

She stretched her hands out beside her, feeling the thick carpet of grass she lay upon. She eagerly splayed her fingers in the silky blades and allowed their energy to seep through her. Her vision began to clear and it wasn't long before her eyes focused on the clear blue sky dotted with bright white puffs of clouds and a brilliant sun whose warmth kissed her face.

A glance from side to side brought a smile to her face. The familiar woods completely embraced her. The tall trees sprouted fresh green leaves, the wildflowers had barely blossomed and the thick green grass was at its freshest.

Spring and Sydney had arrived in the Highlands to-gether.

With one last splay of her fingers through the green grass she pushed herself up. Her vision was completely clear and so was her foggy mind.

"Are you all right?" the soft voice asked.

Sydney turned and her smile widened. The tiny fairy, who expressed concern for her, sat sprawled out on a large stone. Her head wreath sat askew, the tip of her one wing was bent and her soft blue gossamer dress was twisted around her plump little body.

Sydney immediately went to her aid. "I should be asking that of you, Beatrice."

She helped untwist her dress but gave no thought to her bent wing or tilted wreath—both were common traits for Beatrice. The tiny fairy had watched over her and the Wyrrd family for as long as Sydney could remember, and that was a long time considering Sydney was over six hundred years old.

Beatrice brushed at her dress after Sydney helped her to stand and attempted to right her head wreath with no success. It remained tilted, resting just above one of her eyes.

"We made it," Beatrice said joyfully. "And I must say it is good to be home. I do not know why I enjoyed the 1500s so much. It held such turmoil, strife and bloodshed. Yet there was something about the land and the people that was remarkable."

Sydney agreed with a nod. She had been barely two hundred years old in the 1500s. It was a time in her life that held such promise. There was so much to learn, knowledge to gain, life to be lived.

"Of course," Beatrice added with a woeful look, "it was not a good time to be a witch."

"Was it ever a good time to be a witch?" Sydney thought on her own question. Through the years she had learned it was best not to let people know of her true nature, her beliefs, her knowledge. And while in the future witches were not persecuted the way they once had been they were also not accepted, as they rightfully should be.

Witches' beliefs dated back to the dawn of time and if understood and practiced correctly the world would not be in the turmoil it had consistently been in through the ages. But that was not a debatable issue at this time. This was a time she would need to protect herself from the ignorance of common beliefs. Mainly, that witches were in league with the devil.

The answer was obvious and Beatrice gave no reply. She instead addressed their present and immediate issues. "At least Tempest and Michael sent you back dressed for the occasion and placed you not far from home."

Sydney stood and laughed softly. Her dress was familiar though seasoned with her present taste. The dress was of soft cotton in a pale apricot color. It flowed down and around her body, accenting her shape that had shifted over the years but at least had maintained a certain dignity. Her waist remained slim; her breasts, average in size, retained a modicum of firmness and her hips rounded nicely above long slim legs thanks to her five feet, six inch height. She certainly was not a youthful two hundred years old but she held her age nicely.

Pale yellow embroidered Celtic knots trailed along the rounded neckline and down the middle of the long sleeves and then again around the hem. Soft leather sandals covered her feet and her glorious long dark hair lay in a braid to the center of her back.

"What now?" Beatrice asked, rising up to flit in front of Sydney.

Sydney lost no time in taking charge of the situation. "We go to the cottage and then we must discover the date of our return."

Beatrice agreed with a quick nod and flew ahead of Sydney, on the lookout for any possible danger.

Sydney gave thought to her present situation and her reason for returning in time. Two powerful witches and friends—Tempest and Michael—had gifted her with a second chance at love. Tempest was an ancient witch born

with the dawn of time. She was the Ancient One. Her powers were unsurpassed and she took on those students she
chose to teach over the years. Sydney had been lucky to
be one of the chosen ones and Tempest had taught her well.

She had been pleased to be able to offer her own assistance when Tempest required help. A warlock Tempest had
once loved and banished until a time he was given a second
chance had returned to her and Sydney gave wise and much
needed advice to her. In appreciation for all she had done
for the two powerful witches, together they had opened a
portal in time and returned her to a time and place where
she too would have a second chance at love.

Duncan.

Her heart beat with the thought of him. He had been a
clan chieftain, a brave warrior and an honorable man. She
had loved him with all her heart and he her, but when he
had discovered that she was a witch he had warned her not
to use any spells on him. She had attempted to explain that
any spell cast could only prove successful if it benefited
the individual. No spell that caused harm could be cast.

Harm no one was the belief of the Craft. But then there
were those who practiced the dark side of the Craft and
caused the *burning times* to descend upon the innocent.

She thought he had believed her, but something had
gone terribly wrong and she had fled, feeling if she stayed
she would only bring him harm. That had been almost five
hundred years ago. Now she had returned to try again.

Beatrice flitted in her face, her full cheeks flushed and
her smile wide. "The cottage is as it was. It waits for you."

Sydney did not think that the sight of a small, one-room
cottage could cause her excitement. But then it was more
the memories the place held that made the return so pleasant than the actual cottage itself.

She made her way a few feet ahead through the dense
woods to a small clearing and came upon the cottage. She
stared in awe. It was made of stone and covered by a
thatched roof. Windows occupied either side of the thick

wooden door and a stout stone chimney stretched up from the thatched roof.

Several minutes passed before she moved and she purposely took slow steps. She had not expected to see this home again and she had not expected the onslaught of memories.

A tear threatened to spill, but she took a deep breath and refused to give it reign. She had grown in power and knowledge in the last few hundred years and looking back she could understand her youthful mistakes, but then they were necessary. How would she have learned if she had never made mistakes?

And now she had a chance to correct a youthful mistake.

She smiled at the thought and grew eager, her steps hurrying her to the cottage door. Her hand hesitated only a moment on the metal handle and then she entered with a flourish.

Beatrice flew past her, flitting from corner to corner sprinkling the place with a protection of fairy dust. "It pays to be careful." She flew under the narrow bed to toss a handful beneath and was expelled in a flash, her own hard sneeze sending her flying across the room to land in a small black cauldron.

Before Sydney reached her the little fairy stood up and braced her plump arms on the lip of the cauldron. Her crooked wing was a bit more crooked and her head wreath completely covered one eye. She pushed it up and out of her way, forcing it with a hard shove to rest on the back of her head. "Dusting confined places always does that to me."

Sydney laughed. She was so very glad to have Beatrice with her on this sojourn. She did not feel so alone. She had a friend, a good, dear friend who would be there for her when needed.

"The place looks good," Beatrice said and flew up and out of the cauldron.

"I agree." Sydney gave the room a glance, noting that it

looked as she remembered it. A single bed with a straw mattress sat tucked in one corner of the room. Wooden chests in various sizes were spread throughout, a fair-sized one sitting next to the bed with several candles in holders on top of it. A wooden table sat in front of the stone fireplace though there was enough room for a wooden rocker in between. Several barren tree branches rested on the overhead rafters and dried bunches of herbs tied solidly hung down from them. A narrow table to the left of the door held crocks of roots, bark, berries and more. To the other side of the door closer to the bed hung pegs that held several garments.

Sydney laughed again. "My wardrobe certainly has improved over the years."

Beatrice gave her a thoughtful smile. "Do you think you will have a problem with a limited wardrobe? I know how much pride you take in your appearance."

"With a few extra adjustments of my own I think I will do just fine."

Beatrice pushed at her tilted wreath. "Then Tempest and Michael returned you with your full powers intact?"

Sydney's eyes rounded. "I had not given that thought." She felt a brief moment of panic. What if she had returned with the limited powers of a young witch? She had, after all, been given a second chance to right her youthful mistake and wouldn't that mean with the powers she had possessed at that time?

"Only one way to find out," Beatrice said and flew over to plop down on the bed out of Sydney's way. "Make magic."

Sydney did not waste a moment. With a brief wave of her hand the fire was lit in the fireplace, the candles flickered brightly and water bubbled in the cauldron that hung from the hook in the fireplace.

Beatrice shook her head. "Amateur stuff."

For a moment Sydney appeared deflated, but only a moment. She pushed up her sleeves, walked over to the crock of berries, scooped up a handful and marched out of the cottage.

Beatrice followed close behind, rubbing her two tiny hands together. "This should be good."

Sydney stood a few feet from the cottage and extended her hands out. She turned in four directions and gave a respectful nod to the brilliant sun before she cast a spell that only a powerful and knowledgeable witch could successfully cast.

"Hear me forest; hear me call; to all those creatures large and small; come take from my hand so that you may know; I am a friend and not a foe; I will protect; I will provide; know that from me; you need never hide."

Sydney waited for the animals to approach her. If they did not then her powers would be severely limited. She waited patiently, hoping, praying and then . . .

She smiled, for a rabbit peeked his head from behind a thick thatch of bushes. A bird swooped down, ignored the berries but tested her pledge of friendship and snatched a loose thread off her dress. A wide-eyed doe stood beside a tree for a moment, her two fawns tucked safely behind her and when she felt it was safe she and her fawns approached Sydney and fed from her hand. Other animals soon gathered around her and those who feed on berries ate from her hand, those who did not she offered water from the rain barrel beside the cottage.

Beatrice grew teary-eyed, for it took powerful magic to call the animals of the forest to you and offer them protection. Each creature now knew that Sydney would at any time provide for them and protect them.

Sydney sent a silent blessing to Tempest and Michael for allowing her to retain her full powers and with a pleased smile she turned to Beatrice.

All color suddenly drained from the tiny fairy's face and Sydney stilled, knowing something was wrong—then she heard the snarl.

Sydney turned slowly around and her breath caught.

There only a few feet away stood a black wolf. He was the largest wolf she had ever seen. He was well fed, his fur shiny and smooth, his eyes a brilliant green and his teeth sharp and threatening.

He had to be the dominant of his pack and yet Sydney got the feeling he was a loner, traveling a solitary path.

"I offer you shelter and protection when needed," she said softly and picked up the crock she had filled with water from the barrel and that remained half full and took a few steps toward him to place it on the ground. She then backed away.

The black wolf growled for a few seconds more, then accepted the offering. He finished the water, stared at Sydney's bright green eyes then turned and disappeared into the forest.

She knew they would be friends.

Beatrice wiped her perspiring brow as she flitted in front of Sydney. "I was uncertain there for a minute."

"As was he."

"But he accepted your offer and this is good for he will protect you as you will protect him."

Sydney felt pleased. "Yes, we will help each other and I am relieved to know that my powers are fully intact."

"This is good, for we have work to do," Beatrice said, determined. "It is time to reunite you and Duncan."

Sydney placed a hand to her stomach to still the flutter. "I wonder when in my relationship with Duncan Tempest and Michael returned me to. Is it before we met, is our relationship in progress?" She shook her head. "This is what I must discover."

"You have a plan?"

"Better than a plan, I have a spell."

"Wait," Beatrice warned. "Let me check the area."

It was very necessary that Sydney remember where she was and the beliefs of the era. Some believed in the old ways but hid their beliefs out of necessity; others believed the lies they were fed. It was so much easier for the ignorant to lay blame on the innocent when times turned difficult. And how simple it was to use fear to cause mass hysteria thus causing chaos and the *burning times*.

Beatrice lighted on Sydney's shoulder. "The animals linger to watch you, but I neither see nor sense any humans nearby."

"Good, then it is safe."

Beatrice flew off to rest on a nearby tree trunk and watch Sydney cast the spell that would seal her fate.

Sydney slowly raised her hands to the sky, parted them until it looked as though she cupped the blazing sun in her hands and then she spoke clearly and distinctly.

"Powers of light; powers of time; bring to me he who once was mine; have him remember me; and remember the magic that used to be; unite our hearts once again; so that our souls may fully mend; when our joining is as one; know the magic has begun."

She closed her eyes as she lowered her arms to her sides and a single tear slipped from her eye. "I have done it and it cannot be undone. It begins and no one can stop it now. I have one chance, only one chance."

Beatrice watched Sydney walk off into the forest and let her be. She needed time to herself. Beatrice would wait and be there for her when necessary.

Sydney walked into the woods, her thoughts heavy along with her emotions. Was she doing the right thing? And what of Duncan? How would he feel? She had not thought this through. She had simply accepted the second chance given her. She had no choice now but to see it through.

She continued walking without regard to her destination or her surroundings. Her only thought was of Duncan and when she would see him again. It could be weeks, days or minutes.

Her head came up swiftly thinking she heard footsteps. She saw no one, but a tingle ran over her body and she tensed.

Someone was in the woods with her.

Two

Sydney remained still, listening to her surroundings. The wood seemed to accommodate her for it remained as quiet as she did. Not a leaf swayed or a bird chirped or an animal budged. And whoever was in the woods with her listened with the same stillness for not a sound could be heard.

Her only choice was to carefully survey the surrounding area and see if her heightened awareness could help her discover her unknown visitor. Slowly she turned her head to the side and glanced at the strand of trees and flourishing bushes, catching a dark shape hovering near a large stone.

His eyes were sharp and intent upon her.

"You follow me," she said. "I wish to be your friend and I think you want me as a friend."

The black wolf kept his bright green eyes on her, his head hung low, his legs braced as if ready to attack or flee in haste.

Sydney remained calm for she understood the animal meant her no harm; he was but curious and strangely enough protective of her. She sensed it in him and felt the same for him.

"What shall I call you?" She thought on it as he kept a steady eye on her. "You deserve a powerful name for you are a powerful creature. An ordinary name will not suit you." She thought a moment more then smiled. "I think I have a good name for you."

She cautiously approached him, her steps slow yet steady. "Finn. He was a great Irish warrior, a legend, and none could match his daring, magic or knowledge. His power was unsurpassed."

He made no move to run; he remained as he was, prepared to fight or flee.

She moved closer. "You are fearless and daring and yet—" She paused, gently placing her hand palm up near his mouth. "I think you are a loving creature. *Finn.* Yes, I will call you Finn. It is a powerful name and I think that your power may just equal that of the legendary Finn."

He sniffed her hand and just when she thought he would accept her offer of friendship with a gentle lick, his head shot up, he bared his teeth and he growled low and steady.

Sydney tensed herself for she understood it was not her who had alarmed him.

Someone else was in the woods with them.

She remained calm and listened. Although her ears were not as sharp as the wolf's, her senses were and she was fully aware that the intruder stood a distance behind her. She felt no wrong intent from the person and with quick, reassuring words she passed her knowledge to the wolf.

"It is all right. No harm is meant."

The wolf grew silent, though he walked up to stand directly beside her.

"I see that human males are not the only creatures you bewitch."

Sydney grew breathless and her heart lost its natural

rhythm. Anticipation froze her as still as a stone statue, or was it fear?

No. Fear was of one's own making and fear was not at all familiar to her.

With her usual courage she turned, certain she was ready to face the man she had loved and lost.

"Duncan." His name was but a whisper on her lips and the sight of him made her all the more breathless. He was no longer the young man she had known but a mature man in features and form.

His prideful stance had remained the same and made him appear taller than his six feet, almost five inch height. His chest seemed broader, his arm muscles thicker, his legs solid, and he wore the green, blue and yellow plaid of his clan, Tavish, wrapped solidly around him, a white linen shirt beneath it.

His dark chest-length hair bore no signs of gray, but a fanning of lines around his eyes told her he was no longer the twenty-five year old she had once loved. He was well into his thirties, perhaps even forty by now. While she had thought him handsome when he was young the years had matured him beyond handsome. He could steal a woman's breath and heart in one glance.

He remained where he was, staring at her as if he could not believe she stood there a few feet away from him. "Are you real? Or do I imagine you as I have time and again?"

The idea that he had thought about her caused her heart to race. "I am real."

He shook his head. "Nay, I but imagine you. You left—" he paused. "Thirteen years now."

Thirteen years to him, hundreds of years to her. "I have returned."

"Why?"

A fair and simple question that had no fair and simple answer. How could she tell him after all this time how much she had missed him and loved him? It would make no sense to him. He simply would not believe her.

He shrugged at her silence. "It has been thirteen years. What does it really matter?"

How did she explain it had been hundreds of years and that only through divine intervention was she able to return? And yes—it mattered a great deal.

She took a chance and said, "I have missed you."

For a brief moment his guard dropped and he looked as if he wanted, wanted badly to believe her. But he took a firm stance. "Thirteen years is a long time. Much can happen."

"Aye, that it can, but love can survive separation and grow stronger."

"Or it can break a heart and never allow it to mend." He allowed her no time to respond. "Why, Sydney? Why have you returned now after all these years?"

It was her turn to shrug for she had no definitive answer. How could she? He would not believe that she traveled through time from hundreds of years in the future to return to him. It was difficult enough for him to accept her being a witch, but a witch that had lived over five hundred years?

No, he would certainly fear her then.

She followed her shrug with a shake of her head. "I felt the need."

He rubbed his chin and then raked his fingers through his dark brown hair. "I often thought of a moment such as this. A moment when I would meet with you again and I would speak my piece." He shook his head. "Yet words fail me, for your presence as always overwhelms me."

A faint smile appeared on her lips. He had always been honest with her, that was one thing she loved about him. She felt she could trust him for he would always speak the truth to her even if it hurt to hear it.

She wanted to tell him that they could start over again, that they deserved another chance. But there were thirteen years to mend. "Speak, I will listen."

"You never fail to tempt me."

"Is that bad?"

"Do you still claim yourself a witch?"

She recalled how he had always warned her about casting spells on him. She attempted many times to explain that spells were like prayers—if the results were beneficial and meant to be then a spell like a prayer would be successful. If not, the spell was useless. But she also recalled that there were those who would point accusing fingers at those who worked with and worshiped nature. If thirteen years had passed since their first meeting that meant it was 1564 and in 1563 during the reign of Mary the Scottish Parliament had made witchcraft legally punishable. She had returned during the *burning times*.

It would not do her well to admit her heritage, but she found she could not completely deny it.

"I am a women wise in the ways of nature. Does that brand me a witch?"

"You bewitch the wolf." He sounded more curious than accusing. "I know of no wild beast who would stand by a human's side in protection."

She patted Finn's head and his growling ebbed. "We are all God's creatures and as such should treat each other with due respect."

"That is not the common belief." Again there was no accusation in his voice, only curiosity.

"It should be."

He stood silent, staring at her for several moments.

"What troubles you, Duncan?"

"That this is all a dream that I have dreamed before and woke disappointed."

She sensed his hurt and his regret.

"This is the part where I tell you how much I have missed you."

She remained silent, letting him continue.

"You remain silent as always but I see in your eyes, those beautiful eyes that captivate my heart, that you miss me and I wonder why. Why? But there are only more dreams without answers."

"You still believe me a dream."

"Of course," he said, "I would be foolish to think this is real. That I stand here in the woods that I have come to day after day for thirteen years and suddenly you are here. You are real. And though I know it is only a dream, I wish for it to never end for once it does you go away until I dream again."

"I am not going anywhere."

"Familiar words you say often to me and you repeat in every dream."

Had he had repeated visions of this meeting? Had he known instinctively she would return to him? Had he waited for this day? She slowed her chaotic thoughts, for in chaos she lacked insight and now was not the time to lose insight.

"But you always leave."

She smiled. "I always return."

"Aye, you haunt me," he said with a laugh that faded quickly. "I look forward to seeing you even if it is but a dream." He stared at her, his eyes full of sorrow. "You will leave soon. You never stay long."

He actually thought her a dream. He did not believe her real. She doubted there was much she could say that would convince him differently. And having arrived only a short time ago perhaps it would be wise to give herself time to once again acclimate to her surroundings—and plan.

She mentally shook her head. No plan was necessary, she had cast the spell; what was to be would be.

She did not however wish to leave him just yet; after all, it had been hundreds of years since she had last seen him. She wanted to look upon him awhile longer, watch the familiar way he would rake his hair with his fingers or shrug his broad shoulders. And his hands, how she had missed them, long, lean, strong yet gentle. They had soothed her with tender touches and had grabbed at her and swung her around in play. They had tickled her, teased her

and tempted her. And she had loved and greatly missed
every tickle, every tease, every tempt.

"I thought to stay awhile."

His features brightened. "I wanted you to say just that."

"Then I heard you."

He laughed. "But I said not a word."

"I heard your heart."

"My heart betrays me."

"Your heart does not betray you; it is honest and sin-
cere."

He sighed. "How I wish you were real."

"Wishes do come true. All you need to do is believe."

"You speak of magic," he said.

"I speak the truth. Believe and have faith and your wish
will come true."

He shook his head. "Wishes are for children."

"Of course they are." Her soft laugh floated along the
warm spring air like a gentle melody. "Children believe and
have faith so they wish and they wait and they wish again
and then—magic."

"I am not a child and I do not believe in magic."

"A child resides in all of us. Find the child, wish and
believe."

"Help me." He sounded as if he challenged her.

"You do not need my help, you merely need to believe."

He reached out. "I wish to touch you once again, to feel
your soft skin against mine, to have you respond so quickly,
so willingly, so joyfully. I wish—" He closed his eyes. "Oh
lord, how I wish."

He opened his eyes and she was gone.

Three

"I am insane. I talk to a woman who is not there."

The rustle of the leaves and a whisper of warm spring air across his cheek was his only answer.

These visions had haunted him since Sydney had left. They had started when he had come to the woods in search of . . .

Sydney.

He had searched for Sydney day after day, hoping she would return to him, that she would suddenly appear in front of his eyes—and every day she had appeared—and then she had disappeared.

Still he returned, for though she was only a vision, at least he was able to see her, speak with her, but he could never touch her.

How could he?

She was not real.

His sigh echoed deep in his chest. "Why can I not forget you? Why must you forever be in my thoughts?"

He walked over to an old felled tree and sat, the thick

decaying log groaning with the weight of him.

"Perhaps Gwen is right." His sister had insisted that Sydney had cast a love spell over him and that was why he had difficulty letting go of her.

He, however, believed himself in love and remembering Sydney and her honesty he was certain she would not resort to spells with him. Especially since he had warned her that to do so would prove disastrous to their relationship.

She had always been completely honest with him, even in admitting that she was a witch. And she had been good to the clan and those who sought her help. She often would attempt to explain her beliefs, her ways to him. Foolishly he would interrupt her or had only half-listened.

"Damn."

He was angry with himself and with Sydney, angry that they both had been too stubborn to settle their differences.

They both had lost.

He braced his arms on his bent knees and stared out at the woods. This place had become his haven. Oak, beech and birch trees grew in abundance. Ash and willows grew closer to the streams, their roots always thirsty for water. Sparrows were busy with their nests and hawks circled high up looking for prey. Blueberries grew thick and juicy and would soon be ripe for picking and the wildflowers turned their colorful blossoms to the sun for nourishment.

And though the woods teemed with life it offered him solace and solitude. The solitude brought a degree of understanding and a minimum of peace and he anxiously sought both day after day.

He sensed a presence in the woods before he heard the footsteps. Sometimes he thought he could actually hear the person's heartbeat. If the beat was firm and steady then a friend approached, if erratic then a foe hovered nearby. He had always been aware of his surroundings but over the years his awareness had grown and he found himself sensing and knowing much more then was explainable.

"I do not want to disturb you. You look at peace."

Duncan did not look up at his boyhood friend Thomas; he simply slapped the spot beside him. "Join me in peace then."

Where Duncan was a man tall and thick in muscle, Thomas was but five feet, seven inches and solid in his girth. The log groaned, moaned and a snap could be heard here and there when Thomas lowered his weight on it.

"Dora says I am to make haste with the message and you."

Duncan smiled. "And what has this woman of yours promised you if you do as she says?"

Thomas laughed. "You know me too well."

"We know each other well, but how can we not—we were birthed on the same day and have been friends since we could walk."

"Aye, that is why I do not rush you from this place. I see peace in your eyes when you are here, though I do not think it reaches your heart."

Duncan did not know what he would do without Thomas. He was more like the brother he had never had. They talked, laughed and had cried together when Thomas's son was stillborn. Thomas had two daughters and Dora was expecting another babe in summer but Duncan understood that his friend would never forget and always mourn the loss of his firstborn son. Especially since the young son had so resembled his father, a thatch of bright red hair had capped his tiny head and he had had rich dark eyes, almost black. The women had gossiped that black eyes such as his could have only meant doom.

Dora had told them to hush, that he was but a babe, his new spirit free of such nonsense. Later she had confided in her husband that she had wished Sydney had been there, for she had known in her heart that Sydney would have saved little Thomas from dying. Sydney had the power.

"She is always with you, is she not?" Thomas poked at the ground with a stick.

"Thirteen years. You think I would have forgotten her by now."

"Sydney is not an easy woman to forget."

"Nay, she haunts me endlessly and . . ." Duncan grew silent, his own thoughts disturbing him.

"You do not want her to stop haunting you, do you?"

Duncan shook his head and ran his fingers through his hair. "I fear she will stop haunting me."

"Then it will finally be over."

"Aye, it would be done."

Being boyhood friends they could say things to each other that many could not. "It will be done if you foolishly marry this woman your sister has chosen for you."

"Is that the message you were sent to deliver?" Duncan asked with a laugh.

Thomas tossed away the stick. "I am to tell you that Eileen of the clan Carron is expected to arrive within the hour. Your sister wants to make certain you are presentable to your future wife, which means get yourself home for inspection."

"You do not think I should marry this woman?"

"God no!" Thomas muttered beneath his breath, a habit of his when he turned to swearing and one his wife Dora would not tolerate, thus he kept it beneath his breath at all times not wanting to accidentally spew his favorite words in front of her. "You do not love her."

"Love hurts."

"You sound like a woman, do not disgust me."

Duncan punched Thomas in the arm with a firm fist.

"I speak the truth as I have always done."

"The truth you say? Then tell me the truth about love," Duncan challenged.

Thomas threw up his hands. "I cannot answer that and I doubt there is anyone who can."

"Sydney could."

Thomas heard the sorrow in his friend's voice. "Sydney knew much."

"I should have listened more to her."

"Hah!" Thomas gave a hardy laugh. "You were too busy kissing and touching her every chance you got."

Duncan closed his eyes briefly and smiled. "And it felt good, so very good."

"You loved her that is why it felt so good."

Duncan's eyes opened wide. "I thought you knew nothing about love?"

"A little," Thomas admitted. "Very little. I know how I feel about my Dora and that is what I know about love. I look forward to her smiles, her laughter, even when she yells and orders me about I know I cannot do without her. And when I take her thin body in my bulky arms I sometimes shiver with the fear that I may be too strong and hurt her."

"Hurt Dora?" Duncan looked startled. "She is stronger than you think."

"Aye, I realize that, but—" Thomas looked away as though he decided against speaking his mind.

"You love her," Duncan finished for him with a satisfying grin.

"That I do," Thomas said with a thump to his chest. "I love my Dora."

Duncan slapped him on the back. "I am glad for you, for you make a perfect pair."

"We make a perfect pair because we love." Thomas placed a hand on Duncan's shoulder. "Do not marry this Eileen if you have no love for her. You will be miserable."

"I saw Sydney a few moments ago," Duncan confided to his friend.

Thomas ran a curious glance around the area. "Where? Where was she? Where did she go?"

"She vanished into my dreams as she always does," Duncan said, his hand slipping off Thomas.

"You still think you see her?"

"Nay, I do see her, clear as I see you sitting here with

me. Sometimes I think that if I will it enough she will return to me."

Thomas spoke low and cast a glance around to make certain no one lurked near. "Do not speak such nonsense. You have heard the talk that has reached the Highlands. They are burning people who they believe to be heretics. Such talk could bring difficulty and not only for you, those that follow you."

"Witches have always existed and have helped many in the Highlands. Why should we now turn our backs on those who have helped us in time of need?"

"The church claims them evil."

"Do you believe this?"

"I cannot say, for I wonder myself sometimes. Dora went to visit the old woman Elizabeth who lives across the loch just before little Thomas was born. There is talk that the old woman steals babies' souls."

"No one took your son's life, especially not some old woman who has helped birth many fine babies. You are angry with God for taking your son but you cannot admit it to anyone for fear of retribution from the church so you direct your anger on the helpless."

"Aye, I am angry but I do not know who to be angry at and that makes me all the more angry."

"Love hurts."

Thomas nodded. "That it does. So do not marry this woman."

"If I do not love her then I cannot be hurt."

Thomas leaned closer to him. "What if Sydney returned?"

"I have grown old waiting for her to return."

"I am not old and I am thirty and eight."

Duncan pointed to his bright red hair. "I see gray in your hair and lines around your eyes. You grow old."

"I grow better," Thomas said, holding his arm so that muscle after muscle rippled up it.

Duncan elbowed him in the stomach and met with a solid wall.

"I told you, I am better," Thomas said with a huge grin.

Duncan laughed and stood. "Today when I saw Sydney she looked to have aged, beautifully though I cannot tell you exactly how I knew that, perhaps a few fine lines near her eyes, or her body's curves were different though more appealing. Her long dark hair showed not a sign of gray and looked to be as smooth and silky as when I last touched it. Yet there was something different about today than other days when I saw her."

Thomas stood and followed Duncan along the worn path that wove through the woods. "You talked with her?"

"I always do but never at length, though today she seemed to have more to say."

Thomas kept him talking, curious himself.

"I told her that I wished she was real. She told me that I only needed to believe. She told me to believe and have faith and my wish would come true."

Thomas stopped walking. "Do you believe she will return?"

Duncan stopped and turned. "I want to believe."

"There is no harm in believing. I believed Dora would one day love me and she did."

"Dora has loved you since she was a lass of three years and would trail after you and me. You had much patience with her for a lad of ten and three years."

"I think I have always loved her, much the same way you feel about Sydney."

Duncan smiled, recalling the first time he met Sydney. "She put me in my place that day."

Thomas grinned at the memory. "That she did and a pretty sight it was, you eyeing her up and down, judging her in front of the clan when she came at your call."

"I was told by many in the clan that the woman in the woods who had claimed Bridget's cottage was a good healer so I called on her in a time of need."

Thomas muttered beneath his breath.

"What is that you say?"

"You called on her because you heard she was beautiful and wished to see for yourself, and her beauty so surprised you that when she walked up to you in the village you could do nothing but stare at her in awe. And stare you did, walking round and round her until you had your fill."

Duncan laughed. "I was speechless at the sight of her. What else would you have me do?"

"Not make a fool of yourself."

"Which she did nicely," Duncan reminded.

"More than nicely, she did it courageously. What woman, a stranger to the clan, would have the courage to study the laird of the clan in the same blatant manner as he had studied her? She ran her eyes up and down you, walked around you, hands on her hips and even hesitated here and there in her judgment, then when she was finally done she offered you her hand."

"I took it, did I not?"

"How could you deny her?" Thomas said, eyes wide. "All present were impressed with her."

"As was I."

"Hell, you lost your heart to her that day."

"She did not give me her heart so easily." He smiled. "Though it was fun winning it."

"Aye, the chase stirs the blood," Thomas grinned, his dark eyes merry. "That is why I still often chase my Dora."

Duncan's smile faded and he stared off into the woods where he had last seen Sydney. "I chase a ghost. A ghost with a black wolf."

"Black wolf?" Thomas asked.

Duncan began walking again; Thomas followed. "Today when I saw Sydney a black wolf stood by her side."

"Have you seen the black wolf in any other vision you have had of her?"

Duncan thought and shook his head. "Nay, I do not remember seeing a black wolf with her ever before."

"Strange," Thomas said and stopped walking to turn and look back.

"What is strange?" Duncan turned and saw that his friend had stopped. He walked up behind him.

"There has been talk in the village of a black wolf that prowls the woods. A few of the boys that go off to play in the woods have seen him. Some thought the wolf nothing more than their imagination. No black wolves have ever been seen here."

Duncan stood still and glared at the dense stretch of woods before him. "If the black wolf existed and was seen—" He stopped abruptly, almost fearful of voicing his thought.

Thomas was not; excitement filled his voice. "Then he was real, which means Sydney was real."

Four

Beatrice flew with the speed of lightning through the open cottage door, past Sydney sitting in the rocking chair beside the fireplace and straight through the open window on the opposite wall. Her return flight through the window was at a much slower pace and she flitted to a rest on Sydney's knee.

"News." She paused to gain her breath.

"Take your time," Sydney said.

Beatrice shook her head; she wanted to share the news now. "He loves you."

"I know. I saw it in his eyes, heard it in his voice and—" A sad smile touched her lips. "Felt it in his heart."

Beatrice's breathing finally calmed. "Then waste not a moment in letting him know you are here and how you feel, for his sister has made plans for him to marry."

Sydney was stunned silent.

"His friend Thomas joined him to relay a message from his sister about how the woman would be arriving soon and he was to return home."

Sydney shook her head. "But he does not love her."

"That he does not and admitted it freely, but he told his friend that love hurts and it would be easier and wiser, to his way of thinking, if he did not marry for love."

"I hurt him badly."

"There were the two of you in the relationship," Beatrice reminded.

"But I was the wiser one and should have known better."

"Love blinds even the wisest person as it does him now. His love for you does not allow him to see clearly and he foolishly heads into a loveless marriage."

Sydney paused in thought. "I wonder if he wed her and went on to have a family, build a life?" Through the years she had been tempted to find out how he had faired, but that would have been intrusion, or would it have been? Would she have been more upset knowing that he had met another, married, had children and lived a fine life?

"What life could he have had without love?"

"Love is bountiful and can be shared with many, not just one or a few. Good deeds, helping others all involve love," Sydney said in an effort to convince herself that her own life had proved beneficial without a loving partner to share it with.

"True enough words, but we both know that every person looks for another to love. Someone to share the laughter and the tears with, someone to hold hands with, to make love with, to lean on when necessary and to grow old with. That love is as needed as the air we breathe and to deny it is ridiculous."

Silence settled over them for a moment.

"Is it not why you have returned?" Beatrice asked. "To find your love? And have you not told me that sometimes it is necessary and even wise to walk away from love? You learned that the hard way."

"I often wondered what would have happened if I had remained. Now I will not know for I have arrived thirteen years after I had left."

"You expected this return to be easy? To pop back in time to the perfect moment and with almost no effort, recapture the innocence of new love?"

"A silly thought on my part."

"Foolish is more like it," Beatrice corrected. "You are here to learn from your previous mistake, as is Duncan. Since you have wallowed long enough in self-pity for the both of you, can we now get started on reuniting you both?"

"Blunt as usual," Sydney said with an appreciative smile. "It is good to have a friend who offers wise advice."

"That you can always count on," Beatrice assured her. "Now what is our next move?"

Sydney had given the situation thought. She had learned to respond well under pressure. It was a necessity, a matter of protecting herself and her beliefs. Patience, careful thought and awareness were the keys to an agreeable solution.

"Being practical is not going to help you in this situation."

"Sebastian does well with practicality," Sydney said, recalling her nephew-in-law with a smile. Sebastian was a mortal who married her niece Alisande and in joining with her he became a witch in his own right.

Beatrice offered her own opinion. "And if he put some of his practical nature aside he might do better with his witchcraft."

"Someone must have at least one foot in reality between the two, and my niece certainly does not."

Beatrice laughed. "Ali can be a handful." She shook off her laughter and returned to the business at hand. "Reality is that those two are in the future enjoying their newborn daughter. We are here in 1564 trying to reunite you with Duncan, and the practical solution to this situation is to use magic."

"I cast one spell, I need not cast any more," Sydney said obstinately.

Beatrice threw her tiny hands in the air. "Do you think

he will just fall at your feet and declare his undying love?"

Sydney moved to stand, forcing Beatrice off her knee to flit around her as she stood. "I would never expect that of him. I need no man to fall at my feet for I certainly would not fall at his."

Beatrice shook a finger at her. "That stubbornness of yours is not going to help us a bit."

Sydney raised a confident chin. "That stubbornness of mine is what got us through many a difficult situation."

"And into a few," Beatrice reminded.

Sydney prepared to brew a cup of chamomile tea. "But out of all." She glanced slowly around the cottage. "I think this place needs a bit of updating."

"Thank the heavens," Beatrice said. "While I enjoyed this time I have grown accustomed to several amenities I do not wish to do without."

"I agree. A stove and toilet being just two." Sydney prepared to conjure.

Beatrice flew up near her ear and whispered. "What if someone chances in here and sees? You will certainly be declared a witch then."

"Please," Sydney said with a twinkle of a smile. "Give me credit for more intelligence. I will conceal our valuable amenities to all eyes but ours. They will see the cottage as it appears now. We two will be the only ones able to see the updates made to it."

"Do you intend to update yourself while you are at it?" A teasing gleam shimmered in Beatrice's eyes.

"I most certainly do not." Her hands were already at work moving things about. "I have worked hard to become who I am, all of me, and besides—" She paused on a sigh. "If his love is true enough nothing else will matter."

Beatrice rubbed her chubby little hands together. "This is going to be delightful." A sudden thought halted her actions. "I just thought on the outcome of this and wonder to your decision."

It took a moment for understanding to dawn on Sydney

and when it did her hand slowly descended down to rest beside her. The silver tea set with serving tray she had conjured clattered to the table.

"I had not given it consideration. When all this ends I will need to make a decision. Do I remain here in this time with Duncan or do I ask him to return to the future with me?"

"If you remain here you will miss Ali, Sebastian and their daughter and then there is Dagon and Sarina and their son, not to mention Tempest and Michael and your charity work." Beatrice sounded homesick.

"Even if I choose to remain here, Beatrice, you do not have to stay," Sydney assured her.

"I know, but I would miss you."

"There is time to consider the consequences, and besides, we do not know how all will turn out. Only then will a decision be necessary."

Beatrice nodded, concern still evident on her chubby face.

Sydney kept herself busy updating the cottage to a comfortable living level. She could very well conjure up many things on the spur of the moment for herself, food, clothing, lotions, but she preferred taking the time to place a kettle to boil for tea, or baking a tasty loaf of bread or having lotions on hand to soothe her skin.

And she could not be without books. Knowledge gained from reading opened peoples' minds and allowed for more critical thought. It was one way of eradicating ignorance, an evil that needed ridding.

Beatrice yawned; her small body sprawled out on the stack of pale blue terrycloth towels on the table. "Whew, that tired me out just watching you."

"At least we will be comfortable," Sydney said, sitting down in her favorite rocking chair, a cup of chamomile tea in hand. "It is still primitive but livable."

"Looks good to me," Beatrice said, reaching for the tiny cup of tea Sydney had placed beside her.

A small area near the door had been transformed into a reliable kitchen with a modern stove, sink and refrigerator. Several cabinets over the sink and stove held the essentials. Off in a corner was a replica of her bathroom in her home in Scotland, an invisible veil keeping all from prying eyes.

She added a new mattress to the single bed and softer linens and blankets. A larger size table sat beside the bed with a lamp and a stack of books on top; a shelf beneath held more books. A scarred wooden bureau taller than Sydney and with two wide doors opened on several occupied shelves, baskets of wool and various items necessary for life in a single-room cottage stacked neatly.

However, with one wave of Sydney's hand it was instantly transformed into a closet full of clothes and shoes. Of course the clothing reflected the time period, with a few adjustments for comfort and care.

Now that she was settled comfortably in the cottage she could focus her thoughts completely on Duncan.

Beatrice thought the same. "Now it is Duncan's turn."

"Yes, but it cannot be done with a wave of the hand. He is mortal and—"

"You intend to play fair?" Beatrice placed her teacup aside and wagged a finger at Sydney. "Do you think his sister Gwen will play fair when she learns you have returned?"

"Gwen was empathic to the situation the last time. She wants her brother to be happy."

Beatrice wagged her chubby finger one last time. "That woman wants what makes *her* happy."

"You never cared for her, why?"

"I never trusted her."

"She never gave me any reason not to trust her. She loves her brother and I cannot fault her for wanting the best for him and not wanting to see him hurt."

"You are best for him," Beatrice said. "And he will be hurt if he marries someone he does not love."

"I wonder how she will receive my return."

"There is only one way to find out."

Sydney remained silent. She agreed with Beatrice that she had only one choice, and that was to make her return known, but she was nervous. She who possessed the power and wisdom of magic suffered from a mortal condition. And while she understood her reason for her reaction it did not help it any. Her stomach continued to flutter and she continued to feel jittery, uncertain and yet determined in a strange sort of way.

She had advised her niece Alisande on love and had even offered wise words to the Ancient One, Tempest, the wisest of all witches. Now here she was on her own, possessed of the wisdom she had offered them and yet she felt vulnerable and uncertain.

But did not love often do that to you?

"You know, Beatrice," Sydney said with a soft sigh. "Giving advice to others is so much easier than giving and accepting your own advice. Questions invade thoughts and answers seem limited or not quite as clear, though most times it is simply because we fear the consequences of our decisions."

"You are a witch and understand that."

"Yet I hesitate."

Beatrice flew over to rest on Sydney's knee. She gave it a pat. "You loved once and lost that love. You know the consequences and what follows and part of you fears going through it again, so you hesitate."

"It hurt more than I care to remember. I cried until I thought there were no more tears to cry and then I cried again. I admonished myself for not thinking and acting more wisely and then I reasoned I was being unselfish and doing the right thing. Time healed the wound but never fully mended it. I missed him more each day and rarely a day passed without me thinking about him."

"He evidently felt the same. It has been thirteen years for him and still he goes to the woods and thinks he sees you there. And he returns time and again, for even if you are a vision at least he gets to see you."

"I cannot help but wonder what happened to him. Did he marry this woman and spend a lifetime with her?"

"Did you ever try to find out?" Beatrice asked.

"I had thought about it through the years, but then I thought what was done was done and it was best that I did not know. But now I wonder, for I do not wish to rob him of a life he might have enjoyed, might have preferred."

"Then you have only one choice."

"Return now and not pursue this reunion?" Sydney asked as though she posed the question to herself. "A consideration, but one I do not know if I am strong enough to make. I have seen him and realized how very much I have missed him. When I saw him a flood of memories washed over me."

She ran her fingers gently over her lips. "His kisses were magic. I can still feel him on my lips gently nipping, then softly taking and then . . ." She sighed and smiled, keeping the rest of her thoughts to herself.

"That is not the choice I had in mind and you know it was not yours or you would not have returned in the first place."

"You are right and it is about choices. I chose to return when given the chance. I did not think twice about it. I wanted another chance."

"And?" Beatrice waited.

Sydney had to laugh. "Why did you ask me this when you knew that I already knew the answer?"

"You needed reminding, sometimes a nudge. We all do every now and again. Now the answer if you please." Beatrice attempted to sound like a teacher guiding a student but her soft voice sounded more like a concerned friend.

Sydney answered what she knew. "The choice must be presented to Duncan and the decision will be his to make."

"Love always wins in the end."

"It did not win the last time," Sydney reminded, a tear threatening to spill.

"It is not over yet. You have returned."

Sydney patted at her eyes and a soft, radiant smile spread over her face. "I have acted foolishly and it will not do, there is work to be done."

"You act as a woman in love does, confused, determined and confused all over again. It is not the last time you will find yourself this way, but I will remind you."

"I will trust that you do, though at my age you think I would know better."

"Love knows nothing of age," Beatrice said. "It strikes indiscriminately, leaving in its wake confused emotions and a heart filled with joy."

Sydney placed her teacup on the table and held her palm out to Beatrice, who hopped up on it. "It is time for us to strike."

Beatrice grinned and pointed her finger. "We prepare for battle, to the closet."

Five

Duncan sat in the great hall only half listening to the chatter going on around him. He spent as little time in the keep as he could, not feeling at home there. Nowhere felt like home to him, not since Sydney had left.

The keep's construction was finished shortly after her departure. It was not a large keep but sufficient for its purpose. Sturdy in construction, it would survive attacks and keep its occupants safe from harm. He had wisely had it built in a secluded glen, a small mountainous range sitting protectively in front of it. The clan who occupied the land beyond the mountainous range and the clan just past it had joined with his clan for protection. Together they created a mighty force of fearless warriors and being so far up in the Highlands few if any clans warred with them.

He remembered the plans he had of making Sydney his wife and bringing her to live in the newly constructed keep. He had made certain that a smaller room was added off their bedchamber so that she would have privacy when she wished. It sat empty now and had done so from the start. Sydney had not been there to give it life.

His sister Gwen had taken charge as she was so often used to doing and the keep ran smoothly, though he suspected if Sydney were around there would be more laughter, more gaiety, a joyfulness of life.

But then Sydney possessed a passion he had never known before. He felt it in her every time he touched her, kissed her, made love to her. A silent groan rippled through his body and he heard the questions he never seemed to stop asking himself.

Will you ever stop haunting me?

Do I want you to?

"Duncan," Gwen said, turning to her right to where he sat beside her at the table on the dais. "Eileen cannot get over the beauty of the surrounding land. You must take her tomorrow and show her around."

He smiled and sent Eileen an agreeable nod. "As you wish."

Gwen gave his arm a squeeze, a none-too-gentle one. He would hear from her later but at the moment he did not care. He knew Gwen loved and cared about him and had nothing but his happiness in mind, but at the moment he was not feeling sociable.

He had managed to step around Gwen and seat himself beside her instead of Eileen, which is where Gwen had planned on seating him. And while he made the appropriate remark now and again, he was not presently inclined to make light conversation. He actually would have preferred the solitude of his solar. Gwen, however, had gone to a great deal of bother in arranging this meeting. It would be rude and unkind of him to take his leave.

He would let his sister fuss and entertain for a while and then he would make a reasonable excuse and seek the solitude of his solar. He would talk with his sister later and soothe her ruffled feathers.

She was good to him and he did not like upsetting her.

She was his only sibling and older than him by five years. She had looked after him as long as he could remember. She possessed a strong personality and could be demanding at times, though you would not know it by her soft features and short height. She stood no more then an inch or two past five feet. Her long dark hair was kept in a neat braid with never a stray strand in sight. Round, dark eyes kept careful watch over the keep's care and her narrow, delicate lips could spew commands like a battle-worn chieftain.

She had never married and Duncan often wondered if it was because she would answer to no man. She was of an independent nature and possessed a determination to see the clan thrive and that included marriage and children for Duncan.

He could not blame her for wanting to protect their holdings and could understand how Eileen felt when she laid eyes upon her surroundings. They lived high up in the Highlands where the winters were harsh and often unforgiving, but spring and summer brought with them a bounty of beauty and an abundance of life.

The rivers teemed with fish, the forests contained an abundance of game and crops thrived in the healthy soil. Some said as a favor to a friend the Ancient One blessed the land. Others believed that fairies occupied much of the land and their special magic kept the land magical. Whatever the reason it did not matter, for it was his home and he loved every inch of it. He was born here and he would die here, defending it if necessary.

Gwen attempted once again to engage them in conversation. "I have been telling Eileen about the pups recently born. She wishes to see them. Perhaps after the meal you will take her to see them."

His sister was determined and he probably should make an effort. "If you would like I will take you, though once you see them you will lose your heart and take one for your own."

Eileen clasped her hands together. "I would love a puppy for my own."

"Then see which one captures your heart for I am convinced it is the pup that chooses his master, though it will be a week or so yet before they are completely weaned from their mother."

Eileen giggled and clapped her hands, reminding him of a child delighted by a present. He wanted no child for a wife; he wanted a woman. He recalled Gwen mentioning her age, ten and eight years, he thought. Though she was attractive, she was too young and childlike for him, or perhaps Sydney had spoiled him for all women.

Eileen would catch any man's interest with her pretty face, long light red hair and slim body. She appeared to have a pleasant personality and looked as if she wished to please.

A private thought caused him to grin. Sydney pleased in her own special way. She had been strong in character with an independent spirit and passionate about her beliefs, thoughts and deeds. Life had been zestful with her.

Sometimes he had thought himself crazy, for everything around him appeared so much more alive. Colors were more vibrant, scents more powerful, tastes more delicious and touch more pleasurable.

Had that been her magic?

A tankard of ale was slammed down in front of him, the contents sloshing over the rim.

"You need this," Thomas declared from behind him.

Duncan did not reach for it and Thomas dumped himself in the empty chair beside his friend.

"Something troubles you?"

"Of late everything troubles me."

Thomas spoke low. "You are wondering are you not, for I certainly am?"

"It is foolishness to even consider."

"Then I am a fool for I have considered it all day." His

whisper was harsh, letting his friend know he was disturbed.

Duncan attempted to ease his concern. He had seen Sydney every time he had ventured in the woods. Today was no different, or so he kept trying to convince himself. She was not real. She had not returned, not after all this time. She was gone from his life for now and forever.

Thomas gave him no chance. "Do not try to deny it. You think the same as I."

"I think you crazy."

"Then we are crazy together for you cannot tell me you have not thought that Sydney has returned."

Duncan squeezed his eyes shut for a moment, almost trying to hold back the thought, the mere idea that Sydney had returned, it was just too damn painful. "She was a vision of my own making."

"You envisioned a wolf with her this time when there had never been one before?"

"She favored animals and animals favor her."

"A wolf?"

Duncan reached for his tankard.

Once again Thomas did not give him a chance to respond. "Not any wolf, but a black one. Only a black one would follow a witch."

"Hush," Duncan ordered harshly. "You have heard the talk that has drifted through the Highlands. Anyone thought a witch is being persecuted, burned for her beliefs."

Thomas grew excited. "Maybe that is why Sydney has returned, to escape the persecution. She would be safe here." Thomas placed a strong hand on his friend's shoulder. "You would keep her safe."

"I would protect her with my life."

"And your love."

Duncan lifted his tankard then placed it down again without taking a swallow. "How could I chance loving her again only to have her leave? How do you leave someone you love? How do you go on day after day without that person?"

"You have."

Duncan shook his head. "I had no choice, she left me. She had a choice and she chose life without me. How could she have claimed to love me, if she so easily walked away?"

"Ask her?"

Duncan glared at his friend. "Sydney is not here, it is but a vision I see in the woods, and I will hear no more on it."

"Then I will not say another word."

"Which means you have something more to say and you want me to know you have something more to say."

"I will keep my tongue to myself."

Duncan pointed a finger at him. "Say it quickly for my patience runs short."

Thomas wasted not a minute. "Perhaps Sydney returns to make a wrong right."

"Thirteen years, Thomas," Duncan said harshly. "How do you right thirteen years?"

Thomas's eyes had grown wide. "I do not know but you might want to ask her."

Duncan shook his head. "You persist in her return."

"Nay, I know she has returned."

Duncan laughed. "Be careful Thomas; there are those who would call you a witch for making such foolish predictions."

"Not foolish," Thomas said. "And not a prediction; it is the truth. Look for yourself."

Duncan suddenly realized how quiet the hall had grown. Whispers and murmurs were the only sounds heard and they drifted off completely until silence filled the room.

His heart raced, a faint sheen of perspiration covered his skin and a sense of anxious anticipation rushed over him. He slowly turned and raised his head, his glance following the eyes of everyone in the hall.

His breath caught in his chest, his heartbeat swelled to a roar in his ears and his hands gripped the handles of his chair.

Sydney stood at the open doors of the hall.

Six

What reason was there for her to be nervous? She was a powerful witch with powers beyond mortal concept, but here she was a bundle of nerves, feeling like a young girl about to approach a young man for the first time.

Nonsense, sheer nonsense.

Her stomach let her know otherwise, fluttering and tumbling and causing her to feel very human.

She had chosen her clothes carefully, a lavender dress in soft gossamer that flowed gently around her body down to her ankles. The long, wide sleeves ran down her arms, a ribbon in a deeper lavender color entwining with the material to gather at the wrists. The same color ribbon gathered the material low at her chest and crisscrossed around her midsection to her waist. She had pinned up her dark hair, adding a sprig or two of lavender to the mass of curls and waves.

And her feet were bare for a good reason. She wanted, perhaps needed, the earth's energy running through her strongly. It added to her own energy and provided comfort and calm.

She drew upon that energy as she approached the dais.

Gwen stood in a rush. "Sydney." Her voice faltered. "You have returned."

Her shock was obvious and so was her concern.

Sydney stopped directly in front of Duncan. "I thought it was time."

Duncan remained silent, not taking his eyes off her.

"Have I interrupted an important gathering?" she asked, her eyes glancing over everyone who sat at the dais. Her sight caught what was necessary. They were apprehensive and nervous over her appearance and uncertain in their reactions.

Duncan she had carefully avoided. If this was to work between them she could not rely solely on magic. She had to allow love to take its course.

Gwen was quick to answer. "Eileen—" She paused to extend a hand in the woman's direction. "Is visiting Duncan."

Sydney acknowledged the woman with a smile and a nod. Eileen gave her a faltering smile before turning her eyes away. Sydney learned much about her from that brief exchange. The one thing she was certain of was that Eileen was no threat. She was a kind and caring person but she did not possess enough strength, courage, even life to capture Duncan's attention.

"Then I will not intrude; I but wished you all to know of my return." She stepped back away from the dais, and reluctantly away from Duncan.

"Sydney." Her name echoed throughout the great hall and wrapped around her in a mixture of intense pain and anger that almost forced her to her knees.

She turned her eyes on Duncan and waited.

He stared at her. All these years separated and all he could do was say her name. Dozens of questions raced through his mind but none reached his tongue. He could only stare at her like a speechless young boy foolishly in love.

Gwen took charge as was her way. "Do join us, Sydney."

Sydney thought it best to make her presence known and then take her leave. She had startled them all enough with her return and she sensed a feeling of unease from many. She had after all shocked them; it would be better if they had time to consider her return.

"That is gracious of you, Gwen, but another time perhaps."

Gwen looked relieved and sent her a brilliant smile. "You are staying in your cottage?"

"Yes, I am and it is good to be back there."

Gwen frowned strangely, the creased lines between her eyes deepening even more in thought. Gwen had always frowned more than she smiled and the years of frowning had left their indelible marks.

Why the small frown now? In a flash Sydney understood. Her speech was different from when last they spoke. It was more refined and cultured now—and modern. She had all but forgotten the old way of speech, the ayes and nays, the thick accent of the Scots where the words rolled off their tongues in lyrical melody.

She had traveled the world, earned several degrees, spoke various languages, some now forgotten, others that were forever lost and had learned through it all that one had to remain faithful to oneself. She was who she was now; she could not return to who she once was.

A familiar voice broke the silence. "Will you help those who seek your wisdom?"

Sydney smiled widely and turned, her arms outstretched. "Dora."

The woman hurried to Sydney and when she saw that Dora was rounded with child she closed the steps between them. They hugged and laughed softly and hugged again.

"A babe, how wonderful for you," Sydney said, her hand rubbing Dora's stomach. She heard several gasps then whispers race around the room.

"Do not mind the ignorant," Dora whispered. "I am glad you are here for I know I will not lose this child as I did little Thomas."

"You lost a child, how very sorry I am for you," Sydney said with compassion.

No sadness filled Dora's face; it lit in a brilliant smile. "You are here now—that will not happen again."

Sydney had learned much in her long lifetime and she had studied well the past and the reasons for many of the problems and illnesses that had plagued the people. She hoped her knowledge would help Dora and her unborn child, but she needed information if she was to help and she would get it a little at a time so as not to frighten Dora.

"When is the babe due?"

"Sometime near the end of spring, I am not quite sure."

Sydney reassured her with a pat to her arm. "Do not worry, we will be ready for him."

"Oh, a boy!" Dora said in an excited whisper.

Sydney could have kicked herself for not being more cautious. This was not a time to go spouting predictions.

"Thomas will be pleased, though I will not tell him for then he will worry that this son will be born without breath."

Stillborn. With modern technology that would not happen, but here in the past no one had a way of knowing, and Sydney knew all too well that a midwife could be blamed for stealing a child's breath at birth and then be labeled a witch.

"I will visit with you at your cottage tomorrow?" Dora asked anxiously.

"The walk is not too much for you?" Sydney knew the walk would probably benefit her and the child, but she wanted to be certain that Dora was remaining active and therefore capable of the walk.

Dora laughed. "That walk is nothing." She patted her stomach. "Me and the babe walk every morning before the girls rise. It is my time alone, my time to think and give thanks."

"You cannot have her all to yourself."

Sydney laughed as she turned and watched Thomas approach her with outstretched arms. He grabbed her fast and hugged her hard.

"I knew you were no ghost standing at the doors."

"I am no ghost," Sydney said and patted Thomas's solid stomach. "And you grow along with your wife."

"She feeds me well and loves me well."

"Then you are a lucky man."

"That I am," Thomas said, slipping his arm around his wife's shoulders. "Join us, it has been too long since last we spoke."

Sydney was tempted but knew it was best she did not stay. Duncan had said but her name and no more. She could not remain here in the hall with him ignoring her. She was already beginning to wonder if this had been a mistake. Perhaps he was too angry with her to forever forgive and forget or perhaps he was too stunned by her return to respond. Either way she would give him time.

"Thank you but I must go."

"Your wolf needs tending?" Thomas asked so no other would hear.

"Wolf?" Sydney repeated, as if she did not hear him correctly and knowing it was not wise that anyone knew of Finn.

Dora jabbed her husband with her elbow. "Are you mad asking such a question? And what would she be doing with a wolf?"

Thomas looked contrite but continued to probe. "Taking care of a lone one, she always did look after the animals."

"A wolf?" Dora asked as if he were crazy and stepped back from her husband, placing her hands on her hips. "A wolf befriends no one."

Sydney could hear Thomas's silent reply.

No one but a witch.

It was time for her to leave.

"I will see you tomorrow, Dora. It was good seeing you, Thomas." She turned quickly to address Gwen and her breath caught for a moment. Duncan was gone from his seat. "I am sorry for intruding on your gathering, Gwen. May the remainder of your night be filled with joy and blessings to you all."

With that she hurried from the hall, her glance running around the room to see if Duncan was about. She did not see his face, though a few of the faces she caught in her search looked cautious and fearful of looking directly at her. Smiles greeted her as well and she was grateful that there were those who were happy with her return, but it would do her well to remember that there were those who were not happy.

She kept up her hurried pace as she left the keep. Finn waited for her at the edge of the forest; she wanted no one to see him. They had bonded quickly and they protected each other. She would see that nothing happened to him because of her.

The village surrounding the keep was quiet, most being at the hall. The glow of day was fading, casting a range of soft colors over the land. A spring breeze raced along with her and she hugged her arms, wishing she had brought a shawl.

She gave a quick glance around her and seeing no one close by she whispered a quick spell. "Wind above, wind around, please for me, settle down."

The strong breeze slowed its pace and settled in a gentle whisper around her.

"Do you forever use magic?"

Sydney stopped abruptly at the sound of Duncan's accusing voice. She was about to enter the forest; she could see Finn concealed in the bushes waiting for her and she cautioned him with her hand to stay put.

She turned to face Duncan.

He stood a warrior braced for battle, his feet a distance apart for leverage, his arms folded over his broad chest protecting his heart and his handsome features shielded by a strong, hard stare daring her to penetrate his emotional armor.

She dropped her hands to her sides, a sign not of surrender but of a willingness to talk freely and honestly.

"The wind calmed after your whispered words."

"The wind does as it pleases, I only requested that she not chill me so." She intended honesty with him otherwise there was no hope of a relationship between them.

"You speak and nature listens."

"I listen to nature, share with her and honor her as can anyone."

His arms remained tightly folded against his chest. "Why?"

His eyes were filled with pain. Why had nothing to do with her reply. He wanted to know why she returned. She did not think however that her answer would please him.

"I needed to return."

"Why?" He was looking for an answer that would make sense.

Was there one? How did she explain to him that two powerful witches from hundreds of years in the future returned her to him for a second chance at love? He would never believe her. She hardly could believe it herself. How did she explain that they had been given a very special gift? And that they should be grateful, grab hold of each other and never let go.

But a hurt had been suffered, and unless it could be understood and rectified there would be no chance of them coming together again. He had suffered for thirteen years, she for hundreds of years.

And realizing that she knew instantly what was necessary. She would have to teach him what she already knew—that once a true love is found then nothing, absolutely nothing should be allowed to come between it, not even the doubts of the couple themselves.

She would teach as she was taught, through self-realization, for only he would be able to see it for himself. No matter how many times she might tell him, if he did not realize it, he would never understand it or apply it.

"I needed to know you were all right."

"Why care now?"

He would not accept the fact that she never stopped caring; he seemed determined to argue and perhaps it was best if she allowed him his anger.

He went on. "Why did you persist in haunting me in the woods?"

Sydney was glad she could speak honestly. "I did not haunt you."

His arms fell away from his chest, leaving his heart vulnerable. "You did, every day for thirteen years you were there. Some days you said nothing, merely walked in my line of vision, a smile on your beautiful face. Why, Sydney, why torment me?"

"I was not there; the visions were your own."

He paced in front of her then stopped. "Tell me, swear to me that you were never in the forest."

She hesitated for she had been in the forest, but only today.

He raised his voice though it was filled with sorrow. "You cannot."

"Today, Duncan, I was only there today."

"You let me believe you were not real."

"How could I have convinced you otherwise? You believed what you wished to believe."

"Nay, you could have convinced me."

"How, Duncan? How could I have convinced you this time when all the other times you saw me I was not real?"

"This way," he said and marched over to her, grabbed her around the waist and hoisted her up hard and fast against him, his lips rushing to kiss her.

Seven

This is what you've missed.

The reminder resonated in her head and in an instant her arms went around him. She clung to him, never wanting to let him go, never wanting their kiss to end. Through the long years she had fantasized about his kisses and after a while she thought his kiss just that—a fantasy. It could never have felt as good, as right, and as passionate as she had remembered. She had simply made it more than it had been.

Wrong!

It was *more* than she had remembered, much more.

Duncan kissed her with his heart and soul, pouring every ounce of passion, love and tenderness into it. His body became a part of the kiss, pressing firmly against her, the heat of his passion pouring into her.

Then there was the taste of him.

No, it hadn't been a fantasy. It had been real and he was real and she wanted to linger in the taste and feel of him for all eternity.

He ended it on a deep sigh, resting his forehead against hers. "Damn, you are real."

His remark made him gather his wits, and he reluctantly stepped back away from her.

His distance was more than a step away and it disturbed Sydney. They had been parted far too long; she wanted no further distance placed between them.

He shook his head. "This makes no sense, you returning after all this time."

"In some things there is no logic."

"Especially where you are concerned." He folded his arms protectively across his chest once again.

He was locking her out, moving another step away from her. She had to do something and the one thing Duncan thrived on was challenge. "You think you know me?" Her smiled teased. "I am different now, the years have changed me."

"The years have changed us both."

"Then let us discover each other again."

"I am to be married."

His words were a knife to her heart. Had she come back after all this time to lose him to another woman? Or was history to remain the same? Was he to marry and her heart to be broken again?

She retained her composure and charged forward into battle. "Are you afraid of what you will discover?"

"I know what I will discover. Do you?"

He threw her challenge back at her and she accepted it with a smile. "Of course, but it is the path to rediscovery that I so look forward to."

"You tempt me, Sydney, you always tempted me." Sorrow and anger filled his words.

"We tempted each other. It was mutual, always mutual."

Her reminder annoyed him and sparked his anger. "You cannot expect to walk back into my life as though you had never left it. Marriage is in my future, to a woman who wishes to be a good wife and mother."

"Then marry her, Duncan." His words hurt her more than she thought they would. But she would not stand here and argue with him. The choice was his. He loved her or he did not.

"I will," he said obstinately.

"I wish you well then." Sydney turned and began to walk away.

He called out to her in an angry desire, testing her strength. "Give me your blessings."

Did he think she would crumble at his request? Did he think she would curse his union? Did he think she didn't know he wanted her to want him? Sydney turned around slowly and raised her hands to the heavens. A gentle wind descended down around her and she looked directly at Duncan. "*Mother, Father up above; bless this man and his true love; let him taste the truth of life; so his union will know no strife; may their life be rich and long; and may their love grow forever strong.*"

A chill wrapped around him and he shivered.

Sydney pointed a finger at him. "Make certain this is what you want, Duncan, for the blessing I bestowed on you is strong and binds well. And—" She grew silent for a moment. "It must be your true love you marry or the blessing will have little value."

She turned and walked away. Duncan's eyes followed her until she merged with the shadows of the forest.

"Damn you, Sydney," he muttered. He wanted to curse her, hold her, scream at her and kiss her senseless. He wanted to rediscover her just as she had suggested. He wanted to fall in love with her all over again, or did he want to reclaim the love for her that he had never lost?

His pride had forced him to say that he was to be married. Wedding a stranger was not to his liking and he had appeased his sister by agreeing to meet Eileen. One look and he had known there would be no marriage in his future.

He wanted only one woman.

Sydney.

Now she had returned, but why?

The question haunted him. Why had she returned? And why had she left? Those were two questions that needed answers, and he intended to get the answers. He intended to discover her secrets before he rediscovered her. He was certain that there were secrets locked away somewhere. She just did not decide to return after thirteen years. It was almost as if she materialized out of thin air. And where had she been all these years?

He walked back toward the great hall. It was rude of him to leave without a word to anyone but he had wanted to speak with Sydney in private, and he had no intention of waiting until another time.

He had actually feared that if he did not grasp the time with her immediately she could very well disappear again. Now it was necessary to return and tend to proper manners for his sister's sake.

His thoughts, however, would be anything but proper. He could not rid his mind of Sydney, especially the kiss. It had been many years but it seemed merely yesterday once his lips claimed hers. It was as he remembered and so much better than his dreams for she was real.

The warm moisture of her lips, the way she melted against him, her arms circling him with such familiarity, the clean fresh scent of her like blossoming flowers after a spring rain and the softness of her; it was all as he remembered. And his body ached with the need for her.

He stopped before entering the hall, giving himself a chance to focus his thoughts elsewhere. The scent of Sydney was too strong in his nostrils no matter how he tried to chase her from his mind.

She was a part of him and it was senseless for him to deny it. But his warrior side fought the idea as always. He was a man strong in body and temper. He rode into battle prepared, ready to die if necessary, to defend what was his, his honor and his clan's honor.

How then did his strength turn to weakness when it came
to Sydney?

He had been wounded in battle and borne the tremendous pain as it healed and left him with a scar as a reminder
of his suffering. But the scar Sydney had inflicted upon
him was not visible and had yet to heal. It grew deeper and
more painful with the passing days and he had learned how
to live with the constant pain.

He had decided that the pain of battle was preferable to
pain of the heart.

Raised voices, laughter and song caught his attention
and his question was left to wonder with all the other questions that haunted him.

He entered the boisterous hall and walked to his seat,
no one talking to him as he passed table after table. He
wore a look on occasion, not often, but a look that kept
people away. Thomas had remarked more than once that it
was the devil's own expression and anyone gazing upon it
knew that they would be damned to hell if they approached
him or spoke to him.

He had no idea what look his friend spoke of or when
it came over him, he only knew that he must now be wearing it for no one spoke to him and many moved aside as
he passed by.

His sister cast wide eyes on him and tightened her lips,
an indication she was none too pleased with his actions, or
was it his expression that displeased her?

It mattered not. He intended no repercussions for his
actions. He did what he pleased and would answer to none
for it. He sat and leaned near her. "If your intentions are
to give me a tongue-lashing I will leave now."

He could see she fought to hold her tongue.

She whispered so no one would hear. "I do not wish to
see you hurt again."

"That will not happen."

"She has grown wise—you can see it on her face and
in her eyes." Gwen placed her hand on her brother's arm.

"Please be careful. I want what is best for you."

Guilt washed over him. His sister had worked hard to arrange Eileen's visit and it all had been for him and his happiness, though she always kept the clan in mind. She wanted to see it prosper and grow and to do what Duncan needed to wed and have children.

"Keep in mind the talk that drifts up from the lowlands," she said, her voice low. "They are burning witches."

"It is madness," Duncan said with anger and fear; fear that Sydney could meet such a horrendous fate.

"It is the law and for good reason."

"I will not discuss this now."

"Fine," his sister said, "but keep it in mind for your own sake." She turned away from him, joining the conversation going on next to her between Eileen and Dora.

A rage welled inside him though he could not reason its cause.

"I have drunk enough ale and I am feeling no pain so I could throw a few fists if it will help," Thomas said, holding his fist up in front of him as he had done when they were young and itching for a fight.

Duncan laughed as he had done as a young lad, for though Thomas was large and strong he could never best Duncan in a fight. "I do not want to shed a friend's blood."

"And you think you can?" Thomas puffed out his beefy chest.

"Your bravado will do you little good when I knock you on your ass—as usual."

Thomas grinned. "My ass is big enough to cushion my fall."

Duncan slapped his friend on the back and laughed. "When I think there is no reason to laugh, you always give me one."

Thomas grabbed hold of Duncan's arm. "That is what friends are for."

It was Thomas's way of letting him know that he was there for Duncan if needed.

"And you have been the truest of friends."

Thomas thumped his chest then reached for his tankard of ale and raised it high. "That I have."

Duncan grabbed for his full tankard and clinked it against Thomas's. "To you, my friend."

"To me," Thomas said and took a generous swallow. He wiped his mouth on his sleeve and then gave a quick look around to make certain his wife did not see him.

"Dora still hits you in the head when you do that?" Duncan asked with a grin.

"Aye, she says the shirt wasn't made for a wiping cloth. I disagree."

"Though not verbally?"

Thomas shook his head. "Nay, my mind hears my words loud and clear, but my mouth is wise enough to remain shut."

Duncan laughed again.

Thomas leaned over in his chair and lowered his voice. "She is more beautiful than I remember."

A jolt to his heart caught Duncan unaware. Thomas spoke of Sydney and Duncan agreed. "You are right, she is more beautiful."

"Then it was her you saw today?"

"Aye, she admitted it."

"Did she mention the wolf?"

"Nay," Duncan said. "She said nothing of him and I thought not to ask."

"Your mind was busy with other more important questions."

"That found no answers," Duncan said, annoyed.

"She has only returned. There will be time to talk with her at length unless . . ."

Again his heart jolted. He had not asked Sydney how long she planned to remain and now the question haunted him.

Thomas attempted to ease his friend's concern. "She did not return only to leave so soon." He continued on, thinking his words appeased. "Or perhaps she flees and seeks protection from those who fear her ways."

Duncan grew more alarmed. "I had not thought of that."

"And Sydney is too damn stubborn to tell you if she is in danger, and besides, she probably thinks she can handle it all with magic."

Duncan looked about to see if anyone heard Thomas, but everyone appeared lost in their own conversation and the revelry going on in the hall.

Thomas shrugged. "Who knows, maybe she can."

"She cannot," Duncan demanded. "If anyone sees her do magic she will be persecuted for it."

Thomas leaned close to him. "No one sees magic done. Witches are sly in their doings. They mumble some words and it is done."

Duncan was surprised by his friend's remark. "You have never spoken this way before about the old ways."

"I have heard talk. The cleric who passed through the village a few months back spoke of how the old ways are the way of the devil and should be avoided and abandoned."

"You believe this when Sydney has helped so many? You think her evil?"

Thomas spoke low. "Sydney is different."

"Different from who?"

"From that old witch who stole my son's life. She is evil."

"You did not mention this to the cleric, did you?"

"I did not have to," Thomas said, "others told him of her. Does that upset you?"

"We do not need outside influences on our land. We can see to our own."

Thomas nodded. "Aye, I agree, but this is different. The cleric is better able to deal with evil."

Duncan was adamant. "What does he deem evil? An old woman who has helped the ailing?" He placed a hand on his friend's shoulder. "I shed tears with you for your son, but the old woman did not take his life. She has helped birth many babes, has saved many ailing mothers after difficult births and has never turned anyone away seeking help. This makes her evil?"

"You speak as Dora does." Thomas's eyes glistened with tears he fought not to spill. "I still think of how tiny and lifeless he lay in my hands and at that moment I knew no greater sorrow and no greater anger."

Duncan squeezed his shoulder. "You will have another son."

"I tell myself this, but I worry."

"Do not worry, Sydney is here, she will help Dora."

Thomas hung his head for a moment before he looked back up at Duncan. "That was my first thought when I saw her. Not that you would be happy at her return, but that she was here and her magic would breathe life into the child Dora carried."

"I am glad to hear this, for then I know that if Sydney needed protecting you would be there for her."

"You have my word, Duncan. I will see no harm come to Sydney."

"This is good to hear, my friend, because tomorrow I am going to find out the true reason for Sydney's return."

Eight

Duncan held a cloth to his bleeding brow. His plans had gone awry as soon as he had stepped out of bed. He had ordered the morning meal to be brought to his bedchamber, hoping to avoid any confrontation with his sister over his change of plans. His meal tasted stale and sour, and his sister had entered his room with the barest of knocks and had taken a fit when he had made it known that his intention to show Eileen the land and visit with the puppies would need to wait since he had plans that required his immediate attention.

She fussed and squabbled with him until finally, to his relief, she had left in a huff. He wanted to get out of the keep and stay out of the keep for the remainder of the day. And he wanted desperately to see Sydney. Questions or not and answers or not, he wanted to see Sydney.

He wanted to talk with her, spend time with her and damned but he wanted to kiss her again. Hold her. Touch her. Know she was real, actually there and was not going anywhere.

He made it out of the keep and was almost clear of the village when a fight broke out and not a friendly one. He could have slipped away, but he was the clan chieftain and responsible for law and order in the clan. These two men had come to blows on more than one occasion and he was disgusted with their childish actions as were many in the clan.

His thought was to end it quickly, but it turned into more of an altercation than he had anticipated. Both men were beyond reason, their tempers controlling them. He gave them fair warning but they ignored him. Although he was patient, his own temper rose steadily.

A crowd soon gathered, waiting to see what their chieftain would do, and in the end he was forced to enter the melee and put an end to it, but not before receiving several vicious blows.

Thomas joined him where he sat on the low stone wall of the widow Gilda's cottage. She had given him the cloth to staunch the blood that flowed from his brow and a gentle pat on the back and a smile. It was a sign of her pride in her chieftain. She was sixty plus years and had buried two husbands and one daughter. She had three strong sons who saw to her care though she lived alone in her cottage. The clan was her family and her chieftain her protector and he demonstrated his strength today.

She stood talking with others in the clan, all obviously proud of their courageous leader and all ignoring the two men who fought and were now drowning their sorrows in ale with arms hooked around each other.

"They will be at it again in no time," Thomas said and shook his head. "That wound you took to your head continues to bleed. It needs to be looked at."

Duncan swore beneath his breath. "I did not want to go see her in need of tending."

"She will help you. That blood flows too freely and too steadily. It is not good."

He sounded worried, and Duncan removed the cloth.

The pale blue cloth was soaked with blood and the blood flowed down to pool in his right eye. He immediately pressed the cloth to his brow.

"Good lord, you are bleeding!" The high-pitched voice sounded more like a scream and caused the two men to turn in alarm.

Eileen stood beside Gwen, trembling, her hand clutched to Duncan's sister's arm.

"What happened?" Gwen demanded, her hand holding firmly to Eileen in an attempt to comfort. "Who is responsible for this?"

Silence reigned loudly, but Gwen would not be denied. "Who did this to my brother?"

Her strength made Eileen cling all the more to her and the girl continued to tremble.

Duncan stepped forward since many in the clan stepped back away from his sister, who looked about to lash out in retaliation. "It is done."

Eileen spoke up though her voice trembled along with her thin body. "There is much blood."

Duncan took a step toward her but she scurried away from him, hiding behind Gwen. "I am sorry, but the sight of blood makes me fearful."

"What of the wounded in your clan that return from battle? Do you not help them?" Thomas asked, annoyed and surprised by her weakness. His friend needed a strong woman for a wife, not one who cringed at the sight of blood.

Eileen was quick to answer. "We have healers for that work. Do you not have a healer?" She looked to Gwen. "I heard talk of that woman who returned—many say she is a skillful healer." She did not wait for a reply. "Duncan, you must go see her at once and Thomas your friend should go with you."

Suddenly Thomas changed his opinion about the woman. "You are right. Sydney is a skillful healer and

Duncan should go to her immediately, and I will make certain he gets there."

Gwen was fast to interfere. "I can see to his wound."

Eileen remained persistent. "Duncan needs the skill of a known healer."

Thomas went along with Eileen. "I agree."

Gwen turned an angry stare on him.

He ignored her completely. "Come on, Duncan, let us be on our way."

"Aye, be on your way," Eileen urged with a wave of her hand. "And do not return until he has been well tended."

"I will make certain of it," Thomas assured her.

"And that you better," came a familiar voice that had Thomas turning bright red.

He looked to see his wife standing on the other side of the widow Gilda's stone wall, her arms folded over her chest and her eyes solid on him. He walked over to her.

Her voice was low and firm. "I know what you are up to, Thomas, and you make certain he is well before you go leaving him at Sydney's."

"They need to be together," he whispered, wanting no one to know his plan.

"It is Duncan's choice," she said with a wag of her finger at his nose. "And you remember that."

Thomas grabbed her finger, pulled her toward him and kissed her soundly. "And you remember how much I love you."

Dora turned red and slapped him on the back. "Be off with you."

"Aye, Thomas, take good care of him," Eileen called out from where she remained hiding behind Gwen.

"Do not keep him long," Gwen warned.

Duncan listened to it all and graciously accepted a clean cloth from the widow Gilda, who added her own opinion and the one that impressed him the most. "He will do as he will, he is the chieftain."

Not another word was said as Duncan and Thomas left the village and disappeared into the woods.

Sydney rose early, anxious to start her day in this world that was once so familiar to her. She chose a simple brown skirt with a white blouse that tied across her chest. She also tied a pale yellow shawl around her waist, the point hanging down along her hip. She twisted her hair up, pinning it with two bone combs, and she placed a polished bloodstone hooked on a leather string around her neck. The stone was engraved with a protective rune symbol.

She enjoyed a cup of chamomile tea while she gathered her basket and tools for a successful day of plant collecting. It had been far too long since she had foraged the woods for naturally grown plants. She had a plentiful and beautifully arranged herb garden back in the future and could pick and cut from it at any time. But here she would need to use her knowledge and find plants in their natural surroundings. The thought thrilled her.

Beatrice yawned and stretched as she sat up from her soft bed atop the wood-hewn mantle. Sydney had constructed a comfortable bed from a small basket, lining it with cotton balls that she had stashed away in the bathroom that was invisible to all but her and Beatrice. She added soft cotton handkerchiefs as a sheet and a blanket.

Beatrice found it so comfortable she did not want to get out of bed. It was with another yawn she asked, "Are you off somewhere?"

"Plant collecting."

That got her attention. She was up and standing as best she could since the soft cotton kept her on a tilt. "What about Duncan?"

"What about Duncan?"

She wagged a tiny finger at her. "You are back here to get him to love you again."

Sydney sighed and poured herself another cup of tea and a small one for Beatrice. "Make him love me again?" She shook her head, handing Beatrice the tiny cup. "I cannot make him love me—and to love me again? He either loves me or he does not."

"Then do things that will remind him of how much he loves you."

"You certainly are my cheering section."

Beatrice placed her cup aside and flew up out of the bed to rest on the top of the basket on the table. "I remember the way it was between you and Duncan." She hesitated a moment.

Sydney encouraged her to continue. "Go on, I wish to hear what you have to say."

"You two were always together, always laughing, smiling, loving, arguing in a loving way, touching, kissing—"

Sydney interrupted. "All couples in love do the same."

"No," Beatrice was adamant. "You two were different. It was as if you knew something, a secret of sorts that no others in love knew." She paused on purpose and tears pooled in her eyes. "It was as if you captured the essence of love, its truth, its foundation, its spirit."

A chill raced over Sydney and she shivered. "Strange you should say that, for over the long years I had never found what I had shared with Duncan."

Beatrice threw her tiny arms up in the air, shaking her hands. "Then get busy rediscovering it instead of foraging for plants."

"A good thought, but a better one to my way of thinking is to allow him time to think on my return and make a choice of his own."

"I cannot say I agree with you but"—she said with a point of her finger—"I have watched you make wise choices over the years and I will bow to your wisdom."

"Thank you, Beatrice, I appreciate the support."

"That is just for now," the tiny fairy warned. "Do not

put it past me to go whispering some suggestion in his ear if he does not move his backside."

"You forget," Sydney said, bending over and whispering, "he has the ability to see fairies."

"Oh!" Beatrice covered her mouth with her hand.

"You forgot."

Beatrice nodded, her hand falling away from her mouth. "I did. You are right. Even when he was a young lad he could see us, though he made mention of it to none."

"I think he does not believe what he sees and refuses to acknowledge what he sees."

"You are right. He never speaks to one of us but he knows we are there." Suddenly she smiled. "I will befriend him."

Sydney laughed. "I do not think he will acknowledge you."

"I will not give him a choice. How can you not talk with a fairy when she lands on your shoulder?"

"This I would like to see."

Beatrice shook her head. "No, this must be between him and me. It may take some time and patience on my part to get him to accept me. But I have patience and I am determined."

"Determined you are, but patient?" Sydney attempted to hide a smile. "I think you need to work on that a bit."

Beatrice smiled, her chubby cheeks glowing. "Just a bit."

Sydney grew serious. "We must be careful in how we go about our affairs. People will be watching and it will be dangerous for any magic to be performed in front of any mortal."

"I agree. These are difficult and dangerous times, and so many atrocious punishments were suffered by the innocent."

A sound outside the door brought them to silence.

Sydney waved her hand around the room, making cer-

tain particular areas were invisible to the mortal eye as she
approached the door.

Beatrice flew to her basket bed and quickly slipped on
the remainder of her clothes over the gossamer tunic she
wore. She then flew up near the ceiling and over near Sydney, keeping out of view of whoever was at the door but
near enough to assist Sydney if necessary.

Sydney felt secure in her abilities to protect herself yet
a twinge of apprehension filled her as she lifted the latch
on the door.

"Finn," she said with an obvious sense of relief.

The wolf stood, his sharp green eyes focused on her.

"Have you come for breakfast?" Sydney asked and gave
him a gentle pat on the head and a rub behind the ear.

What would sound like a growl to most, Sydney knew
was a friendly response.

She moved aside for him to enter, but he remained
where he was.

"He looks as if he can see to feeding himself," Beatrice
said, flying past Sydney and out the door. "He looks more
to be telling you something."

"Is that it, Finn? Are you trying to tell me something?"

The black wolf turned his focus from her toward the
woods and back to her.

"Someone is out there," Beatrice said.

"Heading this way?" Apprehension again filled her, but
she quickly used her powers to calm her emotions. If she
could not concentrate, she could not sense or be aware; her
own strength would then be useless to her.

She answered her own question, for once she quieted
her mind she instantly knew who was headed her way. "It
is Duncan, and Thomas comes with him."

Suddenly she grew upset and her hands began to shake.

Beatrice flew to her. "What is it?"

"Duncan is injured."

Nine

Finn growled low, and Sydney's hand went to his head to calm him with a gentle pat. "I know who comes and thank you for the warning."

The black wolf paused before leaving to drink from the bowl Sydney kept outside the cottage for him, and being the animal was not in a hurry she knew it would be a few minutes before Duncan arrived.

"Can you sense the severity of his injury?" Beatrice asked, looking to the woods and then to Sydney.

Sydney closed her eyes and concentrated. It was not easy to sense the condition of a loved one. Worry coupled with the desire for him to be all right wages a war in your mind and you never know if what you feel is what is or what you want it to be.

Over six hundred years of practice does help, and while she wished him well she also sensed much blood.

"His blood flows too freely, but he walks on his own."

"That is good." Beatrice was anxious to help. "Are they far? Do you wish me to fly there and return with news?"

Sydney shook her head. "They aren't far and I am certain it is a head wound."

"If it bleeds so much how does he walk?"

"Stubbornness keeps him going, but not for long if that wound is not stitched." Sydney was caught between running into the cottage and preparing what she would need to tend him and waiting there for his arrival. She wanted, actually needed, to see with her own two eyes that he was all right, that what she sensed was correct and a few stitches and rest would take care of the matter.

Her hesitation decided for her. Duncan walked out of the woods a few feet away, followed by Thomas, who shouted to Sydney.

"He has been hurt."

Sydney ran toward them and immediately took charge. "Let me see the wound before you walk another step."

"His step has slowed considerably in the last few moments," Thomas informed her and received a glare from Duncan.

She gently removed the blood-soaked cloth slowly and one look told her it was a deep gash that would require several stitches. The blood loss was another matter that needed immediate attention, and while her actions might prove foreign and frightening to the two men she felt they would not betray her and speak of what she was about to do.

She did not hesitate. "Hold the cloth to your head."

Duncan did as she instructed, a feeling of relief washing over him. He trusted Sydney; she would take care of him and at the moment he was not feeling as strong as he should.

Sydney rubbed her hands together, forming a heated ball of energy. She felt the swirl of heat rage in her hand. It was powerful and ready to do her bidding. With a prayer to the Eternal Mother for guidance and help she directed him to lower the cloth.

As soon as he did Sydney placed her heated hand over

the wound and with her eyes closed she continued her prayers to the Eternal Mother to help her staunch the flow of blood.

Duncan stood perfectly still. The heat radiating through his head comforted and calmed him. He felt as if he were cradled in the arms of a loving mother who protected her child with her whole being, from her heart to the depths of her soul.

Thomas stared in awe as he watched the blood that had begun to flow through Sydney's fingers from Duncan's wound slow to a trickle and then completely stop. He stood speechless.

Sydney felt the energy drain from her to him and her prayers of gratitude continued until her hand tingled with a gentle coolness alerting her that it was done. She opened her eyes and smiled; she could examine the wound more clearly.

A soft touch here and there around the abrasion told her what she needed to know. "It looks worse than it is." She did not sense a concussion, and there would be no point in mentioning it since neither of them would understand. What was important now was to stitch the wound.

"What now?" Thomas asked, reclaiming his voice and concerned for his friend.

"A few stitches should take care of it nicely."

"Stitches?" Thomas asked, bewildered. "You are going to stitch his flesh?"

Medical knowledge was severely limited in the 1500s, a fact she kept forgetting. She thought quickly. "I have traveled much in the last few years and have learned techniques that remain foreign to this part of the world."

"So that's where you have been all this time? Traveling?" Duncan asked, sounding hurt by her remark.

She placed a firm hand on his arm. What did she say? How did she tell him? Not now. Not at this moment. "I wandered; I needed time to think."

She sensed his anger. She understood his need for answers for she had questions herself, but now was not the time. She placed a firm hand on his muscled arm. He was warm and solid and so very real and she was so very grateful to be here with him.

"Let me tend you now; we can talk later."

"You will be here later?" he questioned caustically.

She took no offense; her concern focused on his wound. "As will you, since you will rest until I give you permission to leave."

"Permission?"

Duncan sounded like the warrior she remembered, stubborn, commanding and possessing an indomitable strength.

Thomas laughed.

Duncan shot him a look that would put fear in most men, but Thomas was his boyhood friend and knew him too well for it to have any affect on him—that is except for him to laugh even harder.

Sydney always smiled when Thomas laughed; quite often she would laugh along with him—his laugh was so contagious. It was a hearty laugh, rapid and steady and pulled you in no matter how stoic you attempted to remain.

"Go home, you are useless to me," Duncan ordered him

Thomas staunched his laughter and looked to Sydney. "It is all right that I leave?"

Duncan knew he asked permission of Sydney just to annoy him and he retaliated. "You ask a woman's permission when your laird has ordered you?"

Thomas kept a firm grip on his laughter though it bubbled close to the surface. "She is the healer and Eileen did tell me to make certain you were well before returning."

"Eileen did not see to his care?" Sydney asked, surprised though glad the woman did not tend him.

"She fears the sight of blood." Thomas was quick to inform her.

"She is young," Duncan said.

Sydney felt a twinge of concern. He defended her. Why?

"Age means nothing," Thomas said. "She is weak. Now

for my answer—" He turned to Sydney. "Do I remain or take my leave?"

Sydney knew he asked more of her. He wanted to make certain his friend would be all right. "There is no reason for you to remain. I can see to his care, he will be fine."

Thomas gave a blunt nod and grinned at Duncan. "Sydney's not weak." With that he hurried off, laughter trailing him.

Sydney grabbed for Duncan's hand before he could bring it to his head to rake his fingers through his hair. "Do not. You will disturb the wound."

Duncan stared at her fingers wrapped around his hand. Slim and gracious, her nails long and pale pink, her skin smooth though touched slightly with age by the passing years.

He looked at her. "I sometimes thought you knew my moves or my thoughts before I did."

She slipped her arm around his and began walking toward the cottage. Out of the corner of her eye she caught Beatrice flying away from the cottage and she had no doubt she would be out and about gathering information.

"It is easy to know another's thought when there is a deep concern for that person. You often did the same with me."

"Aye, but it takes a strong bond to form such an ability."

"I agree," Sydney said.

"A bond that is unbreakable."

Sydney nodded.

"A bond that is forever."

"Aye, forever."

They remained silent the last few steps to the cottage, each knowing in their hearts what neither would openly admit. Their love was strong and forever; nothing could tear it apart, not even time.

Sydney positioned Duncan in a chair beside the table, his back to the invisible modern amenities. She had stocked the bathroom medicine chest with several modern medical conveniences. Antibiotics and antibiotic cream, gauze bandages, an emergency stitching kit and much more.

She told him to rest while she gathered the necessary items and offered him a berry drink she remembered he liked and would gladly accept. She dumped the crushed antibiotic in the drink, wanting to make certain he would be protected against infection.

If he saw the modern instruments she used there would be endless questions that she was not yet ready to answer and he was not yet ready to hear. She decided on a plan.

"The wound may begin to bleed again while I stitch it so if you do not mind, I would like to place a cloth with a hole cut out for around the wound over your head. This way the cloth will soak any blood spilled."

"I trust you, Sydney, do as you will."

His words touched her heart and she smiled.

"And do not worry about pain, I am strong and can bear what pain the stitches bring."

"I have a light touch," she said and stared past his shoulder as she draped the cloth over his head at the syringe filled with Novocain. She prepared him well, cleansing the afflicted area with an antiseptic before beginning.

She stitched the wound quickly and skillfully.

"When will you start?" Duncan asked as she tied off the last of the four stitches.

"I am almost finished," she said, disposing of the plastic gloves and the other items that would appear foreign to him and replaced them with a fine bone needle and thread stained with blood.

"I felt nothing."

He sounded as if he accused, and when she removed the cloth he stared at her.

She sighed. "You think I used magic."

"Did you?" He was giving her the chance to speak the truth and he waited.

Sydney spoke honestly. "I used no magic."

"But I felt nothing. How is that possible?"

"I used no magic," she repeated. She did not want to discuss it with him, for if he probed enough he would discover the truth. "Your shirt is bloody, let me wash it for you."

He thought to refuse but then thought better of it. He would have to wait while it dried at least to a point that he could wear it and that would give him an excuse to spend more time with Sydney. Not that he needed an excuse, but one always helped. She helped him out of his shirt, careful that the healing wound was not disturbed. Later she would apply more healing energy so that he would heal fast and not scar.

She stepped away from him and noticed the silver arm cuff firmly wrapped around his upper left arm. She touched it, remembering the day she had given it to him.

Silver for knowledge, she had told him, and the symbols engraved on the cuff would forever protect him from harm and always keep him safe. And beneath the symbols that circled the cuff were smaller symbols that proclaimed her love for him.

"You still wear it."

"Always, I never go without it."

"I had wondered—"

He took her hand. "That I would remove it and never wear it again? Nay, I could not do it. I thought of it but it is a part of me and will forever remain so."

"Duncan," she said in a bare whisper, not being able to say more but wanting to say so very much. She loved this man more than she could possibly say and her heart ached for them to be as they once were.

"Shhh," he said and placed a finger to her trembling lips. "There is much for us to say to each other, but not now. Now it is time for this."

He drew her down onto his lap and cupped her face in his hands. "I have missed the taste of you."

His lips brushed hers, the sweetness of her wafting over him, and he hungered for more. His hands moved down around her waist and her hands slipped to his shoulders.

He tasted every bit of her, his mouth hungry for all it could get and she willing to give him all that he wanted.

He brought his mouth near her ear and whispered, "This is magic."

She nuzzled at his neck and then moved to his mouth. "Yes, magic at its best."

Her kiss was light but not for long; it turned as hungry as his had been and once again they united in a kiss.

Her hands roamed over his chest, his hands slipped along her ribs. The need to taste, to touch, to feel was an unrelenting ache within them both, but doubt and the years of being apart caused them to hesitate and draw back.

She took a deep breath; he sighed and silence reigned.

Hearts raced, emotions soared and words seemed useless.

Duncan broke the tense silence. "Will I be ugly now that I have a scar?"

He could always tease a smile out of her. "You will have a bare hint of a scar."

"So I will remain my handsome self." He squeezed her waist and she laughed softly.

She noticed his shirt on the ground. "I should wash your shirt."

He held firm to her waist. "Nay, you are where I want you."

And she was where she wanted to be. She stayed put.

"There is much for us to discuss."

She nodded.

"Questions that need answers."

She nodded again.

"We must talk."

She nodded slowly, slipped her arms around his neck and rested her head on his shoulder. She heard the steady thump of his heart, felt the breath in his chest turn rapid and relished the warmth of his body seeping into her.

He hugged her tightly. "Damn, Sydney, you feel good."

She said nothing. There was no need for words. She had dreamed over and over of being in his arms just one more time and she wanted this moment and memory to last forever in her mind and heart.

His chest expanded with the deep breath that he took. Then he stood, lifting her along with him.

"I am a fool." He placed his cheek on her head.

"Why?"

"Because I am going to do something I should not."

"And what is that?"

"I am going to love you."

He waited as if giving her a choice and she lifted her head and smiled at him.

He returned her smile and was about to walk toward the bed when the cottage door opened and in walked Gwen and Eileen.

Ten

Duncan sat in his solar, perturbed at the world at large. He wanted solitude from those around him. He wanted and had demanded time alone. The incident at Sydney's cottage had angered him and he was more annoyed that it had been two days since he had last seen her.

He had given no explanation to his sister when she had entered the cottage unexpectedly. He had not even lowered Sydney to the ground; he kept her in his arms, though she squirmed a bit, letting him know she preferred to be released. He had thought otherwise.

He would not have his life dictated to. He had listened to endless opinions the last time he and Sydney were together; this time he would listen to none but his own.

Gwen must have realized his resolve for she turned to Eileen and wisely suggested they wait outside. Eileen followed without protest as seemed to be her way.

Sydney told him to go, there would be time for them again.

He knew she was right but he did not want to think

about what was right. He wanted to be with her. The years apart had taught him much about sorrow and loneliness and he wished to learn no more. She was here now and he did not wish to waste a moment.

Matters and activities at the keep had kept him there and Sydney had not made an appearance and that worried him. Again questions haunted his thoughts and again answers eluded him.

A gentle knock caused him to shout, "Who is it?"

The door opened and in walked Gwen.

"I gave you permission to enter?"

She ignored his rudeness and after shutting the door behind her walked over to where he slouched in a large wooden chair, one of his legs draped over the thick arm.

"You are behaving childishly."

"Be careful where you tread, Gwen, I am in no mood to be chastised."

She sighed and with a shake of her head she pulled a small wooden footstool beside his chair and sat. "You must think as a chieftain and of what is best for the clan. Is loving Sydney best for the clan?"

"Is loving a fearful young girl who cringes at the sight of blood good for the clan?"

"Her clan is strong and borders ours to the south. To unite the two would guarantee our strength in the area."

"What of love, Gwen?"

She placed her small, slim hand on his arm. "What of love, Duncan? If Sydney loved you so very much why then did she leave? Why did she not have the courage to remain and face whatever obstacle was in her path? And," she said with a squeeze to his arm, "if she loved you why, out of concern and safety for you, did she not abandon her magic?"

That brought Duncan to his feet. "And why did I out of love for her not leave my clan?"

Gwen stared at him in horror. "That could not have been

a thought of yours. Tell me it was not so? You could not deny the clan for—"

"Love?"

Gwen stood. "Sometimes it is necessary to do what is right. Think, Duncan, please think. I like Sydney, and she has helped the clan on occasion."

"On occasion?" He ran his hand through his hair, careful to avoid the wound on his forehead that was healing remarkably well. "She selflessly helped countless villagers who were ill or who simply wished a word with her. She never once turned a needy individual away; she never once turned her back on this clan."

"She practices magic, Duncan."

"Is it magic because her knowledge goes beyond what most can comprehend?"

"Why does it go beyond what others can comprehend? Where does she learn all she knows and how is it she can do things others cannot?"

Duncan did not care for what his sister was implying. "I thought you called her a friend."

"I do, but I have concerns."

"Such as?"

"Her way with animals. They were always drawn to her."

Duncan defended her. "She is kind and they sense it."

Gwen grew agitated. "Good lord, Duncan, someone has remarked that they saw her with a black wolf. Wolves are friendly to no human. And she seems more knowledgeable than before. Look what she has done to you, stitched you up and the wound heals almost magically. No fever, no swelling. What did she do?"

"She used her knowledge," he insisted, though Gwen was right. He had been worried about fever, and none came.

Gwen lowered her voice. "Knowledge is one thing, magic another." She held her hand up when her brother attempted to protest. "I tell you this for her safety, for there is talk about your wound and its sudden healing."

He gave her words thought. He did not wish Sydney to be in danger.

"You also have isolated yourself these last two days. You tend to the necessary but seek only your own company. What do you think that makes others think? If you wish Sydney's safety then show that you are not bewitched and live as you should."

"Do you tell me that I sulk?"

Gwen smiled for the first time since entering her brother's solar, glad to see the teasing gleam that was usually present in his eyes. "Did I say that?"

"Quite well I think." He reached out and drew his sister into his arms, hugging her tightly.

An anxious knock on the door sounded along with its opening. Thomas's head peeked in.

Brother and sister immediately walked toward the frowning man.

"You best come, Duncan."

"What is it?" he asked, following Thomas out the door, his sister close behind.

"You need to see for yourself and calm the people."

Duncan did not need to follow Thomas once outside the keep. A large crowd had gathered around William's cottage. William was a good man, with a wife and five sons ages five to ten and four years. He was a skilled bow maker.

William—a man of no more than five feet, eight inches and lean, a full beard well kept and long hair, the sides braided with colorful cloth—made an imposing sight as he hovered protectively over his son.

His five-year-old son John sat in his father's shadow, fear on his face along with a splattering of red blemishes. The red marks ran down his neck and looked to go beneath his shirt.

Duncan heard grumbles and mutterings and he knew if he did not calm things soon people would turn chaotic fearing the worst.

He walked through the crowd with confidence, most

moving out of his way, and those that did not take notice of his approach felt his firm hand on their shoulder and they immediately moved aside.

"William," he said, addressing the man who moved directly in front of his son upon Duncan's approach.

"Duncan," William acknowledged with a nod. "The lad's feeling fine; it is naught but a rash."

"True enough, but I think it best if you have the lad remain in the cottage until it fades away." He stepped closer to William. "For his own safety. You know yourself how some can get."

William looked about and leaned closer to Duncan. "I have kept him in."

"How long?" Duncan grew concerned. Panic could spread if someone thought John carried an illness they could catch from him.

"Four days."

"And it has not gone away?" Duncan noticed his hesitation, but in the end William trusted him.

"It has grown worse, though he has no fever."

"That is good." Duncan rubbed his chin.

"I have sent for Sydney."

Duncan was not sure if that was wise. If something serious happened to the lad or the affliction spread Sydney would be blamed. But then there was the child to consider, and he looked terribly frightened with everyone standing around staring at him.

"What have we here?"

The melodious voice caused all to turn and part, making room for Sydney. Whispers circled the crowd at her approach. She looked stunning though she wore the dress of the other women. A simple brown skirt and pale yellow linen blouse, though she did wear a bright yellow shawl draped around her waist. She walked with confidence, her eyes sparkling along with her smile and a basket draped over her arm.

She ignored everyone but John. She walked directly to

him, stopping and kneeling in front of him. Her hands went to his face without hesitation and he smiled when she touched him.

"No one has touched me since I got the bumps," he said

"They fear they may catch the bumps." Sydney kept her smile bright. She had worried when William's oldest son rushed into her cottage and told her the problem. She had feared small pox or measles, but one look at him and she had her answer.

"You like wild berries, do you not John?"

He nodded his head rapidly and grinned.

"And since the berries are in bloom I would say you have been eating your full."

"Every day."

"Not even one day you skipped?" she asked.

"Not a one," he answered proudly.

He was obviously allergic to the berries and the rash would fade as soon as he stopped eating them. Itching might be a problem but she had not seen him scratch.

"Do the bumps itch, John?" she asked and watched the lad's eyes turn fearful and look to his father. She had her answer. His father had warned him against scratching the bumps.

Sydney ruffled his light brown hair. "I have something that will help the bumps."

"Truly?" he asked excitedly.

Sydney nodded. "But there is one problem."

John turned silent and leaned forward to listen.

"You cannot eat the berries until the bumps are gone and then you can only eat them once or twice a week."

His father had heard and kneeled down beside his son. "The berries did this to him? Impossible. We all eat the berries."

"Not as many as John does." Sydney knew there was no point in explaining allergic reaction to William; he would not understand, yet he wanted a good, acceptable reason for his son's bumps.

"He eats but a few a day," William insisted.

Sydney could tell he wanted to believe her but he had to be certain. "I think he eats more than a few. What say you, John?"

John hesitated.

"Answer, lad," his father said sternly. "How much do you eat from the bucket before you bring it home? A handful or two?"

The lad looked to Sydney then his father. Reluctantly he said, "I eat half a bucket and then fill it again."

Behind her she heard Duncan and Thomas chuckle.

William shook his head. "No more berry picking for you." He looked to Sydney. "He will be fine then?"

"Keep him from eating the berries for at least a week's time and they will quickly fade. I have a salve that will help the swelling and the itch."

"I am grateful for your help. What can I do in return?"

Though she sought no compensation for her help she understood that the clansman's honor would not allow them to take something for nothing.

"Does your wife Martha still bake those delicious scones I have always favored?"

William grinned. "You ask too little, Sydney."

"If you tasted *my* scones you would think otherwise."

William laughed. "I will have my son bring you a batch by nightfall."

"No rush, the anticipation of their taste is half the enjoyment."

William stood along with her and she handed him a small jar, the cork top tightly in place, that she retrieved from her healing basket.

"Put this on the bumps when he complains about the itch or discomfort."

"My thanks again, Sydney, and if ever you need—"

"I will remember your generosity and take full advantage of it if necessary."

William grinned wide, pleased by her response.

The crowd began to disperse, wagging tongues agreeing and some disagreeing with Sydney's observation.

Duncan walked up to her, his voice low. "You are certain of this? There is no need for the clan to worry?"

"No need at all," she said with confidence. "An overindulgence of berries simply does not agree with him."

"It is good you have returned. The clan needs your wisdom."

While she missed her family centuries in the future, she was glad to be where she was, with Duncan. Conditions were challenging and the times uncertain, but she was here with him and that is what mattered the most to her.

"I am glad to be here."

"Come walk with me," Duncan said, eager to have her all to himself. "Let us talk."

Before they could walk off a harried woman, short and round and wringing her hands, approached Sydney.

"You help my daughter, please?"

Duncan shook his head. "Bethany, Sydney cannot help Margaret."

"She helped John, why not Margaret?"

"Margaret has been afflicted since shortly after birth. Nothing can be done to help her."

Sydney wondered if that was the case. So many present-day problems could be easily illuminated and eradicated with modern medicine. It was a shame to see needless suffering.

"What is the problem with your daughter, Bethany?" she asked.

The woman smiled. "Bumps like John, but Margaret did not eat berries."

"Margaret suffers from more than bumps," Duncan said, again concerned for Sydney. Or was he concerned she would help the young lass and then suffer for her generosity and knowledge?

"Let me have a look," Sydney said, ignoring Duncan,

for she knew if she glanced his way he would be wearing a frown.

"I will go with you," Duncan said.

Gwen heard and had her say. "You are needed at the keep."

"It can wait." His forceful tone alerted all that he would have his way and his sister said not another word more.

Bethany's cottage sat nearer to the woods and was well tended. A young lass of about ten and three years worked in the front garden. When she noticed their approach she retreated back into the shadows of the trees.

"It is all right, Margaret, come here. The healer is here to see you," her mother called out.

The young girl hurried forward and Sydney was struck by her beauty, that was if one could see past the redness around her mouth and on her cheeks.

Sydney smiled and offered her hand to the girl.

Shy at first to accept, Margaret stepped back, but Sydney kept her hand extended until the girl crept toward her and took the offer of friendship.

There were several conditions the girl could be suffering from, from simple allergies, to the more complex eczema; Sydney's only choice was to treat each known condition with the appropriate medication. If one did not respond then she would try the next.

She was glad she had stocked her bathroom well with modern medicine; she had the sense that most if not all would be needed, especially the aspirins.

Bethany's mother grew impatient. "Can you help her?"

"I am not certain but I would like to try."

"Aye, try what you will," the woman agreed anxiously.

"Margaret, tomorrow I will bring you a jar of salve for you to apply to your face. We will see how it works."

The girl shyly smiled her thanks and hurried to her mother's side.

"What can I do for you?" Bethany asked.

"Let us see what the salve does first."

"I spin a soft wool," Bethany said with pride.

"I am glad to know this, but we will wait and see."

Sydney joined Duncan where he waited by a large tree at the edge of the woods. He sat with his back braced against the wide base and his legs stretched out in front of him.

He quickly bent forward and looked from side to side. "Is there anyone else who needs saving today?"

Sydney paused, placing a finger to her chin. "I am sure I can find more if I try."

Duncan was swift in his response. He rose up on bended knee, grabbed her about the waist and settled her quickly on his lap as he returned to his perch beneath the tree.

His surprise action stole the breath from her and she took a deep breath as she settled in his lap.

He looked directly in her eyes. "I need saving."

She almost was fearful to ask. "From who?"

He hesitated briefly. "From myself."

Eleven

Sydney gently touched his cheek and was overwhelmed with emotions. It was difficult to distinguish one from another, they mingled and entwined around each other, all leading to one place—his heart.

Her thought was only of him. "How can I help you?"

He closed his eyes, briefly lingering in the tenderness of her touch and recalling past memories of the times they would sit and talk and touch, laugh and smile. He wanted that again. He wanted it so very badly.

He opened his eyes. "Talk to me, Sydney. Help me to understand, to make sense of all that has passed between us."

The warmth and strength of him seeped into her and at that moment she wanted to lay her head on his chest and listen to the steady beat of his heart. She wanted all to disappear and there be only the two of them.

Instead she chose a more reasonable action. "Let us walk in the woods and talk."

When she moved to stand, he held her firm in his lap. "That is not what was on your mind."

She looked surprised. "You know what is on my mind?"

"I know you, and I know when you think a distance is necessary between us."

He had always been perceptive, but then he was a skilled warrior and perception was part of his trade. Or was she attempting to reason when reason was not called for?

"Do you need saving from yourself as I do from myself?" he asked with a smile.

Her laugh was a gentle tinkle.

His finger slowly traced the smile on her lips. "This time it must be different, Sydney. We must be more honest with each other than we ever were. Others will attempt to stand between us; we cannot allow that and we cannot come between ourselves. In the end the choice must be ours alone."

He had grown wise in the passing years and she felt great pride in the man he had come to be. "I agree."

"Then tell me what was on your mind, for it was different from the words you spoke."

She answered without hesitation, for if they wished to rediscover their love honesty and trust would be their greatest allies. "I thought how much I could feel the warmth and strength of you, and I wanted to lay my head on your shoulder and wished for the world to go away so that there would be only you and me."

"If we wish hard enough can we make it happen?"

"Do you believe it could?"

He lowered his voice. "You are asking me if I believe in magic."

"No, I am asking if you believe strongly enough that we can make the world go away if only for a short time?"

"That would be magic?"

"Then magic must be believing for I believe we could."

"Show me," he said and helped her to stand.

She took his hand and they held tightly to each other,

and she led him into the surrounding woods.

The forest was alive with the freshness of spring. Beech, oak and birch trees were in full bloom and the soft chirp of baby sparrows could be heard from the nests that settled comfortably in the trees' protective branches. A golden eagle sounded high in the sky and in the distance Sydney was certain she heard the cry of a hawk.

"Listen," she cautioned Duncan. "We are far from the world and one with nature."

He listened differently than usual. He heard with a warrior's ear, always waiting for an opponent to strike, but this time he listened as if no opponent existed. He heard the whisper of the gentle breeze, the soft steps of the deer, and he felt at peace. It was simply he and Sydney.

He took charge of their direction once his ears grew accustomed to the sounds that were familiar yet not familiar. He made his way around the willow and ash trees and came upon a running stream.

Sydney spotted Finn in the shadows of the trees. He followed them, keeping Sydney in sight at all times. There would come a time for Duncan to meet Finn, but not yet; Duncan was not ready, nor was Finn.

Duncan stood still, taking in the beauty and quiet of the woods. The only sounds were natural ones and a calm drifted over him.

Sydney squeezed his hand. "There is only you and I."

He drew her close to him and leaned down to steal a gentle kiss. "I believe."

"This is good," she whispered, and kissed his lips softly. It was a beginning for him. Believing was magic.

They joined hands and shared a kiss, not of passion but of tenderness, of caring, of new love.

"It is a good time to talk," he said, stepping away from her and sounding excited as if ready for an adventure.

She felt the same. Where before her body stirred with intimacy, she now stirred with a need to share knowledge, to better understand each other. Wasn't that though another form of intimacy?

She smiled at the thought. "Aye, let us talk."

His question was quick. "Why did you leave, Sydney?" He had waited long enough, he needed an answer—he ached for one.

She hesitated, and he continued.

"Day after day I wondered. I had thought that we could talk of anything, that no matter the difficulty or perceived difficulty if we discussed it we would find a way to solve any dilemma."

She spoke honestly. "I am a witch, Duncan."

He could not help but look about and lower his voice. "You place yourself in danger admitting that." He paused a moment. "Is that why you left?"

"The old ways are my belief. My religion." She attempted to explain.

"What religion? Witches practice magic and magic is no religion."

"Is it not?" She extended her hands up and around her. "What of all this? Is this not magic at its finest? Is it not more powerful than you and I?" She walked to an oak tree and lovingly touched a branch. "Look at this tree. It has stood here many more years than we have lived. It grows and thrives and lives on. It receives energy from the earth and the humans that honor it with their touch and in return extends its energy to help life."

"It is but a tree."

"It lives, Duncan. It lives as you and I. It breathes, it feeds, it needs the sun as you and I do. It is life, and is life not magic?"

He shrugged. "It is simply life and has nothing to do with religion."

"Life is magic and magic is my belief, my religion."

"Then you believe that life is religion?"

"Define religion in your heart, Duncan, and you may understand what I tell you."

"Religion is an enduring faith in—"

"Belief." Sydney finished. "If you do not believe, you cannot have faith in anything. You cannot even have faith in yourself, therefore, how can you ever truly exist? Live?"

He shook his head. "You speak in circles."

"Now you understand," she said with a joyous clap of her hands. She leaned down, grabbed a twig and drew a circle in the dirt, its fresh rich scent wafting up around her. "The circle is ever continuous, see." She traced the circle round and round. "Like life, the circle runs forever."

He rubbed his chin. "I attempt to understand but you confuse me. The circle must have a point of origin before it can be ever continuous."

"Yes, it does."

He held up his hand. "Do not tell me—magic. The point of origin is magic."

"And magic is life."

"And life is belief."

"Belief is faith."

He shook his head. "And what does this all have to do with you leaving me?"

She stood, her head drooping. "I did not believe strongly enough."

He walked over to her and lifted her chin. "In who?"

"In myself and my faith."

"Did you believe in me?"

"Always."

"Then leaving was not necessary."

"At the time I thought it very necessary," she said, looking into his eyes and seeing the hurt of the past surface. "You warned me not to use magic on you."

"I trusted you would not cast a spell over me. My love for you was strong, no spell could make it stronger."

Sydney stepped away from him. "Spells are not what you think."

"So you have told me on many occasions."

"They are similar to a prayer sent out to the heavens."

She wished to say universe but Duncan would not understand the vastness of the word. America had barely taken root and galaxies were yet to be discovered.

"They are more than a prayer, Sydney. I recall young women coming to you for love potions."

"And I will tell you what I told them. The potion and spell I gave them would work only if the young man was interested; if he was not the spell was useless. You cannot force someone to love you."

"Then why would you cast a spell on me if you understood that my love needed no enhancement?"

How did she explain? He needed to understand so much more yet. "The circle, Duncan, think of the ever continuous circle."

"I will try," he said seriously and just as seriously asked, "Would you cast a spell on me now if you thought it necessary?"

She was relieved he did not ask if she had already cast a spell and she did not hesitate to answer honestly. "Aye, I would."

She expected him to warn her as he had done that time thirteen years ago, but he surprised her.

He grinned. "But I worry not, for if I do not believe the spell will work, it will not."

"You begin to understand."

He walked over to her and slipped his hands around her waist. "I want to understand."

"I am glad." Her hands went to rest on his arms and the strength of his muscles greeted her.

"But I need you to understand as well."

His concern was not hard to sense; it was palpable and Sydney listened, eyes wide, for he needed her full attention.

"All you say to me of your beliefs interests me and makes me want to learn more about them. But others would find your talk heresy and you would place yourself in grave danger. I could not bear to lose you again, please keep silent about your beliefs."

He could not bear to lose her again. His words resonated in her head and caused her heart to thump rapidly. She however focused on his concern, for she did not wish him to worry needlessly.

"I will hold my tongue."

He shook his head and laughed softly. "Unless necessary?"

He knew her too well. "I will bite my tongue if necessary." And she stuck her tongue out, slightly biting down on it to show him.

"Nay," he said on a whisper. "I will bite your tongue." He leaned down and ran his tongue across the tip of hers where it stuck out from between her teeth.

The intimate sensation caused her to release her hold and allow him to slip his tongue in her mouth, spar with hers until his teeth could lightly nibble at it. She tingled to the tips of her toes.

He did not stop at her mouth; he decided to nibble and taste her lips, then her chin and trail down to her neck and feast on her delicate skin.

"Damn, Duncan," she murmured. "You know what that does to me."

"It makes you wet with hunger for me," he said with a teasing laugh. "I remember well."

She moaned and let him nibble to his heart's content for his action contented her heart as well. But then they always had been extremely compatible sexually. There were no taboos when it came to sex and discussing it. They were comfortable and agreeable in sexual action, thought and deed.

Through the years she had given it thought and realized that what she had shared with Duncan was rare for it had not changed over the three years they spent together. They always wanted each other. They never tired of each other and never grew bored with each other.

His direction changed again and his mouth settled behind her ear and down along the back of her neck and she felt her legs go weak. She grabbed his arms firmly.

"Not fair," she whispered, a moan following.

He laughed again. "You will have your chance not to play fair."

"Promise."

The anxious passion in her voice excited him. "Aye, I promise from my heart."

"Then have your way for I will have mine."

"You know not what you say for I will take full advantage of your willingness."

She rested her head on his shoulder. "You know that I am always willing when it comes to you."

"I have missed you so very much." He hugged her tightly.

"I thought about you endlessly."

He looked down at her. "I do not wish to waste time, too much has already been wasted."

More time than he could ever comprehend. "Much too much time."

He was eager yet hesitant. He fought the past and he fought himself.

She felt his struggle and understood, for she had her own struggle to contend with. What would happen when he discovered she had returned from the future? What then would he think of magic? What then would he think of her?

They both heard the heavy crunch of twigs and leaves signaling someone's approach and stepped apart, turning in the direction of the sound.

Thomas burst through the brush, winded.

Duncan and Sydney hurried to his side.

"Problem," Thomas managed to say, his breath labored.

"Calm down and regain your breath," Duncan urged.

He shook his head. "No time."

Duncan grew concerned.

Sydney immediately sensed the problem. "A fire."

Thomas nodded.

"The keep?" Duncan asked.

It was Sydney who confirmed his question. "Aye, the cook area."

Thomas nodded again.

"How bad?"

"We stopped it." His breath was calming.

"Anyone hurt?" Duncan asked.

Thomas was hesitant.

Duncan looked to Sydney.

"Gwen."

Twelve

Sydney arrived back at her cottage exhausted. The fire in the cook area turned out to be a minor dilemma, though it could have been much worse. If a fire was not immediately brought under control all could be lost. It was contained instantly by Gwen's swift response. Unfortunately she suffered a burn to her arm in the process, and to Sydney's surprise she refused her help. It was actually Eileen's tearful tirade that caused the upset and sent Thomas in search of Duncan.

Gwen had sought Sydney's healing help in the past and often confided in her. She had thought them friends. She had been the one to offer Sydney advice concerning her brother and had been there for her through the difficult time.

"Gwen is upset that I have returned," Sydney said, plopping down in the rocking chair near the hearth.

Beatrice flitted to a rest on her lap, offering a comforting pat to her hand. "You have disturbed her plans for her brother."

"My presence is an interference."

"No," Beatrice said, shaking her head. "Love interferes. Gwen knows that Duncan loves you and that there is no hope for a union between him and Eileen. She does not realize that there never was a chance for them."

"Why do you say that?"

"Duncan is a man of honor and courage, he would dishonor himself if he wed when he loved another."

Sydney sighed and rested her head back. "I had often wondered if his love for me remained as strong as mine for him. Time and absence can sometimes distance love."

Beatrice differed with her. "Not true love. True love grows stronger with the passing years. It does not fade away; it nestles in the heart and waits."

"For?"

Beatrice looked at her oddly. "You know the answer."

"It waits for true love to return."

"You sound doubtful."

"My own fears, I suppose."

Beatrice shook her head slowly. "I do not think so, what troubles you?"

"I'm not certain, but I feel something is amiss. And I wonder if it was amiss thirteen years ago and in blind youth I missed or misjudged the situation."

She rubbed her tiny hands together. "We have a puzzle to solve."

"I feel there is much work for us here, but first a cup of tea."

Beatrice flew up out of her way as she stood. "We must be careful."

"I think the same myself." Sydney prepared a pot of chamomile tea and sliced the honey nut bread she had baked just that morning.

"There will be talk of the magic you performed."

Sydney frowned. "I healed with proper medicine."

"Medicine that has yet to be discovered—that is why whispers of magic will be in the air."

"That does concern me, these are difficult times."

Beatrice shivered and hugged her arms. "And in difficult times people seek to blame."

"When direction, guidance and understanding are necessary." Sydney sat at the table and motioned for Beatrice to join her, a tiny setting of fine china set for her.

Beatrice looked troubled as she sat at the tiny table and chair Sydney arranged for her on the table. "You cannot change their way of thinking, it will take centuries."

"Even centuries are not enough to eradicate greed and ignorance. But," she said with a smile, "I can plant seeds and hope they will flourish."

"Many do not realize that thoughts are seeds."

"All the better," Sydney insisted. "When a person draws their own conclusion because of critical thought, the thought has more impact and causes more thought, thus causing growth."

"Always a teacher."

Sydney cut a piece of moist bread with her fork. "In our own way we are all teachers."

Beatrice furrowed her brow. "Who could possibly teach you?"

"Anyone who causes me to be aware of something."

"Like Gwen?"

"Yes, like Gwen. She has made me aware that something is not right between us. She absolutely refused to allow me to examine her arm. It seemed so strange, as though she feared me examining it."

"Others saw her reaction?"

"Yes, many lingered around. Those who work in the keep huddled in groups, whispering tongues sounded throughout the great hall and Eileen cried and wrung her hands in despair."

"It made for quite a scene then."

"Yes, more than what was necessary. It caused a nervous agitation among many." A yawn attacked Sydney.

"You have had a busy day."

"I did, part of it being extremely enjoyable with Duncan." Her broad smile confirmed her remark. "I sometimes feel as though thirteen years have not passed, that we are as we once where."

"In love."

Her smile faded. "Then I am reminded of the reality of the situation and I tremble at the thought. It has been hundreds of years since last we were together, and when he discovers this what then?"

"The information could place both of you in jeopardy."

"I have considered this, but what to do?" She shook her head. "I think it wise to concentrate on the moment and—" Another yawn stole her words.

"And at this moment I would say rest would be wise."

Sydney agreed with a nod and after cleaning up the dishes took herself to bed.

"Tomorrow is another day," she said, slipping beneath the blanket.

"And I will be watching over you," Beatrice said softly after making certain Sydney was tucked safely in bed.

Duncan stood looking out the window of his bedchamber. It was late, very late, but sleep eluded him while thoughts plagued him. The night seemed darker than usual, which meant a promise of rain during the night or perhaps showers tomorrow.

He watched the distance beyond the dense trees just before the rippling hillside. Sydney's cottage lay nestled there, tucked away from the village and the keep, isolated from the world. He worried about her being there alone but she did not seem to fear her isolation.

She could take care of herself; she knew magic.

Though a thought that no one could hear, Duncan still cast an anxious glance over his shoulder. He shook his head at his own fear.

And what of magic? He heard tales of witches flying on brooms in the sky, cavorting naked in the woods with demons, placing spells on people so they would think and do evil things. He thought it nonsense and gossip spread by wagging tongues, but people listened to wagging tongues whether the talk made sense or not. A good tale was a good tale and with its spreading the tale grew bigger, better and even more embellished.

What troubled Duncan the most was that on occasion he had seen Sydney perform unexplainable feats. Gwen had repeatedly warned him that it was not common for a man to think of his lost love for over ten years and many times had insisted Sydney had cast a spell on him.

If he had confided in his sister that he had envisioned Sydney often in the woods she would have insisted he was under a spell. Sydney had told him she had not cast a spell over him, but then Gwen had advised him to be cautious in his trust.

He had not been celibate in the thirteen years they had been apart; if he had he certainly would have known he was under the influence of a spell. Nay, he had been with many women, though none satisfied him the way Sydney had, and though he cared for each woman he never felt love for any of them.

The shadows of the night crept slowly across the land and rain began to fall. Duncan rubbed the back of his neck and rolled his shoulders, easing the taut muscles that gathered at his neck.

He recalled Sydney's magic touch and how she would rub and massage his neck and shoulders, easing his soreness. He would relax as her fingers worked their magic and then she would gently kiss where her fingers had touched.

He stared at the gentle raindrops beginning to fall and thought of how Sydney's kisses were like those soft drops, one fell, then another and another until she rained kisses all across his neck, along his shoulders, down his back— he shivered.

Sex to Sydney was enjoyable and she placed no restrictions or taboos on what they did. One only needed to be willing, and they both were willing participants. They laughed, they teased, they touched and they tasted and they had done all that often.

She never sought to cover herself in shame or shyness. She was comfortable in her nakedness and in his. They had spent much time in her bed lying there with not a stitch on and talking, then touching and then tasting. In the woods when they were certain they were alone they would make love, the earth their bed.

They would bathe in the nearby stream or the small lake nestled deep in the woods and there were times at night when she would coax him into the woods and make love to him like a woman long deprived.

He had relived those moments time and time again and he had warned himself to let go, release her and the memories to the past where they belonged. It never worked. She would invade his mind be it day or night and he was forced to go into the woods to remember. He would sometimes catch a glimpse of her rushing past a tree, the sound of her laughter drifting overhead, or he would see her reflection in the stream. If he were lucky she would walk out of the woods, smile at him and remain a few moments while he talked nonstop then she would simply fade away.

Had that been magic?

Had she somehow projected herself to that time and space to torment him?

Or was he tormenting himself?

He had no answers as usual, though questions haunted him continuously this night. He felt agitated, unable to relax and free his mind. The incident of the fire plagued him. Gwen had been uncommonly uncooperative. She did not want Sydney to touch her and the more she protested that she required no healing, the more upset Eileen became until her crying went on endlessly.

Sydney had reached out simply to comfort Gwen and

she had retreated as if Sydney's touch had burned her. He had not cared for the reaction or for the scattered whispers that quickly circulated the great hall. There would be gossip of the incident and many would speculate why Gwen would not allow Sydney to touch her.

Wagging tongues would soon spread the word and there was no telling what would come of it, though he sensed it would not be good.

What then?

A soft rap on the door forced him to turn away from the window and the rain that fell in a steady downpour. It was late and he wondered over who shared the sleepless night with him.

He was about to open it when he thought of Eileen. He did not wish a visit from her, especially to his bedchamber late at night.

With his hand on the metal latch he wisely asked, "Who is it?"

"Gwen," came the soft reply.

He opened the door for his sister and stepped aside for her to enter.

She did so quickly, nervously motioning for him to close the door. When he did she hurried over to the warmth of the fireplace, extending her hands out and rubbing the chill from them.

The night air was pleasant, though the keep often retained a chill until the days steadily remained warm. Gwen's chill, however, seemed more from her nervous emotions than the temperature of the keep.

"What troubles you?" he asked. She evidently attempted sleep for her long hair hung down her back in a braid and she wore her velvet robe over her night rail.

"I woke from troubled dreams."

Gwen often had troubled dreams and would speak to him about them. He listened as he usually did.

"I dreamed that there was much dissent and arguing in the village and the keep. It seemed many turned against each other, pointing fingers, blaming and crying over troubled times."

Duncan walked over near the window not far from Gwen and rested his arms over his broad naked chest. "Go on."

"There was concern over an impending visit. Some villagers wanted the visit, others feared it."

"Did you see who was to visit?"

"I think he was part of the clergy for he wore the cloak of religious authority, though I could not say for certain."

"What was the purpose of his visit?" He did not like the implication of her dream. He had no doubt it included Sydney.

She lowered her voice. "I think it had to do with witchcraft."

"Was someone accused?"

She nodded. "It seems so."

"And this religious figure was sent to judge?"

"And condemn if necessary."

"Who was being judged?" He assumed it was Sydney and he waited for his sister to condemn.

She rubbed her hands and stretched them out to the fire. "I do not know. My dream did not show me the poor soul."

Her answer surprised him, though she was quick to prove him correct.

"I can only assume it was Sydney. She is a witch."

"Quiet," he ordered. "That word can prove dangerous."

She lowered her voice. "She all but admits it."

She had admitted being a witch to him, but to no one else. She knew the danger in speaking too freely of her beliefs and he intended to keep her secret safe. "I have not heard her speak such to any."

"She need not say a word." Gwen sounded annoyed that he defended her.

"Then how can anyone speak of her in such a way? What proof do they have of her practicing witchcraft?"

"She heals, Duncan."

"A healer is not a witch."

"If a healer heals with magic she is a witch."

Duncan ran his fingers through his hair in frustration. "Sydney needs no magic to heal."

"Use your head, Duncan, Sydney has healed many remarkably."

"Her herbs do the healing. She simply knows them well and uses them wisely. She has studied and learned and refined her craft."

"Witchcraft."

"Healing craft," he corrected sternly.

"You refuse to see the truth." She threw her hands up as if it was useless for her to continue.

"Do not make something of nothing."

"You know me too well to think I would speak out of turn."

"But you do, and in doing so you place Sydney's life in jeopardy."

Gwen shook her head. "Love blinds you to Sydney's true ways and if you are not careful she will soon have you under a spell you will not be able to break away from."

"Sydney uses no spell on me."

Again her hands went up in the air. "You are a fool if you think that. You have pined for her for over ten years, day and night and you think this is normal?"

Duncan was quick to defend himself. "My love for her is strong."

"See," she said, pointing her finger at him. "You admit you still love her, not a thought to her leaving you, the why and wherefore of it, you simply love her and that is that."

Her remark gave him pause. Was he being foolish? Or was he truly in love? Or was it all witchcraft and magic?

"Think, Duncan, think," she said, walking up to him. "You are an intelligent man. Think of all that has happened. Think of how she so easily knew what was wrong with John and Margaret today and she had the healing herbs needed. Was it knowledge or magic to heal so quickly?"

Duncan had given a brief thought to magic when Sydney spoke with Margaret. John's bump could reasonably be caused by the berries, so he thought after listening to Sydney's explanation, but Margaret? Margaret's problem had existed since a short time after her birth and no one could seem to help her. She lived a solitary life except for family, many avoiding her, thinking her plagued with a disease.

What if Sydney cures Margaret?

Is her healing skill so great or is it witchcraft?

Gwen sighed and placed her hand on her brother's arm. "I only ask you to consider the possibility and be careful in dealing with her. I do not wish to see you hurt. And I fear you will be. Sydney has returned to us with far greater powers."

Duncan frowned. "You believe so?"

"I know so," she said in a whisper.

"What do you know?"

Gwen looked toward the door and then at her brother. "Sydney touched my burned arm."

"I know, I saw her."

"Then look at this." She slowly pulled back the sleeve of her robe.

Duncan stared in bewilderment at her arm.

Her skin was clear and healthy with no sign of a burn in sight.

Thirteen

"I want him to love me." Eileen stood teary-eyed in front of Sydney.

Villagers had been arriving steadily at Sydney's door since yesterday. It seemed that in one week's time John's bumps had disappeared and Margaret's face had cleared and she shined with beauty. All the young men in the village pursued her and she had thanked Sydney personally, bringing a beautiful deep green knitted shawl as a gift.

Many had made reference to her magical touch, though did so in a whisper, and as before they began to request potions and spells.

Eileen sniffled. "Several women in the village told me of your skill. Two insisted that I come see you, for without your help they would never have found husbands. I want a husband; I want Duncan."

Sydney empathized with the young woman's plight. She was desperate to love, feeling incomplete without it. She possessed no courage or strength of her own; she needed another's strength and she believed that to be love.

"A spell cannot force one to love another. A spell only works if it is for the good of both individuals." Sydney did not expect the young woman to understand, but neither could she simply offer her a spell and expect it to work. The success of a spell required that it be beneficial to all. It was simple, but few understood the concept.

It was a deeper form of understanding that most regarded as evil, but then that would mean that knowledge was evil, for the more knowledge gained the more power the individual possessed. And even in the future spell casting was misunderstood and ignored by those who knew no better.

Eileen shed tears, wiping them away with the sleeve of her tunic. "It is good for us both, the spell will surely work."

This was difficult for Sydney, watching this young girl desperate for love, love from a man Sydney herself loved. "You feel this is good for Duncan?"

"Aye, it is. I will be a good wife. I will obey my husband, see to his wants and needs, give him fine sons and please my family with the joining of our clans."

"But will you love him?"

"Your spell will make it so."

"Do you wish to love him? Do you find him appealing?"

Eileen thought over the question, chewing at her bottom lip.

Sydney took a moment to pour them tea. A cup of fine brewed tea could settle the most difficult of problems.

Eileen plopped down in the chair at the table, her elbow resting on the edge and her chin resting in her hand. Tears trickled down her face. "My father warned me that a union with Duncan was beneficial to both clans and I was to do my duty."

"What do you wish Eileen?" Sydney handed her a fine china cup that would not exist for another couple of hundred years.

The young girl did not notice, she simply accepted the

cup and sipped at the comforting brew. Then, after careful thought, she answered. "I favor a young man I have known since childhood. William is his name." She smiled and brightened at the thought of him. "We talk often, share laughter and have shed tears together. He has a spot of land he farms and raises sheep. I spin a fine yarn of wool and we had talked of how we could work well together." Her smile faded. "My father thinks differently. He wants Duncan's protection. Duncan is known for his bravery and his clan has lived in peace for many years. My father wishes such peace."

"Have you spoken of this to Duncan?"

"I dare not," she said with a start.

"Why?"

"He would not understand, and besides, it is not for him to understand. It is for me to see to my clan's safety."

Sydney nodded and knew exactly what was necessary. "Perhaps a spell of understanding should be cast."

Eileen's eyes rounded. "A spell of understanding?"

"As I have told you, a spell must benefit all, and if all understood, all would benefit."

Eileen paused to consider.

Sydney offered further explanation. "The spell would work for the good of all."

Eileen seemed to suddenly understand. "My father would see that I loved William, and Duncan would see that it would be good for our clan to join with his and my father would be pleased?"

"Aye, all would understand, all would benefit." Sydney paused a moment. "You love William?"

Eileen blushed. "I think I have loved William since I was five years old and he picked a flower, though he crushed the delicate petals, and handed it to me." She grinned. "He still picks flowers and hands them to me— but he does not crush the petals anymore."

"He sounds like a special young man."

"Very special." Her smile once again faded.

"You wish to wed this William, do you not?"

"I have always wished to wed William."

"Then it would be beneficial to you both, for obviously from what you tell me he loves you as you do him," Sydney said. "Which means if you cast a spell to love another, it would surely fail."

Eileen sighed. "I was attempting to please my father."

"You need no spell for that, you simply need to talk with Duncan about the clans joining together. He is a fair man and one that understands the strength of numbers. It is better to have many friends than many foes."

"You think this true?"

"I know it is true. Ask him and you will be pleased with his response."

Eileen shivered and hugged her cup in her hands. "I do not know if that is wise." She brightened suddenly. "What if you were to cast a spell over him, then he would accept the joining of our clans without the necessity of marriage."

Sydney realized that the only way to solve Eileen's dilemma was to give her a spell that would suit her need. Her need was to stop worrying and speak with Duncan.

"I will give you a spell, but it is strong and once cast it is done and cannot be recalled."

Eileen nodded vigorously. "It will work quickly then?"

"As quickly as you want it to."

"I want it instantly," Eileen said with excitement. "For then I can return home to William."

"And so you shall," Sydney said. "Cast the spell when you return to the keep and tonight ask Duncan if he would consider joining his clan with yours without the two of you having to wed. Tell him you love another and have since you were young, but you would be pleased if he would remain your friend."

Eileen stared at her with her mouth agape.

Sydney reached out and patted her arm. "You will have cast your spell and Duncan will quickly agree to all you say."

"Truly?"

"I give you my word."

"Tell me the spell," Eileen said softly though eagerly.

"Just before you come upon the keep, near the edge of the woods, stop and extend your hands to the heavens above and recite these words. But—" Sydney warned gently, "you must believe with all your heart."

"I do, I do." Eileen nodded.

"Good, for without belief and faith in the spell it will not work."

"It will work; I know it will."

Sydney heard the conviction in her voice; she believed and would have the strength to do what was necessary. "Listen to me and then you repeat it back."

Eileen nodded again.

Sydney raised her hands up. *"Hear my words for they are true; my heart belongs to another not you; let us forever remain friends; and let our clan ties never end."*

"That is perfect."

"Then repeat the spell to me, so it will set well in your memory."

Eileen repeated the spell with determination.

Sydney squeezed her hand. "It shall work, this I promise you."

Eileen took tight hold of Sydney's hand. "You must come to the keep this evening. I will feel safer and more confident with you there."

Sydney argued gently. "You do not need me. You will do well on your own."

"Please, I so want this to work. I want to return home to William and I wish for Duncan to be happy."

Sydney could not refuse her. She was more courageous than most thought and while the sight of blood might make her cower, she possessed a deep strength in her heart.

"I will tell them I invited you; you will be welcome."

"Should I worry about being welcome?" She had known Duncan was called away to settle a dispute with a nearby

clan. He had sent word he would see her when he returned,
which Beatrice had discovered would be today.

Eileen nervously rubbed her hands together and averted
Sydney's eyes. "There has been talk."

"Talk or gossip? There is a difference."

"A bit of both," Eileen admitted reluctantly. "The villagers talk of how skilled you are and they gossip about
how you acquired your skills. Some believe while you were
gone you learned and others believe that—" She shook her
head.

"Do not be afraid to tell me. I need to know or else I
cannot protect myself."

"Others believe that you work with the devil."

"And you, Eileen, what do you believe?"

Eileen was fast to answer. "I believe you a good woman;
though your ways are strange to me, I do not believe them
evil or I would not have sought your help."

"I am pleased to hear that and I will come to the keep
tonight."

Eileen jumped up and threw her arms around Sydney.
"You have made me so happy. I know now everything will
be fine. It will work out as it should for the benefit of all."

Sydney returned the hug and then bid a smiling Eileen
good day.

"A walk in the woods?" Beatrice asked, flying through
the open window.

"Yes, a walk in the woods is what I need. I have much
on my mind," she said, standing, and as she left the cottage
she grabbed the basket that hung on a peg by the door.

She wore the simple skirt and blouse of a villager, but
in the spring and fall she always draped a shawl around her
waist. Tonight however she would dress as she pleased,
which would probably give tongues more reason to wag.
Not a good idea, but tongues would wag regardless.

Finn approached her as she walked deeper into the
woods. She always waited for him to come to her for she
knew that was his way. She rubbed behind his ear, patted

his head and told him she was grateful for his friendship. He then followed beside her, ever alert to his surroundings.

"What troubles you?" Beatrice asked.

"I do not know." Sydney sat on a fallen tree, placing the empty basket beside her. Finn sat leaning against her leg.

Beatrice flitted down to rest on Finn's head. He seemed not to mind at all.

The three after all were friends, outcasts to most, and they protected each other.

"I feel there is something I should be aware of but I cannot seem to grasp what it is," Sydney said with a sigh. "I do wish Sarina was here. She sees far beyond the ordinary. I sense at times—" She shook her head. "But I do not possess the skill of sight."

"You possess awareness beyond the ordinary," Beatrice reminded.

"If that is so then what is in front of me that I am not aware of?"

"If you have trouble understanding what it is perhaps it is because you do not wish to see it clearly."

"I thought of that, but dismissed it. I have kept an open mind and heart knowing it was necessary. I almost feel as if someone is preventing me from understanding."

"A spell?" Beatrice sounded alarmed. "You think someone cast a spell around you?"

Sydney shook her head again. "I don't know, but I feel there is more going on here than I had thought. I was young and lacked experience the last time I was here. Now I sense something I did not sense before and it troubles me."

Beatrice rubbed her chin. "And do you think what troubles you could have had something to do with why you and Duncan separated?"

"Anything is possible. I allowed my emotions to rule many of my decisions and choices in my youth. Maturity has a way of teaching you otherwise. While my heart aches desperately for Duncan, I know whatever is meant to be will be. And if I must shed tears again, I will, though I will try with all the powers of love to see that I do otherwise."

"You will fight for him then?" Beatrice asked.

"Yes, I will fight, for I know he loves me and wishes the same. I would not force my love on him if I thought he did not love me in return."

"Then who interferes?"

"That is the question," Sydney said. "Who interferes with our love? And did this person or persons interfere the last time?"

"You must think and remember," Beatrice advised.

"And look for someone I thought was my friend."

"But who was not."

"And continues to remain my foe," Sydney said sadly.

"You must be careful," Beatrice warned. "You never know how far this person or persons will go to have their way."

"They got their way the last time."

"And I imagine they plan to have their way this time."

"I think not," Sydney said forcefully. "I am no longer a naïve, young woman in love. I am a strong and wise woman and—"

Beatrice watched her stand and waved her hand in the air while reciting strong words and the little fairy urged Finn to step back. She remained on his head as he stepped behind the fallen log and lay down behind it.

The wind picked up, sending forest debris swirling and a warm, bright light circled the small clearing, causing Beatrice and Finn to squint their eyes and watch, amazed at Sydney's transformation.

Fourteen

It appeared as if the whole village celebrated Duncan's re-turn. There was much food, drink and merrymaking going on and the meal was about to be served when the doors opened and Sydney stepped in.

A hush fell over the crowded hall. All eyes went to her and many a mouth fell open. Whispers flooded the room until it sounded like a buzzing beehive.

Sydney walked into the hall with grace and confidence. She wore a black dress that flowed down around her body, resting gently over her hips to pool at her ankles. The long sleeves fell to points on the back of her hands and on each point hung a tiny teardrop crystal. The neckline scooped low, highlighting her ample cleavage. Her dark hair was fashioned in waves, ringlets and curls and pulled away from her face to cascade in a massive riot down her back. And a crystal pendant hung around her neck on a delicate chain while tiny crystals graced her ears.

To everyone's surprise Eileen stood up. "Good evening, Sydney, I am so glad you came." She courageously announced to all that Sydney was there at her invitation.

Sydney smiled. "I am pleased to join in the revelry."

Eileen glanced around the hall seeing where she could offer Sydney a seat.

Dora settled her problem. She stood and motioned Sydney with her hand. "Come join Thomas and me."

Eileen looked relieved, especially after Sydney discreetly cast her eyes toward Duncan, silently letting her know that now would be a good time to test the spell. The young girl sat and gathered her courage.

Sydney sat between Dora and Thomas at the long table and conversed easily with them as she kept a watch on Eileen.

"Duncan." Eileen feared she spoke too low or perhaps he chose to ignore her when he did not answer or even turn to acknowledge her. She waited a moment and tried again with more gusto. "Duncan."

Duncan was deep in thought. He could not get his mind or eyes off Sydney. She looked amazingly beautiful and damned if he had not missed her. She had been on his mind day and night in the short time he had been gone. He had fought his feelings and his concerns.

Ever since that night Gwen had showed him her miraculously healed arm he had been concerned. Had Sydney's touch healed the burn instantly? And if so, how? Had her magical skills grown more powerful in the thirteen years she had been gone?

He was not certain what to believe anymore. How much was truth? How much was magic? Where had she gone and what had she done in those years?

"Duncan!"

He turned with a start to glare at Eileen. He had never expected to hear her use such a forceful tone, especially with him.

"I do not mean to disturb your thoughts, but there is a matter of great importance that I wish to discuss with you."

He did not know if he wished to deal with this now, but

then he had been putting Eileen off ever since her arrival and she had finally gathered the courage to speak to him. His only choice was to tell her the simple truth. He did not love her and did not wish to wed without love.

His sister Gwen refused to understand the simple concept, but he was adamant. He would not live out his days with someone he did not love. It was unfair to him and unfair to her.

So that she would not be upset or feel foolish he was about to explain how he felt when words rushed from her mouth.

"I was wondering if you would agree to our clans joining forces without benefit of marriage?" She nervously wrung her hands, but continued, determined to voice her concerns. "You see, I love another, William is his name. I have loved him since I was a young lass and I wish to wed him. I have made no mention of it to you because my father expects me to do my duty to the clan as your sister expects the same of you. But I see that you and I are not meant for each other. You need a strong woman who can deal with your strong will. I prefer my William. He is a farmer and strong in ways others are not, but he loves me and I love him. And our clans will benefit from joining forces."

She ran out of breath, giving Duncan a chance to talk. "I agree."

His words stopped her, her mouth agape ready to continue.

"All you say makes much sense." He smiled. "And I do not wish to prevent you from wedding the man you love. Our clans need no wedding vows exchanged for us to join forces. I will decree it and it will be so. There is strength in numbers. And I intend to tell your father how courageous you are and that it is because of your courage that our clans join."

"Truly?"

"Aye, truly," he said, admiring her for speaking the truth and relieved of the burden of a marriage he never wanted.

"I am so happy." In a lower voice she whispered, "It worked, it truly worked."

"What was that?" he asked, not certain of her words.

"Nothing important," she said with a smile.

Duncan felt differently. Somehow he thought it vital he hear her whispered words. "Aye, it is important, tell me."

Eileen became nervous. "It really matters not."

The more she protested the more he felt the need to hear her words.

Her eyes quickly sought Sydney and when Sydney caught them she could see the panic rushing over the young girl.

Sydney sent her a gentle look and softly recited a spell of calm.

Duncan caught the exchange and grew annoyed. Something was not right; he could feel it and he intended to find out. He turned a tender smile on Eileen; after all, there was no point in upsetting the young woman.

She stood before he could say a word. "Excuse me, I must have a word with Sydney."

She moved quickly, giving Duncan no chance to stop her.

Gwen moved into Eileen's seat, an anxious smile on her face. "It is settled then, you will wed. I saw how you both talked and smiled, I assume it is finally done, that Eileen gained enough courage to discuss it with you."

"She has courage all right," he said, watching her hurry over to Sydney and squeeze in between Thomas and Sydney so that they protectively flanked her sides. "She told me how she loves another and wishes to marry him."

"What?" Gwen asked, sending the young woman a scathing look, not that it mattered, she was too busy conversing with Sydney.

"She also wondered if the clans could join without benefit of our wedding."

Gwen huffed. "You told her nay that it is impossible."

"Why is it impossible? Two clans strong is better than two clans alone."

"You gave your consent to this joining?"

"Aye," he said without hesitation. "The joining will benefit both clans."

"But what will keep the clan faithful to us when there is no benefit of marriage?"

"It is what both want and as the clans thrive the commitment will grow."

"Foolish thinking," Gwen admonished.

"You have your opinion, sister, but I rule the clan and the decision is mine."

Gwen held her tongue; her glance settled on Eileen and Sydney. "Many have sought Sydney's help during your absence. They seek spells and potions."

"That is not unusual. They sought the same from her the last time."

"I was told that Eileen went to see Sydney today."

"Why?"

"I do not know," Gwen answered. "Someone merely mentioned it in passing. They happened to be leaving Sydney's cottage when she walked in."

"Are you implying something, dear sister?" He had to ask, for the thought that Sydney had given Eileen a spell immediately crossed his mind when his sister spoke of her visit.

"It makes one wonder, how can it not? Why would she seek Sydney's help if not for a spell or potion?"

"Perhaps she was ailing," Duncan said.

"She has complained of no ailment since her time here."

"That does not mean she was not feeling poorly, perhaps she did not wish to burden you and therefore sought the healer's help."

"You want to believe she went to Sydney for anything but a spell," Gwen said accusingly.

"What need would Eileen have for a spell?"

"The need of you not seeing your duty and wedding her

so the clans would unite in permanent strength."

Duncan shook his head. "No spell would work for I had no intention of wedding Eileen."

"How do you know this? Given more time and thought how do you know you would not have seen the benefit of the union and wed for the good of all?"

Damn his sister for placing doubt in his mind and damn him for doubting. He had been adamant about other decisions but when given time and clear thought he had wisely altered his opinion and ultimately his decision. Still he did not want to believe that Sydney provided Eileen with a spell that was intended for him, for then he would question if his love for her was real—or was it a product of a magic spell?

"I have thought," Gwen said, her voice remaining low, "where Sydney could have been these past thirteen years. Has she become friendly with another clan? Have her travels taken her far? Has she come to know many? We know little about where she has been and what she has done, though I must say she appears more learned. But I wonder where and who she has learned from."

His sister had a way of setting him to thinking. While he had given thought to those very questions he had ignored the answers. He had been so thrilled at Sydney's return, so thrilled at holding her in his arms again that all else was ignored. And that was not his way; he had often demanded answers when necessary and until a satisfactory reply was given he held firm and made no further move. He had not done that with Sydney. He was rushing back into the way their relationship once was without regard to the past thirteen years.

Was he under a spell or was he truly in love?

Gwen placed her hand on his arm. "I want what is good for the clan and I want you happy, brother, though happy of your own accord. And we must consider the consequences of Sydney's presence."

Duncan looked at her strangely.

She lowered her voice to a hushed whisper. "The villagers call her a witch. They believe she heals with magic, and seeing how beautiful Margaret looks I wonder if they are not right?"

Duncan defended her. "She is wise in the ways of healing—that does not make her a witch."

"True, but tongues wag and gossip spreads and it spreads far and wide eventually. Who will it bring to our clan? And will the visit be a welcome one?"

"We are high in the Highlands and left to ourselves. We have our ways, our beliefs, and we will live as we choose. Our healers have always seen to our needs and have done well by us."

"And why is that? Now it is believed that their knowledge comes from evil and they serve that evil so that they may have powers unlike others. I heard of a whole clan that took ill and the only survivor was the healer."

"Nonsense and nothing but gossip that proves to hurt and punish the innocent."

"You think Sydney innocent?" Gwen asked. "Look at her. Do you really believe she is one of us? Do you really think she has gained her knowledge from studies? And if she has walked this land and studied these past thirteen years then why do her feet not bare the signs of wear and why do her hands look smooth and soft? If she has dug in the dirt for plants, roots or berries her hands should show the signs of one who toils in the earth. Unless of course her knowledge comes from elsewhere."

"I thought you cared for Sydney," Duncan said, annoyed with his sister for sounding sensible.

"I do care and that is why I question. Sydney was a good friend and good healer to the clan, but she left and sent no word to us in all those years. Now she returns, from where? And why? You cannot tell me you have not asked yourself the same."

"Nay, I cannot," he admitted reluctantly. He had asked himself the same questions repeatedly. He had intended to get answers, yet Sydney found a way of evading them without him realizing it, until later when he would remind himself he had received no clear answer.

"We have the clan to think of, Duncan."

"So you remind me every day," he said, annoyed.

"While it may seem burdensome to you, it is your duty."

"I need not be reminded of my duty. I place the clan's welfare before my own and I will continue to do what is necessary."

Gwen hesitated a moment. "Even if it means asking Sydney to leave?"

"That would not benefit the clan and the clan wishes her here."

"And if they did not?"

Duncan shook his head, suddenly feeling weary. "I would address the situation if and when it was presented to me."

"And do what must be done?"

"I have never faltered in doing what is best for the clan. Do you doubt me now?"

"Nay," Gwen said softly. "I do not doubt your strength."

"Then why do you sound doubtful?"

Gwen glanced at Sydney, who was smiling and enjoying her conversation with those around her. "I worry about *her* strength."

Duncan rubbed the back of his neck as he relaxed back in his chair. He had so looked forward to returning home—home to Sydney. Now he wished he could escape his home, but then the thought had crossed his mind on other occasions.

What would it be like not to have to worry about the welfare of all? His thoughts could not be only for him and his decisions were never based solely on his needs. He could not complain about clan life; it was good and he had many friends, though he wondered how true their friendship.

Thomas was his one true friend; others respected him

because he was their leader, and then there was Sydney.

Friend, foe, lover; who was she?

He glanced over to where she sat. She looked stunning, and one would think out of place, her dress so different from those around her, but she blended well with the villagers, eating, drinking and laughing along with them.

All were having a good time—all except him.

Gwen had gone off to talk with Bethany and they looked to be enjoying themselves.

He would not sit and sulk. He would seek the night air and think—alone with no one to disturb him. He worked out many problems that way, in solitude. Being on one's own at times was best. You could clear your head and find sensible solutions to insensible situations.

Besides, inaction produced nothing; action produced results.

He stood and waited a moment. No one paid him heed; they were too busy in their revelry.

He left the dais and made his way toward the doors. He was anxious to be alone, eager for the night to swallow him up and grant him solitude. His mind was ready for deep thought, contemplation—answers.

Without thought to his actions he marched over to where Sydney sat and he reached over her to grab her wrist.

She tilted her head back to look up at him, not at all startled by his presence.

"Come with me."

It was an order and all knew it.

Sydney smiled. "Of course, I was waiting for you."

Fifteen

The waning moon was shrouded by clouds and caused the night to appear darker and a bit more ominous. A portent, or a sign of bad weather to come? Or was there a difference?

They walked the outskirts of the keep, the outside torch flames lighting their path and their hands firmly locked together.

Duncan told himself that he held her hand firmly to guide her in the dark, for if she should trip he would already have a firm grasp on her and she would not fall. He told himself this but knew better. He held her hand simply because he liked the feel of it in his.

Her skin was warm, smooth and comforting, and then there was the scent of her. It drifted around him like a gentle breeze. It was a soft sweet scent unfamiliar to him and one that tempted his senses.

Clear head.

The lightning thought cleared his head. He wanted to talk with her and if he did not keep his head clear he would soon be kissing her and touching her and . . .

He let go of her hand. "We need to talk."

"A good idea," Sydney agreed. "Would you like to return to my cottage? We'll have privacy there."

Too much privacy he did not need. "I think here would be fine."

Sydney nodded, hiding her smile with her hand.

Silence reigned for several minutes.

She knew he gathered his thoughts and words and it was time. They needed to talk honestly no matter the consequences, for only in honesty could they find any hope of their relationship surviving.

Though in honesty she might very well lose him.

"Tell me what you have done these past thirteen years."

She tried to remember the thirteen years that followed their separation but they were vague or perhaps she did not wish to recall them. She had missed him terribly and had poured herself into her studies, something she had continued to do all her life.

Where did she start with him?

Slowly.

It was the only way.

"Much of my time was spent in study."

He was glad to hear it, for it would explain why she was an excellent healer.

"I traveled a great deal, learning from various teachers and cultures."

"You left Scotland?"

How did she tell him that she had traveled the world many times—a world unfamiliar to him? How did she explain centuries of change she had witnessed? How did she make him understand the depth of her knowledge?

Time—it would take time to explain it all and his question had been simple and a good place to start. She had to remember he wished to know of the past thirteen years, not the last few hundred years.

"I did not leave Scotland immediately. It was several years before I left its shores."

Why he felt relieved he did not know. After all, she had left, so what difference did it make where she went? But it did make a difference to him, though he was damned if he understood why.

"You remained near?" Why did he feel the need to ask? To know? Would it make a difference?

"Not close by," she said, remembering how Tempest, the Ancient One, had found her alone and heartbroken. She had taken her in and had taught her. Sydney had been privileged to have her for a teacher for there was none as skilled and powerful as she. And she needed to lose her thoughts in something for she forever thought on Duncan. Try as she might she could not chase him from her mind or heart.

"North, south?"

"North."

He almost hesitated before asking, "Were you alone?"

Sydney shook her head. "A wise woman took me in."

Relief rushed over him once again. "She taught you these skills you now use?"

"Much more," Sydney said and paused a moment to remind herself that she had spent many years with Tempest, many more years than the thirteen that he had thought separated them.

"She was a skilled healer and believed as you?"

"Her healing skills far surpassed mine." Sydney recalled watching Tempest lay her hands on an injury and mend it in mere minutes. "Her wisdom goes far beyond the ordinary."

"She is a witch?"

"If you believe a wise woman a witch."

"Does she cast spells, mix potions?"

Sydney thought of the many spells she had seen Tempest cast and those she had heard of and then there was the powerful spell, only one of her strength could cast, on the man she had loved. She had placed him in a void of time to return one day in the future and amend his wrong.

"Aye, and she does it well."

He shook his head and tried to contain his annoyance. "Why would a wise woman need to cast spells or mix potions?"

"Sometimes it is necessary, for it helps another. We have discussed this before, Duncan, and might I remind you at length. I have repeatedly explained that only if a spell is beneficial to all parties can the spell succeed."

"So the love spells you give the village women will only work if the pair wish to love?"

"That is right. If a woman loves a man but he does not love her then the spell will be useless."

"But the women in the village say that the love spells you have given them have found them husbands."

Sydney laughed. "And why do you think that is?"

Duncan thought a moment and then smiled. "You never name a particular man, do you?"

"Exactly. I prepare the spell so that the woman will attract a man who is attracted and suited for her."

"So the spell cannot fail."

"How can it when it is suited for both individuals? A spell cannot harm." She thought about the dark side of the craft.

"Your smile fades."

"There are those who practice the dark side of the craft. They are no different than the evil done by man to the innocent for they both seek the same—wealth, power and control."

"If the dark side cast spells and a spell cannot harm, how can the spell work?"

"Fear."

"Fear makes the spell succeed?"

"Think of it, Duncan," she said, slipping her arm through his and walking along the side of the keep, the torches lighting their path. "When you go into battle if you are not

determined, certain of your cause, does not doubt set in and
eventually fear nip at your heels?"

"There is fear in battle regardless."

"There is fear in death, not the battle."

"True, I cannot say I ever doubted the reason for any
battle I fought."

"The dark side plays on those fears and desires as well,
so when a spell is cast the fear that is already present
grows."

"And gives the spell success."

"Now you understand."

In a way he did, not completely, though he was willing
to learn more. And where he had been reluctant to ask if
Eileen came to her for a spell, mostly because he feared
the answer—that word fear again. He now asked out of
curiosity.

"I heard that Eileen visited with you today."

"Aye, she did. She requested a spell."

He smiled at her honesty.

"That is what you wished to know, is it not?" She
hugged his arm.

He recalled how she would often do that when they
walked and how he looked forward to every hug. "I would
like to know about the spell."

"Since the spell involves you I will tell you, if it did not
then I would expect you to respect her right to privacy."

Duncan shook his head. "You have strange ways and
strange ideas."

Sydney thought of the future and all the changes women
and men would face. "Nay, I have wise ways and ideas."

"We will talk more of these ways and ideas of yours,
but first tell me of this spell that involves me."

"Eileen has spoken to you of her love for another." Sydney knew the young girl had, for when she sat down at the
table beside Sydney she had whispered that the spell had
worked and that she was so very happy to be going home
and home was where she was going as soon as possible.

"Aye and glad I was to hear it. If she had told me sooner her worry and my concern could have been avoided."

"So you do not wish to wed Eileen."

"I have never wished to wed Eileen. I tried to make my sister understand this, but when she feels she is right there is no talking with her. My sister is too strong-willed in opinion and thought and I know she is not always pleased with my decisions. But I lead the clan and my say is final."

"Then it would have been difficult for Eileen to speak of her love for another to your sister."

"Impossible, but not impossible to speak with you. You have a way of listening to people that always amazed me," Duncan said.

"Eileen did speak to me and she was fearful about discussing the matter with you."

Duncan stopped walking, grinned and planted a playful kiss on her lips. "You gave her a spell so she would not be fearful to speak with me for you already understood my response."

Sydney's soft laughter drifted up and around them. "You understand all too well. Are you a wise man?"

He shook his head. "Foolish at times. My first thought, when hearing that Eileen visited with you and could possibly have requested a spell, was not of understanding."

"Your temper ruled."

"I do not have a temper," he said, his grin spreading.

She rested her hand on his chest. "Your temper is infamous."

"Only to my enemy; they need to fear me. You need not fear me." He laughed. "But then you never did, not from our first meeting."

"You did attempt to intimidate."

"I did not, I but looked at you."

Sydney poked his chest. "You looked me up and down. You had called for the new healer who had recently took residence in the woods. I remember it clearly for one of your men did not bother to knock on my cottage door. He simple pushed it open—"

Duncan stopped her, grabbing her hand and returning it to his chest. "Your door was always open, at least before we became intimate."

She shook her head. "My door was closed that day; he pushed it open and demanded that I come with him, that the laird of the clan *demanded* my presence."

"I required immediate attention."

"You had a simple cut on your finger."

He slipped his arms around her. "Aye, but I heard the new healer was a beauty and needed to see for myself."

"And you did. I walked into the village and there you are wrestling with a man twice your size and besting him."

"I stopped and paid you heed."

"You stopped and stared. You were bare-chested, sweat pouring off you, your handsome face smudged with dirt and blood and you stood boldly staring."

He kissed her one cheek then the other. "I was stunned by your beauty."

She laughed again. "Your glance went from the top of me to the bottom as if sizing me up for a hunt."

He kissed her lips and whispered, "The hunt is the best part of the game."

She pulled her head back. "And I did lead you on quite a hunt."

"From the start when *you* boldly ran your eyes over the length of me, to my amazement—and stepped right up to me to have a close look with hands firmly on your hips." His hands slid down to rest on her hips. "Have I told you how much I love your hips?"

Sydney knew her hips had spread some in the years that passed, she was no longer a woman of a mere two hundred years and she had questioned if he would still find her appealing. "Not of late."

His hands moved slowly down her backside. "You feel different."

She tried not to tense but could not and even with all her knowledge, the self-satisfaction and pride with the woman she had become—she was still a woman in love and wanted the man she loved to find her appealing.

He leaned down, his cheek next to hers. "You feel better than I remember and my hands ache to touch you intimately."

She moaned softly, threw her arms around his neck and kissed him like a woman in need.

He eased them into the shadows, away from the light, where they could not be seen. Their kiss turned hungry with passion—passion that had lain dormant and buried with the need to forget. But now they did not have to forget, they could remember and they could allow their passion the freedom that had long been denied.

He pulled her body up against his, his hands enjoying the feel of her soft backside. "Damn, but I want you."

She could feel his need, strong and hard, grind against her and she pressed her body closer to his.

Their kiss turned feverish, their hands explored and their need grew to near out of control.

Laughter and raised voices returned them quickly to reality. They hastily stepped apart, both attempting to calm their raging emotions.

The laughter and voices faded.

Duncan shook his head, "This cannot continue."

"I agree," Sydney said with an unsteady breath and held out her hand. "Come with me. We can continue talking and then if you wish you can stay the night with me."

Duncan smiled and took her hand. "I could never deny you anything."

She hugged his hand with hers. "I know and I am glad for that."

"You take advantage of me, woman."

"All the time."

He laughed, though it faded quickly. "How I have missed you."

She stepped up close to him. "Then let us make up for lost time." She kissed him gently.

They walked away from the flickering torchlight and had stepped into the shadows when they heard Thomas frantically shout.

"Sydney, the babe comes!"

Sixteen

Sydney realized from the start that there was going to be a problem with the birth. She had attended, assisted and delivered many babies over her long life span. She had watched technology advance and save lives that would have been lost in another era. And even with all the knowledge she had gained, the technological advances made, she was limited at this point in time in what she could do for Dora and the babe.

She was frustrated, but hid it well. Dora and Thomas counted on her. They had complete faith in her skills.

"The pain is more than I remember when I delivered the girls." Dora attempted to ease herself up in the bed.

Sydney helped her, making her as comfortable as possible. Thomas had carried his wife to their cottage and told Sydney he would do anything she asked of him, but please, please, please, he had begged of her not to let anything happen to Dora or the babe.

She had calmed him, attempted to ease his concern and chased him from the cottage, sending Duncan, who had followed them, a glance that meant he should keep Thomas company. She had then readied Dora and the bed and gathered the items she would need. She had thought that she would require more modern instruments and had done so, concealing them on a sterile tray, beneath a sterile cloth on the table.

Dora's daughters, Kate and Alice, had wanted to remain by their mother's side, but Sydney had convinced her that it might be better if they were not present. She could not have them there if she had to resort to using modern technology or a bit of magic.

Dora grabbed Sydney's arm as she folded the blanket over her rounded stomach. "Tell me the truth, Sydney, will everything be all right?"

The truth was Sydney was not certain, but she planned to do all she could to see that both Dora and the babe survived. "The birth may prove more difficult than you expected, but I will do all in my power to see that both you and the babe are fine."

Dora sighed and released Sydney's arm. "That is all I need to hear. I have faith in your skills and trust you."

Sydney wished Tempest was there, her skills were far greater, but then Tempest would remind her that she had been taught well and was more than capable of handling the difficult delivery.

She pushed up her sleeves with determination, grabbed an apron from a peg on the wall, slipped it over her head and tied it tightly around her waist. "We have work to do, Dora."

Dora smiled. "All will be well; I know it."

Several agonizingly painful hours later Dora's resolve began to decline and Sydney's worry grew. The babe was refusing to birth and Dora was growing exhausted, a dangerous situation for both. If Dora had been in the twenty-first century she would be having a C-section by now, but this was the Middle Ages, and women frequently died in childbirth.

A soft rap on the door sounded before it slowly opened. Thomas peeked his head in. "Everything all right?"

Sydney waved him in then pressed a finger to her lips to signal him to be quiet.

Duncan followed him in and walked straight to Sydney. He kept his voice to a whisper. "I could not keep him away any longer."

She nodded in understanding and looked to Thomas, who slowly approached his wife.

"She rests?" he asked, seeing her eyes closed and her body still.

"Aye, the babe is being stubborn and Dora grows tired."

Thomas turned and rushed to Sydney's side. "That is what happened the last time, and the babe was born dead."

"No life to the child at all?" Sydney asked. "Not even a stir?"

Thomas shook his head. "The babe looked blue to me and the midwife told me there was nothing to be done. The child was dead."

His words gave Sydney a spark of hope. She had thought the babe Dora had lost was stillborn, but from what Thomas described, the babe's air passage may have been restricted. If that was the case this time then there was a chance for both mother and child.

Dora opened her eyes as another pain took hold.

Thomas immediately went to her side. By the time the pain subsided Thomas and Dora were crying.

Duncan sent a concerned look to Sydney.

Sydney immediately took charge. "Out!" she ordered and began shooing both men out the door.

"But—but my wife," Thomas protested, or at least tried to protest.

"Your wife has a healthy babe to deliver. Now out!"

Duncan smiled and slapped Thomas on the back. "Let us go. Sydney appears to be in control of things."

"Aye she does, does she not?" Thomas said walking out

the door. "This is good, is it not? She knows what to do, does she not? She . . ."

His words trailed off as the door closed behind them, though not before Duncan mouthed to her, "I am here for you."

His silent words touched her heart for she was not alone. No matter what happened, she was not alone.

She looked at Dora. "This babe will be stubborn no more."

Relief washed over Dora. "Aye, he has had his way too long."

Sydney went to work preparing a birthing brew that Tempest had taught her. She had been warned to use it only in extreme conditions and this was an extreme condition.

Dora drank the brew without question.

Sydney then prepared her for delivery, assuring her it would not be long. She knew she took a chance with the brew for Tempest had warned of many things that could happen but being prepared, she had been taught, was the key.

"You will do exactly what I tell you, Dora, understand?"

"Aye, whatever you say."

Dora gave a yell. "I can feel him move."

"Good, now hold tight when I tell you and push when I tell you."

Dora nodded, preparing for another pain, and it came— fast and furious. She screamed loud and long.

Thomas heard her outside and cringed. "This is not easy."

Duncan agreed, for Dora's screams upset him. "Nay, it is not, but Sydney tends her well."

"Aye, this I tell myself."

Several villagers gathered around, offering Thomas comfort and support. But there were whispers too from the women who huddled in small groups.

Duncan felt the whispers did not bode well. He was sure

tongues were wagging and not all were wagging good gossip.

The screams continued at a steady pace and grew in intensity until Thomas could not take it a minute longer and ran toward the cottage, Duncan fast behind him.

Thomas burst through the door as the babe slipped into Sydney's hands.

The tiny baby boy was blue and Thomas gave a cry of rage.

Duncan quickly shut and latched the door behind him for several curious faces attempted to see what was going on.

Thomas's cry caused Dora to cry and he rushed to her side.

"Nay, nay, not again," Dora cried, tears running down her pale face.

Duncan went to Sydney's side. She stood in front of the table, her back to Dora and Thomas, and had placed the lifeless babe down.

"Is there nothing that can be done?"

She did not answer him nor acknowledge his presence. She pulled a clean cloth off a tray and Duncan was shocked by what he saw—instruments or weapons—some made of a shiny metal. He remained silent and watched.

Sydney used one of the instruments to clean out the babe's mouth and then she massaged the babe's chest. She leaned over and placed her mouth to the lifeless babe's mouth, offering him life's breath.

Thomas ran over to her, his hands stretched out ready to push her away. "You will not steal my son's soul."

Duncan grabbed him. "She helps."

"Nay, she does not."

Sydney paid them no mind. She continued to administer oxygen to the child, slowly, for his lungs were tiny. He was premature but not by many weeks and a good size, so if she could get him breathing, keep him warm and nourished he could easily survive.

She continued her effort as the two men argued.

"Thomas!" Dora shouted.

The two men turned and stared in horror. There was blood seeping through the blanket that covered Dora.

Sydney gave a quick look. "Lie still, doing nothing, I will be right with you."

She could not leave the babe now, though she knew Dora needed attention, but she needed one more minute—just one.

"The babe is gone, save my wife," Thomas yelled.

Sydney continued working on the babe and just when she thought all was lost, the tiny babe let loose an ear-piercing scream.

"Come here, Duncan," she ordered.

Duncan went right to her.

She wrapped the babe tightly in a blanket. "Hold him upright and rub his back very gently. His lungs need massaging to help him breathe."

Duncan nodded and did as she instructed, though the thought scared him half to death. He was such a wee bit of a thing. What if he did something wrong?

Sydney hurried to Dora and in minutes had the bleeding under control. It was not as bad as it looked. "Rest while I see to your son, then I will clean you up and you and he can rest together."

Dora grabbed Sydney's hand, though not with much strength. "I do not know how to thank you."

Sydney patted her hand. "It is not necessary. Rest now, you need it." She also needed an antibiotic and fluids, which Sydney intended to give her as soon as she saw to the babe. She was not worried about the blood loss. It was not as much as she had feared and with the proper food and liquids Dora would be fine.

The next couple of hours were nonstop work for Sydney. She had chased the men from the cottage, telling them they could return when she sent for them. Thomas had said nothing; he simply cried as he left the cottage.

Sydney cleaned the babe and dressed him in the tiny garments Dora had stitched for him. She wrapped him in a blanket to keep him warm and placed him in the cradle near the fireplace so the flames' heat would add the extra warmth he needed.

He slept soundly, and from the examination Sydney made using a bit of modern technology his lungs sounded clear and his heart good. He would survive.

Dora took more work, being completely exhausted from the whole ordeal. But Sydney managed to change the bedding, wash Dora and get her into a clean nightdress. Then there was the matter of the antibiotic and fluids. She slipped it into a warm brew that Dora finished without protest. She then placed her son into her eager arms.

"You must promise me you will drink much liquids."

"Aye, I promise," she said, reaching eagerly for her son. "He is a fine looking lad, is he not?"

Sydney touched his tiny fingers. "I think he will be as strong as his father."

A tear slipped down Dora's cheek. "He would not be here, nor would I if you had not been here to help us."

"But I was here to help you and glad of it." Sydney fought her own tears. She was feeling the strain of the long night and difficult delivery. There were times she was not certain if she could save either mother or child. She was glad it was over and bone-tired. She needed rest herself, but first there was the cottage to clean up.

With Dora occupied with the babe, Sydney used a bid of magic to rid the cottage of the modern instruments. They would be cleansed and ready if necessary. Then she went to work on cleaning the room until it smelled fresh and looked spotless. Finally finished, she walked over to Dora. "Your husband is most anxious to see you and his new son as are your daughters."

"I am anxious to see them."

Sydney went to the door and was not surprised to see Thomas and his daughters standing there. Duncan stood behind the waiting trio. "Come in and greet the new member of your family."

They rushed in and soon chatter, laughter and sighs filled the room.

After Duncan wished Dora well he walked over to Sydney. She was busy slicing bread and cheese for she knew the family would be hungry after the excitement of the night.

He placed his hand on hers, preventing her from slicing the cheese. "You have done enough. You look exhausted."

She had not given her appearance thought, but now giving herself a quick glance she saw that her sleeves were still pushed up, her hair had fallen from its pins and her face was probably as pale as Dora's.

Duncan whispered in her ear. "You are even more beautiful right now."

She was grateful for his words and suddenly felt the exhaustion of the night rush over her.

"Alice, Kate," Duncan called. "Come finish this task, Sydney is tired."

Before Sydney could protest the two girls hurried over and took control after repeatedly thanking Sydney for all she had done for their mother.

Duncan turned to Thomas and Dora. "I am going to take Sydney home now. She needs to rest."

"I will see you tomorrow, or I should say today since it is but a few hours till dawn?" Dora asked anxiously.

"I will return around midday to see to you," Sydney reassured her. "Though if you need me before then—I doubt you will—send for me and I will come immediately."

Dora sighed with relief. "My thanks again."

Sydney nodded with a smile and walked out the door, Duncan behind her. They were only a few feet away when Thomas called out to them. They stopped and waited as he approached.

"Duncan," he said. "May I have a moment alone with Sydney?"

Duncan nodded and stepped a distance away, affording them privacy.

"I am not good with words," Thomas said, "but there is something I must say to you. I was wrong to yell at you. You saved my son's life and Dora's too. You are a good woman and a good friend. If you ever need help of any kind I will be there without question for you."

"I appreciate that, Thomas, I truly do. And I am glad we are friends and glad I could help. Now go enjoy your new son and see that your wife rests."

Thomas grinned. "He will grow as big as me, I am sure of this."

"I am too," she said with a smile.

Thomas's grin grew wide and he shook his head. "A son, I have a son and I cannot believe it."

Duncan slapped him on the back. "I think you will believe it soon enough, like when he screams at night to be fed."

"His scream will be a pleasure to my ears." He looked again to Sydney. "Again thank you and remember what I said. *Without question.*"

Thomas turned and hurried off.

"He means what he says," Duncan said.

"I know and I appreciate it, and I hope I never have cause to seek his help."

"But it is there if needed. Now let me get you home."

"It is late; I can see myself home." She yawned.

"Aye, it is late and that is one of the reasons I will see you home. The other reason is that you are so exhausted you might not make it on your own."

She gave a thump to her chest. "I can take care of myself."

"Aye, you can, because you are so stubborn." He slipped his arm around her waist and began walking—she had no choice but to follow.

"My stubbornness keeps me going." Another yawn struck her.

Duncan stopped suddenly when they entered the woods. "What is it?"

"I think someone follows us."

Sydney knew who followed. "He is a friend of mine."

"He?" They continued walking.

"Finn, a black wolf."

"Black wolves do not roam this area. Where did he come from?"

"I am too tired to answer so many questions, another day please?"

He hugged her to him. "No more questions. I will get you home and tuck you in bed."

She sighed. "If I were not so tired I would invite you to join me."

"I would not mind sleeping beside you, Sydney."

She dropped her head on his shoulder as they walked. "I miss sleeping next to you."

"Then let us rectify that tonight."

Her eyes began to flutter. "I am so very tired."

"We are not far from home."

They walked on in silence and when they were but a few feet from the cottage Duncan scooped her into his arms and carried her the rest of the way. He placed her on the bed and latched the door. He thought of removing her dress so that she would be comfortable but then thought better of it.

He slipped off his shirt and left his plaid wrapped around him. He removed her sandals, pulled the light blanket up over her and then climbed in bed beside her, tucking the blanket around them both.

He draped his arm over her waist and rested his face next to hers and sighed with contentment. It felt so very good to lie beside her, to feel her warmth, to listen to her soft breathing, to know she was there, truly there beside him once again.

He kissed her cheek and whispered the words he had whispered to her night after night. "I love you."

Seventeen

*Duncan woke with dawn's first light, as was his way. Some-*times he would dress and go outside to greet the great ball of fire that seemed to rise from the earth itself. It was a spectacular sight and it never failed to make him realize that there were things far greater and more powerful than he.

At the moment though the most spectacular sight was Sydney sleeping beside him. He had dreamed often of her cuddled next to him in bed and woke feeling an emptiness that haunted him for hours. But there was no empty feeling today. Today Sydney was here, her warm body firm against him.

She slept soundly, her breathing light, though an occasional snore interrupted the gentle melody and he smiled. They had both aged in the years that had passed, but the passing years had somehow made her more attractive and appealing. Faint lines framed her lips, though they were as luscious and tempting as ever to him.

And then there was her body.

He slipped his hand beneath the blanket and ran it gently over her midriff, down along her waist, over her stomach that rounded ever so slightly.

She sighed softly and stretched to meet his touch.

She had always responded to his touch—always. There was not a time he had touched her that she had denied him or he her. It was as if they were meant for each other.

He thought to touch her breasts but he wanted her awake and lucid so the choice would be decidedly hers. He braced his arm on his pillow and rested his head in his hand and watched her as he ran his fingers gently over her, wondering if she would react as she had always done to his familiar touch.

"You always knew how to wake me." She stretched like a lazy cat, inching closer to his fingers as they roamed gently over her.

"You have slept barely three hours."

Her yawn confirmed that she had not had a sufficient amount of sleep.

He took his hand off her. "Go back to sleep."

She reached for his retreating hand, holding firmly to it. "You will stay beside me?"

"Aye, I will remain by your side."

Her eyes had barely opened to speak with him and closed quickly, her hold remaining firm on him as she slipped into a much needed slumber.

He rested his head on the pillow beside her and smiled. He liked that she held on to him as if she feared he would leave. It seemed as if nothing had changed in the past thirteen years. They remained comfortable and loving with each other.

Why then the separation?

What had happened to them?

The questions haunted his thoughts as he drifted back to sleep.

Sydney woke before Duncan, realizing that she had only a couple of hours before she would return to see how Dora was doing. She expected all to be fine, Dora and the babe needing rest and nourishment, which she knew her family would give her. But Dora also needed medication to make certain no infection set in and Sydney wanted to keep an eye on any bleeding.

Her stomach growled lightly at the same moment she yawned, and knowing her time was limited she chose to address her hunger. She turned to look at Duncan. He slept on his side, his arm draped over her. He made not a sound, nor stirred; he was in a deep slumber.

She remembered waking up many a morning just like this beside him. She would tease him with her fingers or reign kisses over his handsome face and she thought about waking him in such a familiar way.

Her stomach protested a bit more loudly and she recalled her limited time. When they finally reunited intimately she wanted time—time enough for them to linger and enjoy every moment.

A smile crossed her face when she remembered another way she would wake him. She would make him breakfast, the delicious scent always penetrating his sleep and bringing him fully awake with a smile.

She slipped slowly out of bed so as not to wake him and a bright smile came to her lips. She had modern appliances to work with and the task would not take half the time it once had. There was something to say about modern technology, though she would be wise to leave traces to the contrary.

In no time she had bacon cooking, along with potatoes. She minced fresh basil to add to the scrambled eggs and had biscuits browning in the oven. The scent of the fresh brewed coffee made her all the more hungry as she scooped raspberry preserves from a jar into a crock then scooped the butter from the small plastic tub into another crock. The table was set in no time, with the help of a little magic of course, but then she had been busy cooking breakfast without magic so a little bit of it wouldn't hurt.

Beatrice peeked her head up from her sleeping pallet, looked around and smiled. "I guess I will be having breakfast with the fairies."

"If you don't mind. I packed you a basket to take and share with your friends," she said in a whisper.

Beatrice stood, shaking the sleep from her, then hurried to dress. "My friends will be thrilled. They love your cooking."

Sydney walked outside, handing Beatrice the small basket and sending her off with a smile and a wave. Wild flowers mingled with ferns on the edge of the woods and Sydney walked over to gather a few to put in a vase for the table.

Duncan sniffed the scented air, his eyes inching open slowly. The aroma was heavenly and for a mere second he wondered where it came from and then he smiled. He was in Sydney's cottage and she had cooked the morning meal for him. He had always favored her cooking—actually he loved it. She had a way with preparing food unlike others, especially the morning meal. He hated the heavy porridges, breads and meat the cook at the keep would make, and besides, the food tasted bland.

The food Sydney prepared had flavor and just the thought of its taste had his eyes open wide and him swinging his legs out of bed.

He stopped, his hands braced on the edge of the bed where he sat staring across the room. He closed his eyes and shook his head then looked again.

What were the strange looking objects?

None of what he saw made sense. Where were the chests and pegs and narrow table that lined that wall? And what now stood in their place? He had never seen anything like these devices.

A sudden shiver came over him and he shut his eyes, a thought invading his mind that he would never dare murmur. Did these strange objects have something to do with witchcraft? And if so, were they evil devices?

He shook his head. Nay, Sydney was a good woman who cared for people and helped them whenever she could. So what then did he see?

His warrior instincts took over. He would take a good look at these strange objects and determine for himself what they were and he would ask Sydney about them. There was a reasonable explanation and he would find it.

He opened his eyes as he stood and shook his head again. Sydney stood with flowers in hand and behind her were the chests, pegs and table that had always been there.

Sydney kept her smile bright. She had foolishly forgotten to conceal the small kitchen from all eyes before she had stepped out of the cottage. Duncan had slept so soundly and even if he had woken when she was cooking she could have easily concealed the appliances from him with one simple wave of her hand.

She realized her mistake when she returned to the cottage and saw Duncan sitting on the edge of the bed, eyes closed, shaking his head. He had undoubtedly seen the kitchen and probably right now either thought himself crazy or thought her?

What? What would he think of objects he had never seen before or had no idea as to their purpose or use? She would eventually find out, but not right now.

"Hungry?" she asked and added the flowers and ferns to the empty tankard on the table that would serve as a vase for now.

Duncan sat speechless for a few moments, staring past her.

She could tell his mind was muddled but then how could it not be? He had seen strange things with his own eyes and now they were gone. Did he think it magic? And was it fair for her to keep the truth from him?

Being uncertain was a good reason to say nothing until she could reach a reasonable decision. "The meal is ready." She hoped to clear his mind of the strange happening if only for a while and share a pleasant breakfast with him.

He stood, remaining silent, and slipped his shirt on while glancing every now and then to the far wall. He reached for Sydney's comb that she kept by the bed, noticing she had not changed that habit, and ran the thick bone comb through his hair.

He adjusted his plaid around him as he walked to the table and sat. He reached for the filled mug and sipped slowly, the hot steam rising from it warming him.

He raised his brow. "What is this brew?"

Damn, why had she not remembered that coffee was not a familiar drink to this time period—possibly because she dared not think of a morning without it.

She thought fast. "I discovered the tasty brew during my travels."

He sipped again.

"You can add some milk to it if you like." She held up the small pitcher she had filled with pasteurized milk. Too many years of drinking processed milk made her cringe at the thought of drinking any other kind.

"I will try it." He held up his mug to her.

She poured enough milk for flavor.

He tried it and smiled. "I like it."

Leave it to the morning cup of coffee to make you forget everything—at least she hoped—for now he would forget what he had seen.

Duncan ate with gusto, finishing the last biscuit on the tray. "I have missed your cooking."

And she had missed cooking for him. Their meals together had always been special. They would talk and enjoy or silence would reign for they would each be in their own thoughts. It did not matter for they were comfortable with each other in all ways.

"And I have missed you, but you know this for I have told you often enough."

Sydney hugged her coffee mug. "I have missed you and this you know for I have told you many times." She reached her hand out to him and he grasped hold of it. "We need to talk, Duncan, seriously talk. There is much that must be discussed between you and I."

"I agree." He squeezed her hand. "I know you wish to visit with Dora and the babe to make certain all is well. But there is later this afternoon and tonight."

"I will cook you a special meal," she offered.

"And I will not turn it down."

They laughed and then their smiles faded.

"I will not lose you again."

Duncan was adamant and Sydney only hoped that he would remain so after learning the truth.

"I feel the same," she said, holding on to his hand as tightly as she could.

"I will walk with you to Thomas's and then return later for you. We will then return here together."

"Giving orders are you?" She smiled, for she had to remember men were different in this century and while he was not as demanding as some who told their women to hold their tongue or know their place, he still retained a certain degree of authority when speaking to her.

"You never did take well to orders, did you?"

"Nay, I did not and I never will. Does that upset you?"

"It challenges me to have a woman with such a stubborn spirit."

She laughed. "Then I will challenge you well."

He yanked at her hand. "Then come here and challenge me, woman."

She pulled her hand out of his and stood. She had showered and used a soft peach-scented cream on her skin afterward. She had dressed in a simple skirt and blouse and had pinned her hair up, leaving a few strands to fall freely down the back and sides. She was ready for his challenge.

Sydney was not shy when it came to intimacy, Duncan had taught her that, but then she had been comfortable with him as if they were two pieces that once joined formed a whole. And that is how she felt—whole with him.

She took his face in her hands and leaned down to deliver a kiss that had him hard in seconds.

His hand went immediately to her backside, squeezing and urging her closer to him.

She went willingly, pressing his face between her breasts.

He skillfully used his teeth to separate the ties on her blouse and easily found her nipples, taking one in his mouth to play with.

Her breath caught—there was something to say about not wearing a bra. She wrapped her arms around his head, urging him to enjoy for his enjoyment brought her sheer pleasure.

Her nipple turned hard in his mouth and he continued to roll his tongue over and around the solid orb. She tasted better than he had remembered, but then there was not a time she had not tasted good to him. He feasted like a starved man, though he was full—he was empty when it came to intimacy—intimacy with a woman he loved.

The thought of how much he loved Sydney made him grow even more excited and he moved his mouth to her other nipple, relishing the taste of her.

She moaned and sighed and moaned again. "If you do not stop now I will drag you to my bed and have my way with you."

"A woman who demands I make love to her—you are surely one of a kind."

"I will not be kind about it," she warned and grabbed his hair, yanking back his head and kissing him so that he would know her adamant intentions.

The kiss left them both breathless and sent both pair of eyes toward the bed.

"As much as I want you, I do not want it rushed," Duncan said.

"Aye," she agreed. "It has been too long, much too long, and I want a long night of loving with you."

"Does the talk come first?" he asked.

Did it? She wondered herself.

"Let us wait and see what comes naturally."

He squeezed her bottom. "We both know what will come naturally."

"Then so be it."

Duncan glanced past her toward the wall where the kitchen was concealed. "You will tell me of your studies and who you studied with when we talk?"

"Aye, I have nothing to hide." She hoped to reassure him.

His eyes remained on the far wall and she sensed a spark of doubt.

"You will tell me all."

It was a command, not a request, and she understood why. He needed to know the truth for himself for if he did not know the truth then how could he protect her? But how would he respond?

"All that you wish to know."

His smile was one of relief and he slapped her backside. "You are a good woman."

"You just discovered this?" She laughed and tugged at his long hair.

"You have no shame, thinking highly of yourself," he teased.

"Aye, no shame," she whispered and leaned down to tease his lips with a wicked lick of her tongue.

A soft rap on the door broke them apart.

Duncan moved her aside and went to answer it—Alice, Dora's oldest daughter, stood there.

"Is there something wrong?" Sydney asked anxiously.

She shook her head and her glance went to Duncan. "My father sent me to warn you. There is talk in the village of Sydney."

She seemed reluctant to continue, her glance going to Sydney then turning away.

Duncan encouraged her with gentle words. "Go on, Alice, there is nothing for you to fear." He placed his arm around her and gently urged her into the cottage, closing the door.

The safety of the cottage wrapped around her and she willingly talked. "Some of the villagers think that Sydney performed witchcraft on my mother. They say that the babe and my mother should not have lived—that it was the work of the devil that saved her." She began to cry. "I do not believe this." She looked to Sydney. "I think you know much and that is what saved my mother, your knowledge."

"You are right, Alice," Duncan said. "And I will see to making this right."

Alice looked relieved.

Sydney, however, knew he spoke to ease the young girl's concerns and his own. Once witchcraft was mentioned it was difficult to prevent more talk from spreading.

Duncan took her hand and whispered, "I will protect you."

She nodded and wished with all the powers that be that Tempest and Michael were here to help, their powers being far greater than hers, for she had a feeling that things were about to get much worse.

Eighteen

"I am furious," Dora said, sitting up in bed, her temper causing her cheeks to flame like two bright red spots on her otherwise pale face. Her raised voice did not at all disturb the sleeping babe in her arms.

"And I am about to strangle someone," Thomas said, moving a chair by the bed so Sydney could sit and visit with Dora.

Duncan remained silent and appeared unperturbed, but Sydney knew better. It was when he grew the most silent that one had to be careful. His temper was brewing and the results produced a force not many would wish to face. He stood at the end of Dora's bed, arms crossed over his broad chest, feet spread, expression grim; he looked ready for battle.

Sydney sat in the offered chair and attempted to discover exactly what had upset everyone. She placed her hand on Dora's wrist, offering comfort while checking her pulse. "What is the problem?"

Thomas started. "You think the village women would be pleased and happy for Dora—"

Dora interrupted her husband. "There are a few with sense."

"Not enough," Thomas said. "The sensible ones did what was right. They visited with a gift of congratulations, a loaf of freshly baked bread, a fine stew, and a fine-stitched garment for the babe. The others?" Thomas threw his hands up in disgust.

"What did the others offer?" Duncan asked much too calmly.

Thomas was quick to answer. "They came with gifts and—" He hesitated, casting a concerned eye at Sydney.

"And what?" Duncan urged.

Dora answered without hesitation. "Warnings. They actually sat in our home with my newborn babe asleep safely in my arms and told us that by all that was holy—*holy*— that I, and the babe, should be dead. They claim it was evil doings that allowed us to live and we are not held in God's good graces any longer and—" She could not continue; she was much too upset.

Sydney patted her arm and offered a smile. "It is all right. God knows the truth and that is what matters."

"Then he should knock some sense into some heads down here," Thomas said. "There are those who believe protection from evil is needed in the village. They say that now that evil reigns things will happen—bad things."

"Who says this?" Duncan asked.

"What does it matter who?" Sydney said. "Those ignorant enough to listen to nonsense will believe in nonsense and those who wish to find evil will have it knocking at their door."

All three stared at her in silence and she realized her mistake. She sounded as if she cast a spell on those who spoke against her when all she did was offer a bit of wisdom.

"I have no say in such matters," she said, hoping it

would ease the worried looks on their faces. It did not, and she offered the creed not only witches lived by but wise men and women all through the ages. She expressed it simply. "Harm none is my belief."

Duncan's rigid stance relaxed. "Aye, that is what you have often told me."

"But what of the dark side?" Thomas asked, lowering his voice as if afraid someone would hear him. "The clan speaks of it in whispers and believe it exists."

How did she explain that evil lived if given power? Hate is evil. Greed is evil. Ignoring a starving child is evil. Condemning those who believe differently is evil. Why did humans find that so difficult to understand?

Sydney attempted to explain. "If they give evil power, it will then exist."

Thomas shook his head, confused, and Dora seemed not to understand. Duncan, however, appeared to grasp the knowledge.

"So then whatever happens they will blame it on evil."

"Right," Sydney said.

Thomas grinned. "I see. If a clan member grows ill he will blame it on evil."

"Right again," Sydney said. "When that man or woman may have nothing more than an upset stomach from eating too much."

"Thomas knows about that," Dora said with a laugh.

Thomas patted his bulky stomach. "That I do."

"But such is not the common thought," Duncan said with concern. "The church warns of evil and falling prey to the devil and his ways. The church holds authority and power over the people."

"And so they believe as they are told," Sydney said. "Which has caused many innocent people to be wrongly persecuted."

"There are many that would not agree with you," Duncan said.

"Aye, and so innocent people die and countries war."

"Sometimes it is necessary," Duncan said.

"Aye that it is," Thomas agreed. "You cannot let another take your land."

"I agree," Sydney said. "When someone robs another in the name of greed or righteousness that is evil and it must be stopped. But at the moment we speak of one small clan that has lived in relative peace for many years."

"Aye, we have," Dora said. "But we do live far removed from where many travel."

"And our land does not border with anything but the sea," Thomas said. "An unfriendly sea at that."

"Ours is a mostly peaceful land," Dora said. "The few skirmishes we have experienced, Duncan has quelled successfully."

Duncan looked to Sydney. "You are attempting to make us see something. Tell us."

"Think," Sydney said. "You live in peace, most get along—"

Duncan's arms dropped to his sides. "Where then did this talk of evil come from?"

"That is right," Dora said. "Our clan has always worked together with no word of evil, though plenty of gossip that harmed none."

"Someone spreads this talk of evil," Thomas said.

"But who?" Duncan asked. "And more importantly why?"

The babe stirred and began to cry.

"He has his father's appetite," Dora said, with pride. He wailed continuously until Dora laid him to her breast.

"I have things to see to, Sydney," Duncan said. "Wait here until I return and I will take you home. And do not bother to object, it will do you no good."

"I will wait," Sydney said, not fearful of walking the woods alone; Finn was always close by and there was her magic.

The door burst open and Kate rushed in. "Angus has

fallen and hurt himself badly, Sydney, please come help him."

Sydney reacted as was her way; she rushed over to the young, tearful lass. "Take me to him."

Duncan followed Sydney out the door, Thomas directly behind them, Dora insisting she was fine and could see to herself and the babe.

Angus was Kate's good friend and Sydney suspected they cared for each other, Kate being ten and three years and Angus being ten and five years. He was a tall thin lad with bright red hair and a face that would grow more handsome with age.

Clan members gathered around him where he lay on the ground near his home. Kate had explained as they hurried along that he had been repairing the thatch on the roof and fallen. He was in horrible pain and could not move.

Sydney was concerned. She hoped he had not broken his neck or back, and she hurried up to him, kneeling down beside him.

"Where does it hurt?" she asked.

"My shoulder," Angus said through gritted teeth.

Duncan watched as she examined the young lad with a gentle and concerned touch and he listened to the whispers that floated on the air around him. They were waiting to see what Sydney did. Would they condemn her for helping him? And would they condemn her if she could not help him?

He did not care for the feel around him. They waited, waited either way to condemn. Why? What or who had turned them against her? They had once accepted her as their healer without any doubt. What had changed their opinions?

He had to find out, for he sensed that Sydney faced much danger if gossip continued and opinions grew stronger against her.

It did not take long to realize that Angus had dislocated his shoulder. Sydney was relieved for a quick adjustment, though painful, would set him right again, a bit sore he would be but that was all.

Kate kneeled on the young man's other side, holding his hand and looking to Sydney as if she expected a miracle.

Sydney suddenly became aware of the crowd around her and she knew she was being judged by her actions. The outcome did not matter; she would be condemned either way.

She was damned if she did the right thing, and she was damned if she did not, so she went to work doing what was right regardless of what others thought.

"I need to adjust your shoulder, Angus."

"It is broken?" he asked, fear shining brightly in his green eyes.

Any broken bone at that time could bring permanent disability or death since none knew how to treat it properly, so she understood his concern.

"Nay, the bone is not broken." Sydney tried to explain. "It slipped out from where it should be."

Angus looked confused.

Kate spoke up. "Let her do as she must. She is a good healer."

Her words encouraged him and he nodded at Sydney, though he clung tightly to the young girl's hand.

Sydney wondered if she should seek Duncan's help in adjusting the lad's shoulder, but if she did would she place him in harm's way? Would the clan think that she had made him her consort in evil, enabling him to heal the lad's shoulder?

She could not take the chance; while Duncan was stronger and could more easily repair the dislocation, she could not chance placing him in danger. She would see to repairing the injury herself.

With a quick thought to the best way to proceed, she braced her feet beneath his arm and took a tight hold of his forearm.

Angus looked at her bewildered.

"There will be a moment of great pain and then your shoulder will feel better though remain sore for a week or more. Are you ready?" she asked.

Angus grabbed tighter to Kate's hand and nodded, perspiration beading on his brow.

Sydney did not wait, fearing the lad would change his mind. She gave a firm yank and twist and smiled when she heard the bone pop back in the socket.

Angus let out a loud yell and then fell silent. With a surprised expression he looked to Sydney. "It feels better, sore like you said, but not as near as painful as before."

Sydney eased him up to sit with Kate's help.

"Do not lift or swing anything heavy for several days or the soreness will linger," Sydney said.

"He will not," Kate said. "I will see to it."

Angus smiled at her like a young lad in love. "You do not have to bother yourself with my care."

"I want to," she insisted.

Sydney stood and left the two young ones on their own to talk and fuss. She brushed off the dirt that clung to her skirt and noticed the silence. When had the voices hushed and the whispers ceased?

She raised her head slowly and was not surprised to see the grave faces that stared at her.

"You cause him great pain then take it away with more pain," one man said, shaking his head. "That is not right."

"Why?" Thomas asked. "It worked. You see for yourself the lad is better. Sydney is a good healer."

"Aye, that she is," Bethany said, "We do not need to understand the why of her ways. They work, she heals and we are lucky to have her."

"You care not because she has cured your daughter," a woman said. "But how was she able to take away the marks on her face so easily? Where did she get such power?"

Duncan stepped forward in her defense. "Sydney has traveled and studied, learning more about healing ways."

"Where has she learned and who has taught her?" came a shout.

"Aye, where does her knowledge come from?" called out another.

"She heals like no other," a woman yelled.

"How do we know it is not the devil's work?" shouted a woman.

"You all talk nonsense," Bethany said, shaking a fist at them. "You are all fools."

Duncan leaned over to whisper something to Thomas then shouted to the crowd. "Listen to me."

Thomas hurried over to Sydney. "Come with me." He took her hand and pulled her along, not waiting for a response and expecting no protest.

Sydney listened to Duncan's words as she was rushed away.

"I will not tolerate such talk. The devil does no work here and there is nothing to fear."

"Dora's babe was born dead and Sydney gave it life," a woman shouted, causing the crowd to gasp. "I saw the babe laying lifeless in her hands."

"That is nonsense," Duncan said sternly. "Sydney knew what to do to save the babe. The child was not dead."

"She cured John's bumps fast enough," reminded another.

"And there is Margaret's face, not a mark on it," shouted another.

A raised voice somewhere amongst the crowd cried, "I heard that Eileen went to her for a spell and now she will not wed you."

Another collective gasp sounded.

A raised voice in a fevered pitch screamed, "The witch wants you for her own. We are all doomed."

Nineteen

Duncan marched into the keep, furious. Try as he might, he could not make the crowd see reason. They had worked themselves into worry and fear with each word spoken and would listen to no sensible talk. They were convinced that Sydney worked with the devil and no amount of reminding them how they once trusted her completely did any good.

The workers in the keep were even huddled in small groups, whispering and shaking their heads, and Duncan clearly understood that all of them expected him to do something about it.

Gwen entered the hall and with sharp words sent the workers scurrying. She hurried to her brother's side where he stood, his back braced against the table on the dais.

"This is not good, Duncan."

"You do not have to tell me that, but do tell me who started it."

She raised a brow. "What do you mean who? This has been brewing for some time. Have you not realized it?"

"I must be blind for I did not."

Gwen shook her head. "You give the clan reason to talk."

"What do you mean?"

"It started with the wound on your head. It healed remarkably fast and left barely a scar. Then there was John, but curing Margaret really set tongues to wagging. The lass has suffered with the marks on her face since birth. How could Sydney make them disappear?"

Duncan immediately defended her. "She has learned much in her years away."

"What has she learned, and from whom? Then there was Dora's babe."

"Enough," Duncan said, raising his hand to silence her. "I was there and I saw with my own eyes."

"What did you see?" Gwen asked, lowering her voice. "Have you asked yourself? And have you been truthful with yourself?"

Duncan stepped away from his sister. "You speak against, Sydney; I thought she was your friend."

"She is my friend and I tell you what I hear, what is being gossiped about behind your back. If this continues we will have a cleric at our doorstep before we know it and then Sydney will be in serious danger."

Duncan shook his head. "This does not make sense. The clan cared for and protected Sydney. Why suddenly talk of evil?"

"Gossip drifts in from the surrounding area. There is talk of witches doing harm to the innocent, villagers falling ill, crops failing and babes dying. The church is busy investigating and punishing the guilty." She looked about, then whispered, "There have been burnings so that the witch can be freed of the evil that possesses her and she can die whole in God's good graces."

"Nonsense, pure nonsense."

"Do not speak against the common belief or you will be accused accordingly," Gwen warned.

"And who will dare speak against me?" Duncan crossed his arms over his chest in defiance.

"Fear causes many to talk nonsense."

"As they do now."

"The clan has a right to fear, Duncan."

"What right?" he demanded. "Sydney has done nothing but help them."

"Her ways are strange since her return. She even speaks differently at times, using unfamiliar words. And Eileen made mention that she drank a brew at Sydney's cottage and though she had never tasted it before, it was delicious and that the cup she drank it from was like none she had ever seen, beautifully crafted and delicately light in weight. What did she really offer Eileen to drink, and did it change the young woman's mind toward you and marriage and make her think she loves another?"

Unwanted thoughts forced themselves into Duncan's mind and he recalled the strange instruments he had seen Sydney use on the babe and the odd objects he had seen in her cottage.

"You have your doubts, I see it on your face," Gwen said. "I accuse Sydney of nothing, but I do wonder where her new knowledge was acquired and if evil had any hand in it."

Duncan rubbed the back of his aching neck. "I cannot believe she has anything to do with evil."

"Why, because you love her?"

Duncan stilled all movement and glared at his sister. "Aye, Gwen, I love her with all my heart."

"Be sure you love her of your own free will and not because of some spell she has cast over you."

He was quick to defend. "She would not do that."

"You know her so well?"

He hesitated for he knew her well once, but that was thirteen years ago. How well did he really know her now?

Gwen placed a gentle hand on her brother's arm. "Be

sure, that is all I ask of you. Be sure. I do not wish to see you hurt again or the clan suffer."

"Have no fear, I will not see the clan suffer," he reassured her. "I know my duties."

"Then do what you must. What you know is right."

A young woman entered the hall, rubbing her hands nervously, and approached Gwen reluctantly.

"What is it?" Gwen asked when she stopped a few feet away from her.

"A problem with the food."

Duncan recognized her as one of the cook's helpers.

"What problem?" Gwen asked.

"Insects," the young woman said with a shiver and crossed herself, mumbling a prayer.

Gwen looked to Duncan and he understood her silent message. The clan would assume that Sydney had something to do with the insects. She expected him to do something.

He gave her a nod and she hurried off with the young lass.

What now?

He did not hesitate. He marched out of the keep directly to Thomas's cottage.

Sydney was just placing a freshly bathed babe into Dora's arms when the door to the cottage was thrown open.

Duncan stood in the doorway like an avenging warrior and Sydney instinctively knew something was wrong—very wrong.

Dora hugged the babe to her and remained silent.

"There is a problem with food at the keep," he said, entering and shutting the door behind him.

"Something that needs my help?" she asked, untying the apron she wore and slipping it from around her neck to hang on a peg.

"Insects!"

The one word delivered so vehemently made Dora shiver.

Sydney stared at him. "Am I being accused of something?"

"Many will see it as such."

"And you?"

Duncan noticed how Dora squirmed uneasily in the bed. "Let us discuss this elsewhere."

Sydney nodded, then turned to Dora. "Rest, you and the babe do well."

"Thank you for everything, you are a good friend."

Sydney smiled, pleased that Dora trusted her and wanting Duncan to know it.

Sydney followed him out the door and to the small garden behind the cottage. It was out of view of many and would give them a bit of privacy to talk.

He was blunt. "You did not cause the insects?"

Sydney sensed his doubt but also sensed his inner struggle. Part of him believed in her and another part needed to believe in her. Doubt was a powerful weapon, and someone was skillfully using it against him.

A sudden thought jolted her before she could respond. *Was there another witch working dark magic against her?*

"You need to think on the answer?"

"Nay," she said, shaking her head. "I did not infest your food with insects."

"Could you? Are your skills that powerful?"

She would not lie to him. "Aye, my skills are that powerful."

"Why would you learn to inflict insects on food?"

"It is not something you learn in particular; it is more the dark side of magic, and it takes fear to give it life."

"Are you telling me that fear needed to be present for the spell to work?"

"If it is a spell," she said. "Perhaps it is not."

"Can you determine if it is a spell or not?"

"Aye, I can, but do you trust my word?"

He did not answer; instead he asked, "Can you remove the spell?"

"It may be possible." If the one who cast the spell, if it was a spell, was more powerful than she then she could do nothing, but now was not the time to explain that to Duncan. And besides, what if the witch was more powerful than she, what then would she do?

"Come with me to the keep?" He gave her a choice.

She did not hesitate. "Of course, anything I can do to help."

The cook area was in chaos. Many stood aside looking fearful, while others attempted to rid the grain of a plethora of crawling, squirming insects, an impossible task from what Sydney could tell.

"The insects attack the stored grain," someone shouted.

Some began to shout, others cried and many attempted to work faster under Gwen's urgings.

She and Duncan had not been spotted yet.

He leaned down and whispered. "Can you help?"

"I can try, but not with so many present."

"The witch!" a young woman shouted, and pointed at Sydney.

"Silence!" Gwen ordered sharply.

Duncan took command. "All of you leave."

No one challenged him. They hurried out of the room, all except Gwen.

She stood with her hands on her hips, a warning that she would not move.

Duncan looked to Sydney. "Do what you can."

Sydney knew she took a chance performing true magic in front of him and Gwen, but he would witness her power sooner or later and it was time he began to understand and hopefully accept. She went to the center of the room, stood perfectly still for several moments then turned in a slow circle.

She listened and sensed and knew that a power much less than hers had been used to cast a spell of blight. She would have no trouble discharging the spell. She did however wonder who had cast it, for undoubtedly it was meant to make her look the culprit.

She raised her hands above her head and recited with a clear and strong voice, *"Heaven above; earth below; this blight is wanted no more; and must immediately go; it vanishes quick and fast; and leaves behind no trace that will last; and if who sent it attempts a return; she will forfeit the knowledge she has learned."*

She lowered her arms and looked to Duncan. "It is done and the bugs will not return."

Gwen hurried around the room checking all the places that had been infested. "It is all clear." She glared at Sydney. "You truly are a witch."

Duncan stepped forward. "What you have seen here, no one shall hear of, is that understood?"

Gwen appeared stunned and did not immediately answer.

"Promise me this, Gwen," her brother urged.

"I will say nothing, but—" she raised a shaking finger to him. "Remember what I told you." She left in a hurry, visibly shaken and upset.

"We need to talk, Sydney. I think there is much you need to tell me."

She agreed with a nod. He needed to hear the truth, but would he accept it?

They left the keep and made their way through the village, grumbling and stares following them. Sydney paid them no heed, knowing that often what was not understood was feared.

Duncan, however, was a warrior and he felt as if he prepared for battle, though this battle was unlike any other he had ever fought. His opponent apparently was magic and how could he fight magic? Was it even necessary to fight it?

They walked in silence, the woods awash with the rays of the late afternoon sun. The leaves rustled in the warm breeze, birds chirped in busy chatter, animals scurried around and all seemed as it should be—but it wasn't.

Duncan stopped suddenly. "With all that has passed between us, my love for you remains adamant. Why? Have you worked your magic on me?"

"Love has its own unique magic. Spells are not necessary."

"A simple aye or nay will do."

His frustration was obvious and she was not sure if any answer would appease him or if he would truly believe her.

"I think love worked its own magic on the both of us. You are forever in my heart and mind. The time spent without you—" She swallowed back the cry that rose in her throat, recalling all the empty years spent without him. She had been foolish when last they were together and she blamed herself for what had passed between them. If she had been stronger they may have had a chance.

She did not intend to make the same mistake again.

She raised teary eyes to him, though she refused to shed a tear. "I found life empty without you. I missed the way you would tease me awake with your touch, the laughter we shared, the long talks and even the silent times. I realized I missed every part of you and I ached to have you back again." She took a breath then continued. "I thought time might heal my heart, but it did not. Time only served to make me miss you more and more. And finally, after years of attempting to deny the obvious, I realized that I was deeply in love with you and would always be deeply in love with you." She squeezed her eyes shut to stop her tears from falling. "I hoped, lord how I hoped, that you loved me at least half as much as I loved you. And I hoped that one day we would have a chance to love again and that nothing or no one would ever come between us."

His arms wrapped around her and she laid her head on his shoulder. "The strength of my love for you is like nothing I have ever known. I ache inside when you are not near. My thoughts are filled with you. You are a nourishment to my soul."

She lifted her head and he pressed a finger to her lips.

"Why—has haunted my thoughts since you left and I swore that if one day you returned I would have answers to my endless questions. Now I realize that to question my love for you would be foolish." He shook his head. "Perhaps I have thought you cast a spell over me because I could not believe I could love you as strongly as I do— and what else could it be but magic. I love you, Sydney, and I do not wish to ever stop loving you."

They kissed, wrapping their arms around each other as if fearful to let go.

Duncan reluctantly eased away. "There is time for talk later. It is time for us to once again love."

She smiled.

He took her hand and tugged. "Let us hurry."

She laughed softly and pulled him toward her. "Aye, let us hurry." She wrapped her arms around him and raised her lips to his. "Close your eyes and we will be home."

"Magic?"

"Does it matter?"

He smiled, closed his eyes and pressed his lips to hers.

Twenty

Duncan opened his eyes and found himself standing in the middle of Sydney's cottage, his arms still wrapped around her. He thought to ask her how she managed such extraordinary magic, but there was time for that later. At the moment he wanted no answers to questions; he simply wanted to love her.

"Are you sure of this?" she asked, slipping out of his arms to take a step away from him. Why she felt the need to ask him she did not know, but the need was there and she could not ignore it.

He smiled and began to undress, reaching to unwrap his plaid. It was a smile that had long haunted Sydney's dreams. He wore the audacious grin when his intentions were for them to make love, and it never failed to excite her as it did now, though she remained a bit apprehensive.

"It has been some time—"

His actions silenced her for his plaid had dropped to the floor and his shirt was off in no time, which left him standing naked, gloriously naked. He had aged well, his muscles thick, his waist filled out some and his stomach solid. He was a mature man in mind and body and his body told her the truth of his desire.

Why then did *she* feel vulnerable?

He stepped toward her; she stepped back and wondered why.

She had dreamed endlessly of this moment, this reuniting and the consummation of their love—so why then did she hesitate?

He reached out and brushed a stray hair from her face. "Are you sure?"

The tenderness of his touch, the concern in his voice, the way he stood without doubt and filled with such passion for her made her realize that it was her own feelings of inadequacy that caused her apprehension.

Would he find her as desirable as he once did?

She was no longer the young woman he once knew, but much older than he realized and while she had remained in relatively good shape, age still had a way of leaving its mark.

But then as she had often told those who sought her advice, true love sees through the eyes of love and accepts with the deepest of hearts.

She pressed her cheek to the palm of his hand. "Aye, I am sure."

His hands slipped to her waist and began to pull her blouse from her skirt. "Then it is time to shed all that stands between us."

He referred to more than clothes and Sydney silently agreed. At this moment in time there could be no other thought but the two of them. Nothing else mattered, only that they loved, for in their joining was their beginning.

Her blouse fell to the floor; her skirt followed and she stood naked before him with pride and an excitement that showed in her generous smile.

He scooped her up into his arms, hugged her to him and kissed her lips as he walked to the bed and lowered her down, following along with her. He stretched out beside her and with one finger began to explore her slowly, starting on her face.

"You are more beautiful than I remember."

He captured her response with a kiss, a long lazy kiss that heated her body and melted her mind—thought, at least rationale thought, was impossible—and she did not care.

His finger drifted down along her neck, to her chest, to lazily circle her breasts. His lips followed, lingering at her neck.

She attempted to reach out and touch him for her hands ached to feel the familiar touch of him.

He denied her. "Do that, my love, and we will finish much too fast."

She pouted teasingly. "But I want to touch you. I want to feel the strength of you grow in my hand."

He shivered and kissed her, stealing her pout away along with her breath.

She moaned when he was done and continued moaning when he took her nipple in his mouth to tease, taste and tempt beyond reason. And damned if his finger did not continue exploring—whispering across her stomach and inching slowly down between her legs.

He brought his lips to hers once again and kissed her gently. "I love touching you. Your skin is so soft." His hand slipped between her thighs, gently spreading her legs and running his fingers delicately over her inner thighs.

Gooseflesh ran over her and she shivered.

He laughed. "You have not changed; you respond to me as you always did."

She sighed. "That is because you have a magic touch."

He kissed her cheek. "I possess magic?"

She nodded. "In you hands, your lips and your—" She reached down and wrapped her hand firmly around him.

He grinned, shook his head and whispered, "A warrior is always prepared." With that his finger slid up along her thigh and gently into her warmth to relentlessly tease her.

She released him and writhed in pleasure as his fingers worked their magic.

He whispered in her ear, "I have missed the feel of you and the taste of you."

She barely got out, "Duncan."

He moved down over her to intimately torment her with his tongue and she was flooded with a passion that consumed her mind and body, and there was nothing—absolutely nothing—that she could do but surrender to the exquisite pleasure of it.

And she did, climaxing over, over and over again.

When she thought herself spent, unable to move, he lowered himself over her and gently entered her, slipping his arms beneath her and pulling her up against him so that their bodies seemed as one. Then he began to move and she joined him as she had always done in a steady rhythm that grew stronger and stronger, her moans filling the air as they climbed together higher and higher.

They both held tightly to each other as the explosion came in unison and their moans blended together as one as they experienced the overwhelming joy of loving.

They remained locked in each others' arms while their breathing and bodies calmed and returned to normal, though both knew at that very moment that nothing would ever be normal again.

"I love you, Sydney, and always will."

She almost cried for it had always been his way to tell her so after they had made love and she had wondered if he would remember. She recalled her own response.

She cupped his face in her hands. "Not half as much as I love you."

He smiled, kissed her gently and slipped off her, taking her in his arms to rest against him. "I have learned much about love."

"Tell me." She snuggled against him. She had loved this time with him when they would lay naked beside each other and talk. They would laugh and smile, debate and lovingly argue and then love again.

"Love comes when it wishes to come. It cares naught for the time or place. It simply arrives unexpectedly and surprisingly."

"Aye, it does and it captures your heart—"

"It strikes your heart like an arrow," he said. "And you suffer in many ways from its never-ending wound."

"You suffer only if you refuse to accept the love."

He shook his head. "I do not believe it is that easy."

"Aye, but it is. Love is simple, it is what surrounds it that makes the difficulty."

"People."

"For one, thoughts for another."

He groaned. "Thoughts can make one crazy, especially when you are in love. Love seems to invade your thoughts like a foe bent on destruction. And you war with yourself, for at the time you are your own worst enemy."

Sydney laughed. "It sounds like a battle that saw no victory."

He gave her a gentle squeeze. "I think the battle is turning in my favor."

She tapped his chest. "You think you can be victorious over love?"

He turned to kiss her lips. "I think love is always victorious, even when we think it is not."

She faintly traced his lips with her finger. "I am impressed. You understand much about love."

"It has not been an easy lesson, but it has been a worthwhile one. Have you learned about love?"

Sydney rested her hand on his chest over his heart. "I learned that if you do not accept and fight for the true love you find then you will forever regret it and never know such a strong love again."

"You have loved no other."

"Nay, Duncan, I have loved no other. You reside forever in my heart and there is no room for no other there."

"This is good," he said with a teasing smile, feeling pleased that there had been no other.

"And you?" she asked with a poke to his ribs. "Have there been any others you have loved in my absence?"

He scrunched his brow and eyes. "Let me think."

In a flash she straddled him and began to playfully punch his chest. "I best receive an acceptable reply or you will soon be bruised and battered."

He laughed heartily and grabbed her flying fists by the wrists. "You think you are capable of making me surrender to your demands?"

"Aye, that I am," she insisted.

"You are not strong enough," he said, continuing to laugh.

"Strength comes in different ways." She leaned down and teased his lips with her tongue.

"You think to seduce me?"

"You think I cannot?" She went to his neck and nibbled with her teeth, his warm skin tasting ever so tempting.

"You can try."

"Release my hands."

"Nay, make me release them." He defied her with a hearty laugh.

"I will." She did not bother to raise her head from where she nibbled at his neck, though she began to move her body where it nested comfortably against his groin.

His laugh subsided though his smile remained. "You will not win."

She laughed this time. "I win either way for I am enjoying myself." With that she began to move down along his body, her mouth tasting every inch of him as she went along.

"I can stop you with one yank of my arm." He gave a tug of her wrists to prove his point.

She simply smiled. "Stop me anytime you wish."

She inched down lower and lower and lower, nipping and tasting like a lover long deprived.

It was not long before he released her wrists with a soft "Damn."

She laughed and took him in her mouth, tasting and licking, prolonging his pleasure and hers until she brought him to the edge of surrender.

She looked up at him. "Have you loved another?"

"Now you ask me?"

"You have a choice—surrender or not?" She licked her lips slowly and squeezed the length of him.

His answer came on a moan. "Nay, witch, I have loved no other but you."

She smiled. "I am so pleased to hear that and now I intend to make you surrender completely."

And he did with no regrets, only never-ending pleasure.

They slept afterward wrapped in each other's arms for an hour or so past midday. They hurried to dress and grabbed bread, cheese, fruit and a jug of ale and rushed into the woods to their favorite secluded spot, where they had spent many a time together.

They were like young ones in love, laughing, hugging and kissing as they hurried along.

Beatrice smiled and watched them from where she sat perched on the top of Finn's head. The wolf's green eyes kept a steady glare on the couple, making certain they were kept from harm.

"They do well," Beatrice said to the animal. "It is good for it grows dangerous for Sydney. She cannot remain here much longer and—"

A low growl from Finn interrupted her.

"What is it? What do you hear?" She listened, placing her hand behind her ear and straining to hear what the wolf heard. "I hear nothing."

His growl continued.

"You must sense something." She tapped him on the head. "Let us follow them and make certain they are in no danger."

Finn followed slowly, keeping the couple in view, but himself and Beatrice concealed.

Duncan spread a blanket on the ground and Sydney soon had the food out and arranged on white linen cloths. She took two pewter goblets from the basket and poured them ale.

Duncan shook his head and smiled. "You amaze me, you make everything so appealing and enjoyable."

She kissed him before handing him the goblet. "You have seen nothing yet." How true were her words, she wondered, and how would he react to all he learned?

He raised his goblet. "To us—" He paused but for a moment. "May we never part and always love."

She smiled and raised her own goblet, tapping it lightly against his and then raising it toward the sky. "May we never part and always love." She kissed him. "Your spell is cast."

He placed his goblet to the side and reached for a piece of bread. "A spell you say? And cast that easily?"

"Do you believe it so?" She placed her goblet down and reached for a piece of cheese, handing him one as well.

"Aye, I believe, at least I want very much to believe."

"But do you believe, truly and honestly from the depths of your heart?"

"Aye," he said. "I believe strongly for I have no intentions of letting you go again. One mistake is enough. We shall not make another."

"I agree, but we must remain firm in our belief or it will not see fruition."

He brushed the crumbs from his hands. "Let me understand this, though you have explained it many times. All I need to do is believe, really believe, and what I believe comes to pass?"

"Within reason."

"Nay, you have repeatedly told me, believe and it is so."

"Believe, take action and it is so," Sydney said.

"Fine, then let us test this theory of yours."

"If you wish."

"I do," he said, "and I know what I believe."

"What is that?"

"I believe that people will drop from the heavens."

Sydney laughed. "That is not reasonable."

"You told me to believe and it would be so."

"Believe for a good reason. What reason could you want for people to drop from the heavens?"

He thought and then smiled. "Anyone that comes down here out of the heavens must be wise and would therefore help us with our dilemma."

Sydney shook her head. "And you believe the heavens will send someone?"

"Not one, but one or two more. I believe it so, I believe we require as much help as we can get."

Sydney shook a finger at him. "Be careful what you ask for!"

Duncan stood, stretched his arms upward and said, "Heaven please send us wise ones, make it fast, for we are not sure how much longer we can last."

Sydney laughed and shook her head.

"It is my first spell and I think a good one," he said with a smile.

"Aye, a good one," she agreed, though continued laughing.

Duncan stared at the sky. "So how long before they arrive?"

Sydney's laughter subsided. "You truly believe?"

"Aye, and I think I hear a rumble."

Sydney listened and heard it as well. It sounded like distant thunder approaching them.

"They arrive soon." Duncan laughed.

Sydney jumped up and poked his chest. "You tease me."

He grabbed hold of her and hugged her to him. "Do you

really think people can fall from the heavens?"

The thunder suddenly roared, the ground shook and Duncan held tightly to Sydney, forcing her to move away from the clearing to stand beside a large stone.

No sooner had they moved then a gigantic hole tore open in the sky and out fell six people one right after the other.

Twenty-one

"Did you have to make that landing so hard, Tempest?" Ali asked, standing with the help of her husband Sebastian. She immediately brushed off dust and forest debris from her long black skirt and peasant blouse. Sebastian did the same to his plaid and white linen shirt.

"What did you expect to happen when you travel through a hole in time?" Sarina said, standing with the help of her husband Dagon. Sarina plucked leaves and twigs from her brown skirt and pale yellow blouse.

Dagon simply removed debris from his plaid and shirt with a flick of his finger.

Sarina quickly grabbed her husband's finger. "Remember the time we are in. It is not safe to use magic."

Ali pointed to a couple standing on their feet, his arm wrapped around her, and they were smiling. "Tempest and Michael landed easily enough."

Sebastian grabbed his wife's pointing finger. "Sweetheart, their skills and powers far surpass any of ours."

Ali pulled her hand from her husband's grasp and walked over to Tempest.

The woman stepped forward, a gentle smile on her beautiful face.

"I'm worried about my aunt Sydney," she said, explaining her reason for complaining. "We all sensed something was not right and I'm concerned."

Tempest placed a comforting hand on her arm. "We are all concerned, Sydney being a true friend to us all, but I told you we would find her and make certain she was well."

"Will it take us long?" Ali asked anxiously. Sebastian walked up beside her.

Tempest smiled, took Ali by the shoulder, turned her around and pointed to a large stone.

"Aunt Sydney!" Ali yelled, and ran straight into the woman's arms.

Duncan stepped out of the screaming woman's path. He was too stunned to do anything else but stand there and listen. Their talk was foreign, their actions strange and they had fallen out of the sky.

Had he brought them here?

The two women hugged, and Duncan listened to the young blond woman chatter without taking a breath. She used strange words and phrases. She was not from these parts or anywhere known to Duncan. Could she possibly be from the heavens?

Sebastian stepped forward and extended his hand to Duncan. "I'm Sebastian and the woman who you probably think is quite insane is my wife Ali."

Duncan was not certain if he should touch any of the strangers, though the decision was made for him since the chattering woman named Ali flung herself at him, hugging him tightly.

"I'm so glad to finally meet you. My aunt's love for you has survived countless years and never once did she ever stop loving you. You were always in her heart—always."

Duncan did not return the hug. He stood with his arms at his sides. "We have been separated only thirteen years."

Ali immediately grew silent after a whispered "Oops." She stepped back and took her husband's hand.

"There you go," Dagon said with a laugh. "Leaping before you look."

Sarina defended Ali. "She is happy for her aunt and cannot help but demonstrate her feelings of joy."

Finally someone who spoke with sense and clarity, Duncan thought. But then her dark eyes seemed as if they could see and understand much. Her features were soft and appealing and she wore her long dark hair in a braid.

Ali smiled. "I like your wife more each day, Dagon, even though she knocked my husband down and landed on top of him when they first met, and then of course she dumped him in the fountain and—"

"That all was my fault."

Duncan was startled at the beauty of the woman who stepped forward to take the blame. Her long blond hair was sparked with streaks of fire running through it, her voice was delicate yet strong and she walked with the courage of a warrior confident of victory. She looked young and yet seemed so very old.

Sydney approached her with a gracious smile and arms extended.

Duncan could tell that Sydney admired and respected the woman and he grew all the more confused.

They hugged, spoke softly and then turned toward Duncan.

"So this is Duncan," Tempest said and extended her hand.

Duncan took her hand without hesitation.

"I am Tempest, an old friend of Sydney's. She has told me much about you and I am pleased to finally meet you."

"And I you, Tempest," he said, at least he thought he did. If Sydney was aunt to one and friend to the others then he did not summon them from the heavens, yet they fell from the heavens. None of this made sense, but it certainly intrigued him besides causing him concern.

Tempest motioned to the man who had stood beside her and he joined them. "This is my husband, Michael."

Duncan determined the worth of a man in a quick glance and one look told him that Michael was more powerful than any man he had ever met. It was not only the scars on his face, which told of his courage, or his height and the solid strength of him, or the way he walked with confidence— the man exuded a power that in battle would frighten the most fierce warrior.

Duncan respected strength and offered his hand to Michael.

"It is good to meet you," Michael said and shook his hand.

Quick introductions followed, and Duncan learned that Sarina appeared the easiest to understand; Ali loved her aunt dearly, which endeared her to him; Tempest was wise in all her words, causing him to wonder the most about her and her husband Michael. Dagon, Sarina's husband, he had no trouble understanding. He had the arrogance of the nobility, the strength of his convictions and a caring heart. His handsome features would capture any female heart and though tall and lean he looked to be a worthy opponent.

But it was Sebastian, Ali's husband, who he found the most interesting. He was friendly and inquisitive, asking many questions, though at times his speech could confuse. He was a man determined to know all he could, though he already possessed a good degree of knowledge. He was tall and muscular and would hold his own in a fight. His dark hair was shorter than that of the other two men and he wondered if it was the way of his clan.

All of them were concerned for Sydney; they apparently cared for her very much. Now all he needed to determine was where they came from and their means of transportation?

Duncan took charge. "The sun will set shortly. I think it wise if we seek shelter."

"The cottage," Sydney suggested.

"Is too small to accommodate all comfortably," Duncan said. "And I do not think it is wise to take them to the keep."

Michael solved the problem. "I know of a large cottage not far from here."

"I know these woods well," Duncan said. "I know of no other cottages nearby."

"It sits secluded, hidden by trees and brush," Michael said.

Duncan accepted his explanation reluctantly, while the others understood that Michael had conjured up a place for them to reside while here.

A short walk and pushing past overgrown foliage brought them to a large cottage that could easily accommodate the three couples.

Duncan remained skeptical, especially when they came upon the place. It was a good size and looked well-lived in—wood stacked nearby, a barrel full of rainwater, flowers growing around the front and smoke puffing steadily from the chimney. "This is large for me not to have known it was here. I have walked these woods every day. And it looks to be already occupied."

No one commented; his remark was best left ignored so that it would soon pass out of his thoughts.

"Tea, I need a cup of tea," Ali said, entering the cottage. "Where's the kettle?"

"What is tea and what is a kettle?" Duncan asked and glanced at each of them. "And where did you all come from? You fell out of the sky right after I cast a spell."

Ali realized her mistake and took immediate action, focusing the attention on Duncan. "You cast a spell, how wonderful."

"You summoned us, we felt it," Sarina added with excitement.

Sebastian slapped him on the back. "Good for you. It took me a while to get the hang of it."

Before Sydney could advise all of them that Duncan knew nothing substantial about spells or about her circumstances, Duncan spoke.

"You are all witches." His voice quivered, though only for a second. He would show no fear, there were too many witches around him.

They all looked to Sydney.

Sydney looked at Duncan and smiled. "I told you to be careful what you wished for."

Her humor relaxed him, though the warrior in him kept a slight guard up. "I brought them here then?"

Sydney looked to Tempest for an answer for she was not certain what had brought her niece and friends here.

Tempest suggested they sit at the large table and said to Ali, "Why don't you brew us all a drink."

Four voices, Sebastian, Dagon, Sarina and Michael, called out, "No!"

Ali placed her hands on her hips. "I can handle a brew without a problem. Where's the stove?"

Heads shook, Duncan stared and Sarina saw to settling the problem.

"I will help you, since I could use a soothing brew myself."

"You will find what you need in the other room," Michael said.

The two women nodded, knowing that Michael had probably provided the modern necessities for everyone's convenience.

The others all gathered around the table, with Sydney sitting next to Duncan and taking his hand.

"I think it would be best if first I properly introduced everyone to Duncan. This must be confusing to him, your visit being so sudden and unexpected."

Duncan turned wide eyes on her. "Sudden? Unexpected? They dropped out of the sky."

"We will get to that," Sydney said. "But first let me make certain you know everyone."

He nodded with reluctance. "But I will have my answers."

"Aye," she said with worry in her voice. "You will."

He squeezed her hand, realizing he had upset her and wanting to reassure her that it was all right. They would make it so.

Sydney started with Tempest and Michael. "Tempest is a good friend of mine." She made no mention of Tempest having been her teacher or that Tempest was called the Ancient One and was born with the dawn of time and was considered the most powerful of all witches. She did not think he was ready to hear all that just yet. "Michael is her husband and also a good friend." Again she did not mention that Michael had once been a warlock and in love with Tempest. She had to send him away in a protective spell for him to return at a future date in time and attempt to make his wrongs right if their love was ever to be. He could learn all that later.

"Your speech is strange to me," Duncan said, looking to Michael.

"I come from a distant land and doubt you have heard of it."

"Your way of travel I have not heard of either."

"In time," Sydney assured him.

Ali and Sarina entered the room, carrying trays.

"Brews and bread," Ali said with a smile, and placed the tray on the table. The delicious aroma drifted in the air and noses sniffed with appreciation and anticipation.

Sarina placed her tray down and the scent of mulled cider was strong though a hint of chamomile tea could be detected.

"Honey bread and berry bread," Ali said and squeezed in between her husband and Dagon.

"Did you make the bread?" Dagon asked with a grin.

She jabbed him in the ribs. "I have gotten better at cooking."

Dagon looked past Ali at Sebastian, who shook his head.

Ali turned around fast but Sebastian was faster and had stopped shaking his head.

He smiled and kissed his wife's cheek.

Everyone helped themselves to the bread and herb-flavored butter, tankards were filled with cider and chamomile tea was poured in china cups.

Duncan sat staring, wondering how bread could be baked so fast and wondering over the easy and comfortable camaraderie that existed between the three couples. They teased and poked fun at each other, but they cared—they cared deeply—and that caring had brought them here to Sydney.

Sydney arranged several slices of bread on a pewter plate and Sarina filled a tankard with cider for him.

When everyone had finally settled, Sydney continued as though she had never been interrupted.

"Ali is my niece—"

Duncan interrupted. "I did not know you had a family. I had thought you were all alone."

That he was upset was easy to see and it disturbed her. She was not being fair to him, but how did she explain a niece who was born a hundred years or so after they had met? It was becoming more and more difficult to keep the truth from him and that was not good. He deserved the truth; she would want it from him.

But what would the truth bring?

Decisions for both of them.

"Ali is my sister's daughter." The more she explained, the more needed to be explained.

"Ali speaks in the same strange tongue as Michael. They come from the same land, the same clan?"

"The same land," Sydney said.

Duncan shook his head, obviously confused and frustrated. "Sarina and Dagon's tongue while not exactly like ours is similar. Tempest's tongue changes depending on who she speaks with, that is all strange enough, but—" He took a breath and raked his fingers through his hair. "What confuses me the most is, how you all fell out of the sky to the earth. Where did you all come from?"

Sarina stood suddenly, knocking over her half-filled teacup. "Something is wrong. There is danger."

Dagon stood, his arm going protectively around his wife. "Where does the danger come from?"

"Close by." She shivered.

Duncan stood. "Can you tell me more?" He understood that she could see what others could not.

Her hand flew to her chest. "They want to hurt him."

"Who?" Duncan demanded.

Before Sarina could answer Beatrice flew through the open window and flitted in Sydney's face. She sounded angry, though on the verge of tears.

"Men have cornered Finn; they intend to kill him."

Sydney stood in a rush, her chair crashing to the ground. "Show me."

Beatrice landed on Sydney's shoulder and with a snap of her fingers the two disappeared.

Twenty-two

Sydney materialized along with Beatrice behind three men who had Finn cornered against a cropping of large stones. The fierce animal growled and snarled, keeping the men at bay, though they readied their bows and took aim.

Sydney burst past them, knocking one to the ground, and took a protective stance in front of the large black wolf. He calmed considerably, though his growl remained menacing.

"Put your weapons down," she ordered with such fierceness that one of the men shivered.

"The witch," one whispered, and all three men crossed themselves for protection.

"He hunts our animals," one man said in defense of their actions.

"He seeks his food in these woods," Sydney said.

"Then why do our animals disappear and why are their bodies found torn apart?" asked another man.

"He is a demon," shouted another.

Sydney stood tall, her head high, her shoulders back.

"The wolf is a friend of mine and I will not allow you to hurt him. And the only demons around here are ignorant men who hunt senselessly."

One man grew angry and drew his bow back, pointing the arrow directly at Sydney. "Move."

Finn growled louder and paced restlessly behind Sydney, sensing the danger around them.

Sydney threw her arms out wide, presenting an easy target. "Shoot if you dare."

Silence reigned—even Finn's growling ceased. The man waited, his hand trembled, causing the bow to quiver.

"Shoot and it will be the last thing you ever do."

The strong voice echoed through the woods, and the man immediately lowered his bow and his face paled to a deathly shade when Duncan stepped out of the woods into the clearing.

The shortest man of the three spoke up. "What are we to do, Duncan? Four animals have disappeared—" He paused to point an accusing finger at Sydney. "Since she has started practicing her magic."

The taller man joined in. "Two of the animals were discovered torn apart, their entrails removed and their carcasses left to rot."

"Why has this not been brought to my attention?" Duncan asked.

Their eyes widened when Sebastian, Dagon and Michael walked out of the woods to join Duncan.

"Friends of mine who have arrived for a visit," he said, setting the men at ease for strangers always caused one to pause. "Now answer me."

One finally spoke up. "You are bewitched by a witch, what good would it have done?"

Duncan lost his temper. He had had all he could take. He was tired of everyone calling Sydney a witch when he had seen her endlessly offer her help to the ailing. And her love of animals would never allow her to hurt one.

"Look," Duncan pointed at Sydney. "Look at the way

she defends the wolf. She does not wish harm to come to any animal."

"The wolf kills for her," one man said, "and she gives him her protection."

"Enough!" Duncan shouted. "You have no sense. I will bring this madness to an end by finding out who is responsible."

The three men nodded firmly.

"Aye," one said, "find him and all will be settled."

"What if the witch is responsible?" one man asked, staring at Sydney.

Duncan marched right up to him. "Sydney is not responsible for the senseless slaughter of your animals and she is a healer who has helped many in the clan, or do you forget that, Robert?"

The man's shoulder's drooped and he shook his head. "Nay, I do not forget how she saved me from fever those many years ago, but strange things have happened since her return and many talk."

"Gossip that stirs the discontent—those looking for excuses instead of sound reasoning."

Robert nodded, then returned to shaking his head. "Gossip grows strong about Sydney's powers. Some insist that they have seen it with their own eyes. Some—" He looked around Duncan at Sydney then stepped closer to him to speak low. "Some say they saw her in the woods with the devil, working magic."

"Go," he said. "I will hear no more nonsense."

The men did not hesitate to leave. When Duncan's voice rumbled like thunder everyone knew it was not a good time to defy him or ignore his orders. They hurried off without another word, the woods swallowing them up and their footsteps soon a faint echo in the distance.

The women stepped out from the covering of the woods as soon as the men were gone.

Duncan ignored them all and walked over to Sydney. "You were foolish for attempting to handle this situation on your own. You could have been harmed, and do not tell me you have your magic to protect you, for that can bring you harm as well."

"He is right," Tempest said, stepping forward.

"At least one of you is sensible."

"We are all really sensible," Sebastian said. "That's why we've come here. We sensed Sydney needed help."

Dagon moved to Sydney's side. "And from the looks and sounds of things, it's obvious you could use our help."

Sydney smiled. "Thank you, dear heart, for being there for me."

"You have been there for us more times than we deserved."

"He's right," Ali said. "Whenever any of us were in need you were always there. Now it's our turn."

A low growl from Finn reminded everyone of his presence.

Sydney turned her attention to the wolf and gave him a pat on the head and moved aside so that he could run off. The wolf did not favor people and she could sense his anxiousness to leave, knowing the danger had passed.

With one quick look at Sydney to make certain she was all right, Finn took off into the dense forest.

Part of her felt like running herself for she feared that things would worsen before they improved. But then she had family and friends with her now and with their help perhaps all would turn out well.

Tempest walked over to Sydney. "You have been here almost three months and already gossip spreads about you being a witch?" She shook her head. "That does not make sense. I know you and you would not place yourself or others in jeopardy. Something is not right."

"I have questioned the very same thing," Sydney said. "And stranger still is that a blight of insects was brought down on the keep's grain."

"A spell?" Tempest asked.

"Yes, but I have had no time to investigate or determine its origin."

"A blight of insects?" Tempest asked to be certain.

Sydney nodded.

"That is a spell that is purposely meant to harm, which would make it a—"

"Warlock's work," Michael finished.

"Not a strong warlock," Sydney informed them. "I was able to discharge the spell and keep it from returning." She suddenly realized that Duncan stood staring at them all.

All eyes followed hers.

Duncan looked from one to the other. "You are all witches." It was not a question or an accusation, simply a confirmation.

They all nodded.

Sydney went to him and slipped her arm around his.

"You come from a long line of witches?"

"A long line, Duncan, and I am proud of my heritage."

"It grows late," Tempest said. "And we are tired from our journey. We will talk tomorrow."

No one disagreed; they all understood that Duncan and Sydney needed time alone.

The three couples walked off hand in hand, soon disappearing into the dense woods, though Duncan had a feeling they did not walk back to the cottage.

He took Sydney's hand. "Let us walk back to your place."

Sydney smiled, squeezed his hand and began to walk with him. "Perfect, the sun will be near setting when we return."

"The church tells us to beware of magic, that it is evil," Duncan said, enjoying the warmth of her hand in his. Her touch always felt good and it had nothing to do with magic. It had to do with love.

"Magic has always been a part of life in the Highlands. Your own culture and heritage is steeped in it. If I recall correctly you told me that your grandmother had the gift of vision."

"Aye, she did." He laughed. "Thomas and I could not hide a thing from her. She always knew what we were about, and knew about others. But is that part of magic, and what really is magic?"

"I do not think there is a simple definition of magic, though magic does entail making the unbelievable believable."

"A power of suggestion, as with the spells."

Sydney nodded. "Thoughts are powerful. They are filled with an energy that can create amazing things and have us do amazing things. It is understanding that energy and using it correctly."

They came upon the cottage, the sun slowly fading on the horizon.

Duncan stopped and took Sydney's hands in his. "Will you teach me what you can about magic? I feel powerless to protect you when I see the feats you are capable of. And I need to protect the clan from their own ignorance."

Joy raced through Sydney. "You truly wish to learn of my ways?"

He stole a quick kiss from her. "I love you and I wish to know all I can about you. Of course—" He grinned. "It will probably take me a very long time to learn it all."

She slipped her arms around his waist. "Many, many, many years for sure."

"So we will need to remain together."

"Aye, we must remain together; it is important that you learn."

"Very important." He kissed her again, lingering at her lips.

"Stay with me tonight?" she whispered when their lips briefly parted.

"My very own thoughts, witch."

"We can make magic."

"You will teach me?"

"That magic you already know."

They laughed and hurried to the cottage.

They came to an abrupt halt when they looked at the front door.

Sydney took a closer step, but Duncan held firm to her hand.

"I will take a look."

"No need, I know what this means."

Duncan stepped forward to take a closer look. "It is a strange symbol written in blood."

Sydney went to his side. "It is a symbol many believe to protect against evil, though it is also the very symbol evil uses to gather strength."

"The power of suggestion."

"Aye, by placing it here; it informs all that evil exists and they must beware, be cautious of who they trust, and so they fear and strike out at the innocent."

"I will clean it off," Duncan said.

Sydney nodded. "I will help."

Sydney poured a cleansing liquid in the bottom of the bucket before adding water from the rain barrel to it, knowing the heavy duty cleaner would remove most of the wet blood. Tomorrow she would paint the door a bright white and add a protective rune script across the top.

They scrubbed the mess with coarse cloths.

"Tempest and you seem to be concerned of a warlock. Is a warlock different from a witch? I have heard the term used and for some reason connect it to a powerful witch."

"A warlock is a witch who practices the dark side of our ways."

"And you think a warlock is responsible for the infestation?"

"I believe it is a witch new to the ways of the dark side, on the verge of becoming a warlock."

"Tempest appears a powerful witch."

"Why do you think that?" Sydney asked, tossing the cloth in the bucket and grateful that the door cleaned up well, with only a minor trace of the symbol remaining. Paint would cover the rest.

Duncan dropped his cloth into the bucket. "She remains calm and in control when the others do not. She does not look as if she fears and she speaks with a gentleness that soothes and captivates. She knows and therefore fears little."

"You are very observant." Sydney emptied the bucket and tossed the cloths in another bucket she had filled with hot water and detergent and left them to soak overnight.

Duncan opened the door for her. "I lead a clan, I must be."

She went straight to the fireplace to set a pot of water to boil. She needed tea and they needed a solid meal. "Everyone should be observant, then they would not be so easily fooled into foolish thinking."

Duncan laughed. "Can you teach that to people?" He sat at the table, his laugh turning to an appreciative smile when Sydney began placing food on it.

"People can teach it to themselves, but first they must realize they need to learn and that is the most difficult part."

He reached for a slice of meat and bread. "You learned from Tempest, she was your teacher."

Sydney turned wide eyes on him. "How did you know that?"

He grinned. "I observe well."

Sydney smiled and joined him at the table. "Tempest was a wonderful teacher and as I have told you, now a good friend. She taught me how to think differently and therefore become more knowledgeable about life and the craft. I will always hold fond and grateful memories of the time spent with her."

"How much time did you spend with her?"

"Not long, only fifteen years." She realized her mistake too late.

"Fifteen years? But we have been apart thirteen." He shook his head. "You studied with her before we met?"

"Nay, I did not."

He rubbed his chin. "I am confused."

Sydney reached out and placed her hand on his. "There is something I must tell you. It is time you know the truth."

"Good, I would like to hear it."

"But will you believe it?"

"I believe people dropping out of the sky," he said.

"But you have many questions about their arrival, do you not?"

"Of course I do, how could I not? But I am willing to listen, observe and learn, especially if it will benefit everyone concerned." He squeezed her hand. "And especially if it will keep our love strong and keep us together."

She hesitated for a moment, her own fear keeping her silent.

"I love you, Sydney. There is nothing you can say that will change that."

With that reassurance she spoke bluntly, wanting it to be done. "I am six hundred years old and I have returned in time from the twenty-first century to reunite with you."

Twenty-three

The piece of bread dropped from Duncan's hand at the same time an urgent pounding sounded at the door.

Duncan stared at her. "Six hundred years old?"

The pounding sounded again, this time followed by an insistent Thomas. "I cannot leave without you, Duncan, or your sister will have my head."

"The future?" Duncan paid no heed to his friend, who pounded on the door again.

Sydney stood. "I know it sounds strange." She walked to the door. "A moment, Thomas."

"Aye, a moment then," he said impatiently, and the pounding ceased.

"We have no time to discuss this now." Sydney remained as calm as possible, though she felt anything but calm. "You are obviously needed at the keep."

Duncan stood, upsetting his chair, and walked up to her, grasping her by the shoulders and almost lifting her off the ground. "You tell me you are six hundred years old and have returned from the future to me and I am to leave without a word being discussed?" He shook his head. "I think not."

"Thomas waits."

"Let him. I want answers."

"But Thomas—"

"Will wait," he finished impatiently.

She had little time to explain, for Thomas was certain to start pounding on the door again.

Duncan released her and raked his fingers through his hair then shook his head again. "That would have made you over one hundred years old when we first met."

"A bit older," she said.

He could not stop shaking his head. "How can this be?"

"It is our way. Our knowledge has enabled us to live longer lives than mortals."

A pounding at the door caused Duncan to raise his voice. "When I am ready."

Silence followed, and Sydney knew that Thomas would wait as long as was necessary after hearing Duncan's forceful edict.

Thoughts raced through Duncan's mind, some he cared not to think of, some were simply curiosity and some were simply unbelievable.

"I know this may seem difficult for you to accept."

"Difficult?" Duncan said. "Today I have witnessed you heal a broken shoulder, clear the grain of insects, then I watched as witches fell out of the sky and I listened when you told me you are—" He threw his hands up in the air. "Difficult? It is unbelievable and I must be a fool to even consider it the truth."

"You do believe me?"

He reached out and grabbed her, hugging her to him. "I believe that I love you, therefore I must believe in you, and as crazy as all this sounds I believe that somehow I will come to understand it all—though do not ask me how."

Sydney wrapped her arms around him and squeezed tight. "I do love you so very much."

He rubbed his cheek against hers and held her as tightly as she did him. "We must hold on to that love, Sydney, for I fear it may be the only thing that saves us."

Prophetic words? Or was it his own doubt and fear speaking? Sydney could not be sure herself; her own thoughts were as chaotic as his.

He gave her a hug and stepped away. "I want nothing more than to be able to discuss this matter with you for I have endless questions. All my beliefs have suddenly been challenged and I find myself starving for answers."

"We have time to talk," Sydney assured him.

"I worry that we do not. The men who you confronted over the wolf today have probably already started tongues wagging, and then there are the strangers who have come to visit. Gossip will spread fast."

"We will do our best, that is all we can do."

Duncan walked to the door and stopped when his hand touched the metal latch. He turned to look at Sydney, his eyes filled with concern. He seemed about to speak then held his tongue for a moment before saying, "I love you, Sydney. I always will."

He walked out, shutting the door quietly behind him and Sydney felt her legs go weak. She hurried to sit in the closest chair, her hands trembling and a chill causing her to shiver.

Words were not necessary; she understood his concern. If she actually returned from the future to him, would she return to the future without him? The question haunted her as well. What would she do? Remain here and live in constant danger? Would he consider returning to the future with her?

There were so many possibilities, but merely one decision.

She yawned. The day had been long, but . . .

She smiled, recalling her time with Duncan. Intimacy with him had always been special. It was warm, satisfying and loving. She had always felt so very loved by him. His love was in his every touch, his every kiss and his every glance.

Love was a constant between them. She did not have to search for it, wonder over it or concern herself with it. It simply was there for her to grasp onto when needed or simply when she wished to feel its warmth and comfort. That had been the way of it and that was how she wished it to continue.

There was no doubt that she loved him and no doubt that he loved her. It was all that surrounded them that threatened their love, and together they could conquer anything that stood in their way.

Another yawn warned that she was dangerously close to falling fast asleep in the chair. She stood and began to clean off the table.

Beatrice flew in the open window and shook her tiny head as she settled on Sydney's shoulder. "You are tired, use your magic."

"It is dangerous for me to use my magic right now. I sense that someone keeps a close watch on me." She stifled a yawn. "Thank you for keeping watch over Finn."

"Finn and I were keeping watch over you and Duncan." Beatrice smiled. "Though things looked to be going just fine."

"We love—it is that simple."

"This is good, and it is good to know you have family and friends here now to help you."

"They were a surprise."

"Quite a surprise for Duncan I can imagine." Beatrice yawned along with Sydney.

"Wait until he recalls seeing you. With all the excitement he made no mention of your appearance, but when things settle in his mind and he recalls today's events, he will remember seeing a fairy."

"And think what?"

Sydney sighed. "That magic is a wonderful thing."

"It is, but not here in this century or for centuries to

come. Even in the twenty-first century there are those who
still think witches and fairies are evil."

"They simply do not understand, perhaps in time they
will, but for now—" A yawn rose up to interrupt. "For now
I go to bed."

Beatrice flew off her shoulder to her bed on the mantel.
"Before returning here tonight, I paid a visit to the keep.
There is much whispering and rushing about. Eileen prepares to leave tomorrow, a few days earlier then she had
planned. Something is amiss."

Sydney crawled gratefully beneath the soft wool blanket.
"Gwen sent Thomas to get Duncan. He insisted he would
not leave without him."

"Something is going on. Something unexpected."

"I am sure Duncan will tell me about it tomorrow." Sydney's eyes began to drift closed. "I must rise early; I have
much to do. Paint the front door, write a rune script, visit
with my niece and friends, and I must talk with . . ."

Beatrice watched as Sydney's words faded and she began to snore lightly. She worried over the woman. She had
not liked the feelings she had sensed around the keep. It
was not good, and she was relieved that the Ancient One
had arrived.

She hurried under her small blanket and settled down
for the night. She would rise early with Sydney and help
her. All would be well.

Why then did the whispers in the keep disturb her so?

The great hall was quiet when Duncan entered. His sister
Gwen stood by the dais talking with Eileen, who looked
visibly shaken.

Thomas had informed him that Gwen insisted that he go
find Duncan and have him return to the keep at once. There
was an urgent matter that needed to be discussed. She had

refused to confide in Thomas about it, but stressed the importance of Duncan's return.

Thomas had also informed him that Eileen had decided to leave a few days earlier than planned and her decision had been sudden. The young lass seemed anxious to be on her way, as if she feared remaining at the keep.

"I am sorry to hear that you are leaving us so soon, Eileen," he said, approaching the dais.

Her smile was nervous and forced. "I feel the need to return and talk with my father about the change of plans."

"Tell him the truth," Gwen urged, her hand reaching out to comfort the upset lass.

Duncan stood ready to listen, his arms folded across his chest. "Do not fear to speak with me, Eileen. I am your friend and wish you no harm."

"It is not you whom I fear." She looked around her as if worried that someone listened and she lowered her voice. "It is the—" She bit her tongue, preventing herself from finishing.

Gwen finished for her. "She fears the cleric's arrival."

"Cleric?" Duncan asked.

Gwen nodded. "There is talk of sending a message to the abbey near Loch Catherine and requesting that a church official be sent to investigate the possibilities of witchcraft in the area."

Eileen rubbed her hands nervously. "I have heard tales—" The young woman could not finish.

"I will send my clansmen along with your own clansmen to guarantee a safe journey home," Duncan said, hoping to calm her.

"Nay, nay," she said quickly. "The men who came with me will be sufficient protection. I need no more. We will leave at sunrise. Please excuse me—I have much to do." Eileen hurried off.

"She wants no one from the clan to accompany her for fear the magic may follow," Gwen said, shaking her head.

Duncan was annoyed. "This is all absurd."

"Is it?" his sister asked. "This day Sydney has all but proven herself a powerful witch."

"Why, because she healed a young lad's shoulder?"

Gwen lowered her voice though it remained harsh. "You know what I speak of, only a witch of great strength could rid the grain of insects. And I also heard that she protected her black wolf in the forest today."

Duncan feared that talk would spread rapidly and with what he had just learned from Sydney herself—he did not know how he would ever be able to protect her if someone discovered the truth.

Gwen placed her hand on her brother's arm. "Sydney must leave here and the sooner the better—for her sake."

The thought had crossed his mind, but he had attempted to ignore it. He did not want Sydney going anywhere. He did not want to lose her again, but was he being selfish? Her safety should be his first concern.

"Let her go if you love her."

He could not fathom life without her. He did not want to. "I will see if I can calm those who seem to think that witchcraft is afoot."

"Most think that witchcraft is afoot and fear what will happen. Do you not fear yourself?"

"You fear, Sydney?" he asked incredulously.

Gwen sighed and turned to fill two tankards with ale from the pitcher on the table. She handed her brother one, but he declined with a shake of his head. "She is different than before and I know you see it yourself. Her strength has grown considerably." Gwen shivered. "I cannot believe how easily she dispelled the insects from the grain."

"She uses her strength for good. She harms no one."

"So she says, but tell me this, brother, who infested the grain with insects?"

A warlock was Duncan's first thought, though he wisely kept it to himself. If word spread of another witch's presence chaos would reign.

"Did she dispel the infestation so easily because it was her own spell she dismissed?"

Duncan had heard enough. "You speak ill of Sydney, why?"

"I worry over you."

"I can take care of myself."

"Not against a powerful witch."

"Be careful what you say, Gwen, I love Sydney."

Gwen sighed and shook her head. "I feared this. I feared she would work her magic on you and you would foolishly defend her."

Duncan walked up to his sister. "You think my love for Sydney is not true?"

"She is a witch and cast spells. Love spells. The women talk of her skill. Look what she did to Eileen."

"She listened to Eileen. The young lass never wished to marry me in the first place. She loves another and has for some time."

"You know this for sure?" Gwen asked, her voice trembling with anger. "In all the correspondence I had with her father he never once mentioned a young man his daughter fancied."

"Why would he? He wanted our clans united and his daughter would do as she was told."

"Which she intended to do until she visited Sydney."

Duncan spoke with an angry rumble. "Do you help to perpetuate lies about Sydney?"

Gwen held firm to her own anger. "You defend and protect her no matter what is said. Do you not see she has blinded you to the truth?"

"What truth, Gwen? We love, she helps heal the ill and guides the lovesick. She has done only good and has caused no harm. And yet you speak of her as if she is pure evil."

"I want what is best for you," Gwen said, softly, her slim shoulders sagging as if weighted by a burden.

"Sydney is best for me."

"And what is best for Sydney? If gossip continues and

if a bishop should arrive here to investigate witchcraft, what then? How safe will Sydney be? How well can you protect her?"

"I must quell the gossip and reassure the clan that all is well and they have nothing to fear." A task that sounded simple to his ears, but in his heart he understood it would be near impossible.

"But they do fear, and that fear has taken firm root and grows wildly. Sydney is in danger and you know it, but you refuse to acknowledge that she would be safer if she went away."

"I do not want to lose her again."

"You have a responsibility to this clan and must see to it. You also have a responsibility to the woman you love, to protect and care for her. To achieve that your only choice would be to send her away."

Duncan made no comment; he stared at his sister with eyes that warned she tread on dangerous ground.

Gwen persisted, reaching out to lay her hand on her brother's arm. "If you truly love her you will let her go, insist that she go—if you truly love her."

Twenty-four

Sydney rose with the dawn. The stunning sight never failed to steal her breath away. The bright orange ball would rise as if it was being born from the depths of the earth. Fresh and renewed it would cast its brilliance and offer the same renewal to anyone who cared to observe its magic. After centuries the whole process still amazed her and filled her with joy. Every day was a new beginning.

She wore an old beige cotton shift, had left her feet bare and pinned her dark hair up and set to work on the front door. She now wore traces of the white paint on her shift along with the purple paint she used to write the protective rune script over the top of the door. She felt good examining the results of her labor.

The front door now welcomed with its brightness and would soon welcome with a spring wreath. She had taken time to hunt the woods for branches, berries and herbs to make the wreath.

With coffee and a cinnamon bun in hand she walked over to where she had arranged a blanket on the ground with all the material and tools needed to make the wreath. She sat down and went to work on the wreath.

She favored time alone now and again. It gave her time to think, clear her head, sort things out and reach reasonable solutions to any concerns at hand. And then again it was a time to simply favor the peace and calm of solitude.

Beatrice startled Sydney when she suddenly flitted in her face.

"Gwen heads this way."

Sydney nodded and knew her time of solitude was at an end and the day had started anew.

Gwen entered the clearing of Sydney's cottage and stopped when she spotted Sydney sitting on the ground, her hands skillfully working slim branches into a wreath.

Sydney smiled and waved to her, sensing her reluctance to approach.

Gwen stepped forward with caution and determination. She wore her plaid high and tight around her pale yellow blouse and brown skirt. She was proud of her heritage and her plaid announced it.

"I have come to talk with you," Gwen said once she stood in front of Sydney.

"I am glad. We have had no chance to talk since my return and I have missed our conversations." Sydney patted a spot on the blanket. "Join me."

Gwen looked hesitant but sat. She eyed the nearby coffee mug suspiciously.

Sydney picked it up. It was too late to hide it, so better to offer it. "A brew I discovered on my journeys and grew fond of. Would you like to try it?"

Gwen shook her head. "The smell is strange."

"The taste is not." Sydney took a sip of mocha chocolate-flavored coffee and sighed appreciatively.

"You make a wreath?" Gwen nodded toward the lean branches that formed a circle.

Sydney proudly held it up for inspection. "A spring one

for my door. A few more branches and it will be ready to decorate with berries and herbs."

"Will it hold magic?"

Sydney expected the question and suspected that the questions to follow would be more challenging. "How could a wreath formed from the wonders of the woods not be magical?"

"You always managed to dance around answers, never speaking straightforward."

"An art, do you not think?" Sydney asked, smiled and placed the wreath in her lap, continuing to work on it as they talked.

"Or a way to conceal the truth?"

Sydney was a young woman when she had known Gwen, now she was a mature woman steeped in much knowledge and a woman who did not intend to play games.

"What truth, Gwen?"

"The truth to questions you want no one to have the answers to."

"What questions do you speak of?" Sydney's hands skillfully worked on the wreath, though her mind remained steady on the subject at hand and Gwen. She seemed rigid and tense, nothing like she had once been. Once she had laughed freely and lived life fully, making many smile along with her.

"Magic and witchcraft. You have returned with much power. Power I never imagined possible. You were but a simple healer when you left here and now—" She shook her head and crossed herself. "And now—" She shook her head again.

"I mean harm to no one." Sydney wanted her intentions clear, whether Gwen believed her or not. What had happened to Gwen in the past thirteen years? She was not at all as Sydney recalled and the thought troubled her.

"Yet the clan grows fearful and restless with the spells they have seen you work."

"I have cast no spell on anyone since my return."

Gwen turned wide eyes on her. "How can you say that when you healed those who should not have healed?"

"Knowledge healed Margaret's face and Angus's shoulder, not magic."

Gwen spoke low. "Where did you learn this knowledge?"

Sydney offered the truth. "In my travels I met many wise men and women and I studied and learned."

"How do you know where they got their knowledge? How do you know it is not the work of evil?"

Sydney remained patient, understanding how her advanced knowledge could appear evil to the less educated. "Margaret is happy and prospers. Angus is healing well and will be able to use his arm without a problem. How can such good results come from evil?"

"The two could be beholding to an evil source they have no knowledge of and will discover their debt at a later time."

Sydney shook her head. "They owe no debt. They heal because someone studied theories and methods and reached conclusions." She avoided saying anything about experiments. Science could not have progressed without them, but if not understood, an uneducated mind might view them as evil.

Gwen grew frustrated with Sydney's reasonable answers. "What of the infestation? Did you rid the grain of insects with knowledge?"

"A partnership of knowledge and belief rid the grain of the infestation." She wanted to avoid any reference to magic though she doubted Gwen would let her. It was almost as if Gwen wished to judge and condemn her.

"What belief is that?"

"Belief in the old ways."

"Magic," Gwen said in a whisper.

"Call it what you will, but in your heart you know the truth of the old ways."

"I do not." Gwen sounded insulted.

"But you do," Sydney said. "Your heritage is steeped in such beliefs. Your ancestors believed in the old ways, in the cycles, in magic. And it worked for them, so why now are those same beliefs that thrived for centuries evil?"

"We know better; we have learned."

"I have learned as well, but I do not disregard the knowledge or beliefs of my ancestors. Your own grandmother believed as I do."

"Hush," Gwen snapped. "I want no retribution brought down on me if a church official should come."

"Church official?" Sydney asked, concerned. There was sure to be trouble if the church was sent to investigate.

"There is talk that someone has advised the abbey at Loch Catherine that witchcraft is suspected here."

"That is not good."

"Nay, it is not and I worry about the clan, but mostly I worry about my brother." She reached her hand out and grasped Sydney's wrist. "I fear that his love for you will bring him harm."

Gwen was filled with fear and a chill raced through Sydney, knowing what she was about to say.

She released Sydney's wrist and stood looking down at her with condemning eyes. "If you love my brother leave him."

Sydney spoke with strength and conviction. "I will not run away again."

"You will see my brother suffer?"

Sydney moved the wreath off her lap and glared up at Gwen. "I would never wish suffering on anyone."

"You brought suffering down on this clan."

A gentle voice entered the heated debt. "Ignorance brought the suffering."

Gwen jumped, startled not having heard anyone approach, and turned, her eyes spreading wide when she looked upon the beautiful woman standing behind her. Her long hair was a golden red, and she wore a blue skirt with a pale blue blouse and a bright purple shawl was tied around her waist, the point falling comfortable over her right hip.

"Good morning, I am Tempest," she said and held out her hand.

Gwen hesitated and took a step away.

"Tempest is a friend of mine," Sydney said, realizing too late that connecting Tempest to her would only make Gwen more suspicious.

"You are a witch?" Gwen asked candidly.

Sydney spoke up. "She is a friend and a good, kind woman."

"Do not let your own fears and the ignorance of others blind you to the truth," Tempest said, lowering her hand so the woman did not feel obligated to accept her offer of friendship.

Gwen shook her head. "I am not certain what to believe anymore. I only know that since Sydney's return nothing has gone right. I have planned and worked hard and have given up much so that this clan would thrive. And the fruit of my hard labor was about to see fruition with my brother's marriage."

"The clans will still unite," Sydney said. "You achieved what you planned."

"Nay, I did not. It was a marriage for my brother and children so that the clan would continue."

"The clan will always continue," Sydney said, knowing for a fact that it had. The clan name had taken on different variations through the centuries, but it had remained strong.

"All your learned knowledge confirms this?" Gwen asked.

Sydney heard the sarcasm in her voice but chose to ignore it. The woman was upset and rightfully so. "The leadership of the clan confirms it."

"Aye, the leadership of the clan—Duncan. But he cannot continue to lead if faith in his leadership is lost, and at the moment that faith is fading quickly."

"Your brother is strong and courageous and knows what to do."

"He knows what to do, but love blinds him. I only hope his love for you does not bring the downfall of the clan and his demise." Gwen marched off, leaving the impact of her remark to settle in.

Tempest joined Sydney on the blanket. "Her concern is understandable. So many innocent people suffered needlessly and horrendously through this period in history."

"I remember taking refuge far north where the old ways were treated with respect, and the news that trickled in now and again from the outside world was studied with interest. And the knowledgeable ones cautioned all that the old ways must survive and be protected."

Tempest nodded. "So we turned silent, kept the old ways strong within us, teaching those who followed. It was ages ago and yet here we sit in the midst of it all."

"We need to be careful."

"Were you not careful on arrival?"

Sydney shook her head. "I did nothing that would cause anyone to think me other than a healer, though those I healed were healed with knowledge yet to be learned."

"And what one cannot understand, one fears, so the clan gossips about your *strange* healing powers."

"I can say that it is not the entire clan. Many continue to seek my help with ailments and approach without fear."

"Then someone must be fueling this fear, but who, and more importantly, why?"

"I know another witch is around this area. I sensed the spell and dispelled it easily. This is not a powerful witch, though I think he or she tends more to the warlock ways, the darker side of magic."

"You have had no success in discovering the identity of this person?"

"I have only recently discovered that another witch is present and I have had no time to investigate."

"We are all here now and will help you," Tempest said,

"though we must be careful to not raise anymore suspicion."

A rustle of leaves and crunch of twigs surrounded by busy chatter caught their attention, and out of the woods stepped Ali and Sarina.

Ali called out as she hurried over to her aunt, "Please, please tell me you have a bathroom."

Sydney nodded and Ali rushed past her toward the cottage. "It is invisible to the unknowledgeable eye."

Ali waved a hand and hurried into the cottage.

Sarina joined the two women. "This time is difficult for her. She is very much a modern woman."

"And she is very much a witch," Tempest reminded. "She is three hundred years old and has no doubt used the woods when necessary."

Sarina laughed. "Which I reminded her, and I must say in her defense she tried."

"What happened?" Tempest asked, certain that if it involved Ali something went amiss.

"She did not take a close look at where she squatted and received a surprise from the nesting animal beneath her."

The women laughed.

Ali joined them, plopping down beside her aunt and picking up the wreath. "Go ahead, have a good laugh at my expense, but I'm telling you right now, when you're bent over, bare bottom up, looking into a pair of beady black eyes and sharp teeth you realize the woods is no place for bare bottoms."

When the laughter finally subsided, the talk turned serious. Sydney and Tempest explained to the other two women what they had been discussing and the seriousness of the situation.

"We must remember the present time period and the ramifications of being suspect of practicing witchcraft. We have all lived during such horrendous times and witnessed the atrocities that went on. If our ways, manners and speech appear foreign we will cause suspicion. We must be vigilant in all we do."

"I worry about Sebastian," Sydney said, looking to Ali. "Your husband only knows the modern world. He truly is a foreigner here and he is still a novice to the craft, and that can cause him problems."

"He is sensible though and realizes the situation, for he has warned me that my tongue sounds too modern and that I should weigh my words well before speaking."

The women laughed.

"What was your response?" Sarina asked, knowing Ali did not take well to dictates.

Ali grinned. "Let's just say he knows that I am in full control of my tongue."

The women roared.

Beatrice flitted down in the middle of them, visibly upset. "It is good to see you all."

"What is wrong?" Tempest asked.

"Duncan has attempted to quell the gossip, talking with the clan, reassuring them that all was well and that no magic was afoot."

"Something happened," Sarina said, sensing the problem. "It troubles many."

Beatrice nodded. "Duncan did well turning frowns to smiles and doubts to belief. The clan even welcomed Sebastian, Dagon and Michael when they entered the village and Duncan introduced them as friends."

"Tell us what happened," Ali said impatiently.

Beatrice did not hesitate. "Right in front of many eyes a small log suddenly turned into a frog and then another and another and another."

"Sebastian!" Ali said, and jumped to her feet.

Tempest stood quickly and prevented Ali from running off. "Your husband may be a novice when it comes to spells but he is not ignorant. He would never have attempted a spell in front of so many."

"Tempest is right," Sarina agreed, as did Sydney.

"This is the work of a witch who wishes her or his magic to be purposely seen and for it to be blamed on Sydney. We must find out who," Tempest said.

"Where do we begin?"

"With our strengths," Tempest said, and the women smiled.

Twenty-five

Duncan stood in the middle of at least fifty frogs and a group of hysterical people. He was a warrior skilled in battle. He had faced dangerous enemies many times and death twice and had triumphed, but logs turning into frogs he did not know how to combat.

Michael made his way through the crowd of frogs. "I could easily get rid of the frogs but that might cause a bigger problem."

Dagon and Sebastian joined the two men.

"It is the witch's doing," cried out one young woman.

"It is not," Bethany said in defense of Sydney.

Duncan sent her a grateful glance.

"This will get out of hand if we do not quell it," Dagon said.

"A reasonable explanation for the frogs' sudden appearance would appease the people," Sebastian said.

"True as that may be," Duncan said, "where is the reason in a log turning into a frog?"

Sebastian remained patient. He had learned the necessity

of patience in dealing with his newly acquired witchcraft skills, and patience was definitely a requisite in his profession—security. He owned the top security firm in Washington, D.C., and dealt with many politically important people who were forever impatient. They wanted results and they wanted it immediately. This was such a case.

Expedient resolve was in everyone's best interest.

The people continued to complain, many in loud angry voices.

"This will turn disagreeable soon if we do not do something," Dagon said. "And that something must include drawing the blame away from Sydney."

"Magic," Sebastian said with a nod.

Dagon shook his head. "Poor choice."

"I'd agree with Dagon," Michael said.

Duncan listened, realizing the three men had more power to combat this situation than he did.

"No, not true magic—Hollywood magic." Sebastian smiled.

Duncan did not understand Sebastian, forget that his accent was difficult to comprehend, but some of his words were completely foreign and made no sense.

"Think about it," Sebastian continued. "Hollywood magic is making one believe what they see is real when it is—an illusion."

Michael grinned. "Good thinking."

Dagon agreed. "I do believe you are right."

"I do not understand," Duncan admitted, "but if it will help settle this crowd and help Sydney I am in agreement."

The three men nodded.

"A bit of real magic will be necessary," Sebastian said.

"Are you up to it?" Dagon asked with a grin.

"Frogs are no problem," Sebastian said. "Just don't ask me to materialize a person." He nodded toward a log beside a woman who looked to be complaining to two other women. "I'll start with that one."

Michael walked up beside Sebastian. "If you need help—"

"I won't, this is an easy one." Sebastian focused on the log, and a small frog hopped out of it. Another followed, then another and another.

"Well done," Michael said in a whisper and turned his attention to another log a few feet in the opposite direction.

One of the chattering women caught sight of the frogs. "More!"

The other nearby women screamed.

"Over here as well!" shouted a man.

"An evil omen," cried out another.

"Logs with frog nests in them," Thomas yelled, holding a log up and tipping it.

Frog after frog fell out and hopped off.

One brave woman picked up the log near her feet and did the same. A few more frogs fell out and then there were none. "Empty." She grinned in relief.

"I saw a log turn into a frog," said one insistent woman.

"This log?" Dagon asked, picking up one he had materialized among the hopping frogs around his feet.

The woman stood speechless, staring at the log, though another spoke up in her defense. "But I saw what she saw."

"This log?" Dagon asked again, shaking it and causing the frog he had magically placed inside to drop out.

The two women's eyes turned wide.

"Foolish women," a man shouted and threw his hands up into the air before turning and walking away.

"Losing your sight, Abby?" laughed another man.

"More like her mind," said another, joining in the teasing.

The short, round woman glared at the men. "I saw what I saw."

The men dismissed her insistence with a hearty laugh.

Abby would not be disregarded that easily. "You are all fools if you allow yourself to be tricked by the witch."

"Sydney is not here," a man called out.

"How do we know that?" questioned another. "She could be nearby."

"She does not need to be here to perform her magic," shouted a woman.

"What goes on here?" Gwen pushed past people, making her way toward her brother, then stopped when she caught sight of the plethora of frogs. She met her brother's eyes in silent question.

A thought struck Duncan. "Where have you been, Gwen?"

"I visited with Sydney."

A sudden hush fell over the grumbling crowd.

"Sydney remained at her cottage?" Duncan asked, relieved that he could finally prove to the crowd that their fears were unfounded.

Gwen nodded. "Aye, I left her visiting with a friend."

The crowd grumbled once again and he wished his sister had kept that bit of information to herself. Any friend of Sydney's would fall suspect to witchcraft, but he could not worry about that now. Now he needed to make certain that Sydney was not blamed for the frogs.

"Sydney then remains busy speaking with a friend?"

"And making a spring wreath."

Her remark caused many women to smile and Duncan's concern to lessen at least a little.

Bethany spoke up. "Sydney always crafted beautiful wreaths, their rich scents lasted months."

"Magic," Abby said, refusing to change her opinion.

"Herbs," said another woman. "Sydney uses an abundance of herbs and adds more every few days to keep the scent strong. She advised me of this when I inquired about her fragrant wreaths."

Duncan took command. "You all now see for yourself that Sydney performed no magic. She visited with my sister and now visits with a friend."

Most of the crowd nodded and began to turn their attention elsewhere, disregarding the frogs hopping off in all directions while many more frogs disappeared with the help of a little magic from Dagon and Michael. A few persistent people remained firm in their opinions, though they moved off, busy in their gossip.

Gwen marched up to her brother. "What is this about?"

"Misunderstanding." He had no doubt that he spoke the truth. It was not magic but simply fear of what one did not understand.

Gwen did not easily accept his brief explanation. "There is more you do not tell me."

"I tell you what I know."

The strength in his voice warned her that she would get no more information from him, and when she attempted to discover the identity of the three men around him Duncan informed her that they would speak later. She had no choice but to nod and take herself off, leaving the men to talk in private.

"A place where we can speak?" Michael asked.

"My solar," Duncan suggested, and motioned to Thomas that he wished to speak with him.

Thomas hurried over and Duncan quickly introduced the three men as friends of Sydney's. Thomas immediately understood. "Keep your eyes open and your ears strong. I need to know what is about. I will be in my solar."

Thomas nodded. "We will speak later."

His remark told Duncan that he would have news for him when they spoke. He was glad there was one person he could trust beyond a doubt, for at the moment he was not certain who was trustworthy.

The crowd had dispersed and only a few disgruntled villagers remained busy in gossip. Duncan paid them no heed; he walked with the three men into the keep and straight to his solar. He ignored the curious stares and hushed whispers, more intent on finding out as much as he could about these witches who fell from the sky.

With tankards filled with ale and seats taken in front of

the cold fireplace, the four men were ready to discuss issues at hand.

Duncan was blunt. "Sydney tells me that she has returned from the future to me. You all come from the future as well? This is where she knows you from?"

Dagon and Sebastian purposely remained silent. Michael and his wife Tempest had opened the portal in time to return Sydney to the past and they had done so again when Sarina, Dagon's wife, had insisted that Sydney was in danger and required assistance. Michael would therefore be best in explaining it all to Duncan.

"Sydney has discussed this with you?" Michael asked.

"I know little of it since we have had limited time to discuss it at length, and I understand even less."

"I imagine it overwhelms you," Michael said, realizing that much must be left for Sydney to discuss with him. He, Dagon and Sebastian could only help prepare him for what was to come.

Duncan took a generous gulp of ale then shook his head. "I think I am a fool for believing this all possible." He shook his head again. "Witches falling from the sky?" He looked from one man to another. "Are you all as old as Sydney?"

Dagon answered first. "I am around three hundred years old."

Duncan took another gulp of ale.

"I'm the youngest and a novice to the craft," Sebastian offered. "I'm only thirty-nine years old and I converted when I pledged my love to Ali; I have no regrets."

Duncan appreciated his honesty and looked to Michael, expecting, for some unknown reason, that his tale would be the most challenging to accept.

"I am young and old at the same time and it is a tale left for another time."

"You are the most powerful?" Duncan asked, having noticed how the other two men deferred to him when it came to magic.

Dagon grinned and raised his tankard. "To the most powerful witch among us."

Sebastian joined in the toast, holding his tankard high.

Duncan respected Michael though he had only met him. He appeared honest and loyal to his friends, so it was not difficult to raise a glass in his honor.

Michael raised his own tankard. "To my wife—the Ancient One."

The three men downed a gulp while Duncan stared at Michael. "The Ancient One is a myth."

"You have heard of her?"

"Who has not in these parts? It is told that the Ancient One was born with the dawn of time, that she walks this land and protects the innocent and that her magic is—"

Michael finished, "Pure love."

"She is a myth, a mere legend."

"No, I can assure you she is not a myth. She is real; she is my wife."

Duncan grew silent for a moment. "I am honored by her presence."

"Thank you," Michael said with relief and surprise. "I thought perhaps you might fear her as some do."

"Those who lack understanding fear," Duncan said. "In the years Sydney has been gone I thought much about her words and her beliefs and I am now beginning to realize how much knowledge she left with me. Knowledge for my own protection. It took time for me to realize it, though I thought it only thirteen years. It has been much longer. How is this possible? How did you all travel here?"

Some questions Michael could answer easily; others involved an understanding of true magic. "I will attempt to explain it."

Duncan moved to the edge of his seat, anxious to hear his words.

"Thought is energy and energy is ever continuous, thereby allowing all time to exist simultaneously. The wisdom contained in that energy can find a portal in time—

the opening between the worlds—allowing a person to travel in time."

"Tempest possesses such wisdom?" Duncan asked, attempting to understand.

"Yes, she does."

"But both of you opened the portal on two occasions, not only Tempest," Sebastian said, curious to understand and learn along with Duncan. "Once when Sydney was sent back and then again when we all took the return trip."

Michael explained, "It takes much energy to accomplish such a feat, two powerful energies make it a bit easier." He pointed to Sebastian then Dagon. "With focus, deep concentration and belief you both could do it."

Sebastian laughed along with Dagon.

"We are both novices when it comes to such a powerful feat," Dagon said.

"More because it is an unnecessary feat," Michael said. "There is no reason to travel in time. The time you are presently in is the important time. Your concentration should be focused on present purposes."

"Then why did Sydney return to me?"

The three men looked at Duncan.

"That is a question for Sydney to answer," Michael said. "My main concern is your understanding of Sydney's ways—our ways—and Sydney's safety."

"That is what brought you here? Sydney's safety?"

Dagon answered. "My wife, Sarina, is a powerful seer. She can see much and she warned us that Sydney was in danger and someone was requesting help from wise ones."

"It was but a jest," Duncan said.

"Was it?" Dagon asked. "Sarina told me the message was sent with great concern and a strong belief."

Duncan turned quiet.

"You want to believe but you fight it," Sebastian said.

"You are a seer too?" Duncan asked.

"No, a man who once felt as you do now. I wanted to believe, and the more I fell in love with Ali the more strongly I wanted to believe. Then my own ego interfered and I foolishly believed the spell she had cast on me had caused me to fall in love with her."

"A spell can bring no harm and a love spell can only work if it is good for both," Duncan said.

Sebastian raised his tankard to Duncan. "You're a wiser man than I was."

"Sydney is a good teacher," Duncan said with pride.

"I agree," Sebastian said, "so don't be as foolish as I was—believe in her with all your heart and soul."

Duncan collapsed back in the thick wooden chair. "I believe in her, but I worry for her safety. Though we live high in the Highlands, far removed from much that goes on, gossip still travels."

"I am surprised that your clan fears the old ways," Dagon said. "I recall this area being steeped in the old beliefs, magic, fairies and myths."

Duncan scratched his head. "I think I recall seeing a fairy."

"Beatrice is her name and you will see her again," Dagon assured him. "But tell me, for I am curious, what caused your clan to fear the old beliefs?"

"I cannot say for sure or point to one particular thing. It seemed that things happened. Thomas's son died and the old woman who tended to the birthings was blamed. Crops failed one year, some animals turned ill another and then we heard that a law was passed by the Queen outlawing the practice of witchcraft. More gossip followed with tales of those burned for being witches after admitting under torture to consorting with the devil and practicing the black arts. More and more people began to fear the old ways."

"Maybe it wasn't the old ways they feared," Sebastian suggested. "Maybe it was the new ways and how they were forced upon them."

Duncan nodded. "That could be. I have heard that many who held firm to the old beliefs fled north where the land still holds many mysteries and where few wish to go."

"These problems started after Sydney left?" Michael asked.

"Aye," Duncan confirmed, "though I thought nothing of them. Crops do fail, animals grow ill; it is the way of life."

"The clan thought otherwise?" Dagon asked.

Duncan thought. "They grumbled now and again."

"About witchcraft?"

Duncan stared at Dagon. "You try to determine if witchcraft was present before Sydney returned?"

"Yes, if witchcraft was responsible for anything that had gone on before then—"

"Sydney would not be responsible for the present difficulties," Duncan said, a sense of relief rushing over him. "It is not easy being in love with a witch."

"Tell me about it," the three men said in unison.

Duncan laughed. "But you are witches yourselves."

"That doesn't make it any easier," Michael assured him.

"At least life is never boring when you're married to a witch," Sebastian said. "There's always some surprise, like traveling back in time and learning what it truly means to live life without a toilet."

Dagon and Michael laughed.

"What is a toilet?" Duncan asked.

"A device that tends to convenience and unpleasant odors and once used is difficult to do without." Sebastian raised his refilled tankard.

"Here, here," agreed Dagon and Michael.

A reminder that these men he conversed with came from the future brought an unwanted question to mind, though Duncan felt compelled to ask regardless of the answer.

"You will all return to the future?"

"When we are finished here," Michael answered.

Duncan looked directly to Michael for the answer to his next question. "Will Sydney return with you?"

Twenty-six

Duncan lay in his bed, his thoughts chaotic and the hour late. His bare arms cushioned his head and a light blanket was drawn up to his waist. His chest was bare, though the heat from the low burning fire in the hearth kept him comfortable, the cool night air causing several hearths to be lit throughout the keep.

His thoughts troubled him since speaking with Dagon, Sebastian and Michael, and he had grown more troubled after speaking with Thomas. He had successfully avoided Gwen, not wanting to discuss the frog matter with her or Eileen's departure that morning. The young woman was happy to leave and he was relieved to see her go, wishing her well with the man of her choice.

She would be happy he had no doubt, but then she loved a mortal, not a witch from hundreds of years in the future.

Michael had answered his question honestly, though with understanding, and his words remained constant in Duncan's mind.

That is for Sydney to say.

He had thought to go see Sydney this night, but time did not permit it and he had wondered if his own fear of the answer had kept him away. It disturbed him that he was a fearless warrior who feared confronting a woman, but it was actually the answer he feared.

How did he prevent her from going away? Or how did he prevent himself from sending her away when he knew she would be safer far from here at this time?

He felt as if a knife twisted in his stomach when he thought of a day without Sydney. He had spent too many years without her and she had spent far too many years without him.

But what was the best answer to their problem?

If she remained here the danger would worsen and her life would surely be in jeopardy.

Thomas had made it worse when he had informed him that many of the clan felt that when Sydney left thirteen years ago she had left a spell on the clan, causing the various problems that had plagued them from time to time.

Duncan found that odd since Sydney's name had not been mentioned once when a problem had surfaced in the years she was away. And the clan had suffered no major problems in her absence, a few illnesses, a crop that did not produce as expected and various other annoyances. The only problem that had caught the clan's attention was when gossip spread about Thomas's son being born dead.

It was then witchcraft was mentioned, and news began to trickle up into the Highlands about witchcraft being considered the work of the devil.

Michael had asked many questions after avoiding answering Duncan's question, but they were pertinent questions concerning the problem at hand. It was concluded that another witch was present in the nearby area and was causing the commotion in the village.

The reason for the witch's antics seemed to be directed at Sydney, unless of course the unknown witch had bumbled all her attempts and accidentally caused chaos.

Dagon could relate to such a theory since his wife, Sarina, had experienced a problem with her powers due to a spell, so there was that possibility.

The men attempted to determine the best approach. Naturally the less attention drawn to Sydney the better, so they agreed that their presence in the area would remain limited. The clan did not need strangers, especially friends of Sydney suddenly appearing out of nowhere.

In the meantime they would use their abilities to see if they could discover the identity of the witch and put an end to her troublemaking.

So why did Duncan find no relief in these decisions?

He wished at that moment Sydney was with him. They could discuss at length all the troubling concerns like they had once done. There had not been an issue they had not discussed when last they were together. Sometimes they did not agree and a heated debate helped to sway one or the other's opinion. Other times they would laugh at their differences, for they would see how foolish they were, and of course there were times they agreed on things, which had been most times.

At first he had thought it odd that they got along so well. She was a healer, a woman, and yet she had become his best friend. Even when he had discovered she was a witch it had not disturbed him.

A witch after all had been considered a wise person, who many in the clan would seek advice from and that advice always proved helpful. So her beliefs had not bothered him as long as she cast no spell over him, and she had given him her word on it.

He shook his head and stared at the wooden rafters high up. Where had things gone wrong between them? Why had she felt it necessary to leave? Had their love not been strong enough to survive any problem?

"I want you here and now, Sydney," he said, frustrated. "I want to talk with you, to hold you, to love you, and damned but I never want to let you go."

He sighed, releasing as much of his annoyance as possible, though more remained locked inside him.

A low rumble of laughter escaped him. If Sydney were here she would bombard him with endless questions in an attempt to reach the root of his annoyance and then she would help him to understand it and lastly urge him to do something about it.

Think it through, take action, and solve it, she would say to him.

"Think it through," he said out loud. How could one think through falling in love with a witch that returns to him from hundreds of years in the future?

"Fool," he whispered.

"Would that be you or me?" came the soft voice from the dark corner.

Duncan sprang up in bed. "Sydney?"

"You did summon me, did you not?"

She stepped forward and his breath caught.

She wore a long, black silk garment, two thin straps over her shoulders held it on her body while the soft luscious material fell over her breasts, down along her curvy hips, spreading generously out until it ended at her ankles.

He found his breath, actually it found him, for he gasped a bit then spoke. "You heard me?"

"Aye, I heard you call, softly at first and then a bit more adamantly. Since your summons seemed urgent I thought it best I come to you."

Duncan smiled and sat straight up, throwing his arms out wide. "Then come to me."

She laughed and approached his bed slowly. "That is not the urgency I heard."

"It is an urgency now, woman, come here." He summoned her with the sharp wave of his hand.

She stopped and crossed her arms over her chest. "You think to command me instead of woo me?"

"Do not make me get out of bed," he warned with a teasing grin.

"Are you naked?" She sounded like she challenged instead of questioned.

"You will find out soon enough if you do not come over to me right now."

She laughed slowly as if she found his statement amusingly foolish.

"I will not warn you again, woman." He could not keep his smile from growing.

She remained were she was—laughing.

Duncan waited patiently like a warrior who knew the exact time to enter battle, and in this battle victory was assured.

Sydney kept her eyes on his eyes, knowing they would warn of his move and she intended to be prepared—at least she thought she would.

He sprang out of the bed so fast that Sydney jumped in surprise, which gave him time to reach her and sweep her up into his strong arms while he laughed as he hurried back to the bed with her.

They fell on the bed together in a tumble of laughter and teasing.

"That was not fair," Sydney insisted, attempting to free herself from his strong embrace, though not very forcefully.

"It was fair enough," he reasoned, throwing his leg over hers to settle her struggling and finding he very much enjoyed the soft silky feel of the black garment she wore. "You met my eyes and waited for me to alert you to my move."

"Huh!" she gasped. "You tricked me. You knew I would keep a keen eye on you."

"It is what you have always done. A good warrior learns his opponent's moves and makes use of them when in battle. That is why I am always victorious."

She ran a finger lazily over his lips. "What makes you think you are the victor?"

"I have got you where I want you." He sounded smug and ever so confident.

Her finger continued its lazy pace down along his jaw. "Are you sure of that?"

He looked down the length of her from where he hovered over her. "You lay beneath me exactly where I want you to be."

Her fingers roamed down along his chest. "And you are on top of me, exactly where I want you to be. So who is the true victor?"

He brought his lips to hers. "We both are victorious."

Their kiss was a blend of gentleness and passion and it captured their hearts and stung their senses. They lingered in their kiss, feeling deeply of all they shared and knowing there was more yet to come.

Duncan eased his mouth from hers. "I want to talk with you and yet I want you."

"We can talk later," she said, her own desire running rampart as her hand stroked his naked body.

"Later never seems to come with us." He shivered as her sensuous touch fired his already heated passion.

She ran her hands over his shoulders and slowly forced him onto his back. She crawled slowly over him, her hands touching and tormenting in the most intimate places. And when she took him firm in her hand she said, "This needs attention first—talk can wait."

He did not argue with her, and he certainly did not deny her when she climbed over him, settling herself comfortably against him.

He reached up and lowered the thin straps of her black gown. "I want to see your breasts. I love to look at them and feel them and most of all taste them." He rose up, his arms going around and up her back. He eased her toward him and took her nipple into his mouth and gently suckled the delicate nub.

His words and actions caused her passion to leap. Her breasts lacked the firmness of youth and she had assumed also lacked appeal, but she failed to realize that when one looked through the eyes of love everything appealed.

She rested her cheek on the top of his head and was grateful for this moment she shared with him. They would love strong and hard. They would talk. They would touch. They would rest beside each other in sleep. And they would hold on tight and never let go.

She eased him away.

He protested. "I am not finished."

"I find I cannot wait."

He laughed and nuzzled her neck. "You want me that badly do you?"

She moaned for her neck had always been sensitive to his playfulness, and then she wiggled her bottom against him. "I think you want me that badly."

He nipped at her neck several times, causing her to moan, sigh and whimper—all the sounds that had once excited him to a fever pitch—and still did.

"You will ride me?" He fell back on the pillow, secure with the answer.

"With pleasure."

"Take your gown off, I want to see all of your lovely body."

She lifted the nightgown off without hesitation. She felt comfortable in her nakedness, secure in his love for her, and she leaned down to give him a kiss.

Her words were simple. "I love you."

He captured her face in his hands. "Always, Sydney, I will always love you."

For a moment they remained as they were, peering into each other's eyes, realizing the depth of their love and knowing that not even centuries could have kept them apart.

Sydney rose then and took control, teasing and tormenting with nips and kisses, touches and strokes and a generous movement of her body against his.

When he finally could not stand it a moment longer he took command and settled himself deep inside her, and with his hands on her hips he took control of her ride, though in bare seconds it took control of them both.

Sydney bit her bottom lip, not wanting her screams of pleasure to echo throughout the keep, and when Duncan saw how she struggled to keep quiet, he lowered her down so that she could bury her face in the crook of his neck.

She held firm to him, enjoying every thrust and grind and wiggle and the sheer delight of loving him. It was not long before they both exploded in a blinding climax that had them both fighting to contain their screams of pleasure.

Sydney collapsed against him, her breath labored, her body completely relaxed and she completely satisfied.

He hugged her like a man unwilling to let her go and that was all right with her, for she was right where she wanted to be.

After several minutes Duncan noticed that her backside was turning cold and he eased her off him and eased them both beneath the soft wool blanket, where they snuggled in each other's arms.

"You will go nowhere," he said firmly.

"I had not planned on it," she said. While she could have argued and insisted it was her choice, she understood his demand. He wanted her there with him without worry or concern that she would leave. He knew the choice was ultimately hers and had often given her choices, something most men of that era did not often do. But then he was a man ahead of his time.

"This is good." He relaxed his embrace.

"Though I do not think it wise for anyone to know I am here."

"The clan knows I spent the night at your cottage." He did not care to hide his love for her though he could understand the wisdom of her words.

"My cottage is one thing, the keep is another. Until things settle I do not think my presence in your bedchamber should be known."

"I suppose you are right, and besides there are more other important matters to discuss."

"Where do you wish me to start?" Now it was time for them to talk.

"At the beginning of all this, thirteen years ago when you walked away from me, and I do not want to hear that you did what was necessary. I want to know why you thought it necessary and how when you loved me so very much you could turn away from me."

His words pierced her heart and tears threatened her eyes. "I loved you so very much that I never wanted to let you go."

"But you did."

"Please, Duncan," she pleaded softly. "This is difficult for me."

He hugged her. "I will listen."

The hurtful memory was hard to discuss, but it was necessary, as she hoped he would see. "I knew that you would grow old and I would not and the thought tore at my heart that one day I would lose you."

"So you robbed us of what life we could share?"

"You said you would listen," she reminded.

"I am sorry, but part of me remains angry at losing you."

"I understand since part of me remains angry with myself for being so very foolish." Before he could say another word she continued. "You see, there was a spell I could have cast that would have sealed our love, but only if our love was true and real would it have worked."

"We needed no spell to seal our love—it was sealed tightly from the moment I admitted my love for you and you for me."

"True, but this spell would have allowed for a more magical joining."

"But I had warned you about casting a spell over me. You left for this reason? Why not remain and see if you could have changed my mind? We were young, there was time."

"You had a duty to your clan, and once I heard that the

clan did not look favorably on our involvement I realized the difficulties that lay ahead for you."

"I heard no grumbling from the clan, all seemed pleased with you."

"But not for you to take as your wife." She paused and spoke softly. "You thought the same yourself but said nothing to me."

Duncan raised himself up on his elbow. "What nonsense do you speak? I never thought such a foolish thing."

"Gwen told me how you were duty bound to the clan to marry and have fine sons to carry on the clan name and that you understood it could not be with the likes of a *witch*."

Duncan frowned. "I told her no such thing."

Sydney turned wide eyes on him.

"Gwen attempted to convince me of such nonsense but I argued with her. I intended to marry for love, not for duty. I refused to be bound to a woman I cared naught for, and besides, I could never find another woman as special as you."

Sydney shook her head. "I do not understand. Gwen came to me frantic one night, telling me how you intended to leave the clan and go away with me and that if I loved you, truly loved—" She stopped suddenly and shivered.

"What is wrong?"

"When your sister visited with me yesterday morning she told me that if I loved you, truly loved you, I should leave you and bring an end to the difficulties."

"She told me that if I truly loved you I would send you away for your own good."

They both turned silent, and then Duncan spoke.

"She used our loved against us."

Sydney felt the hurt in his heart and tried to soften it. "She probably thought she was doing what was best for all."

"She knew how deeply we loved each other. She knew I planned to make you my wife; I told her often enough.

She made me believe she was happy for me, while behind my back she plotted to destroy my plans. She lied and manipulated both of us. She made you think she was your friend."

"I truly thought she was. She seemed happy that we loved, though . . ."

"What is on your mind?"

"If I remember correctly, a few months before I left she began to talk incessantly of you and the power of the clan and how important it was. There was a decisive change in her and it makes me wonder."

"Wonder what?"

"Wonder if the witch we seek has influenced your sister."

Twenty-seven

Duncan walked through the woods, his mind flooded with thoughts. He walked the familiar path to Sydney's cottage without thinking of his destination. He ignored the touch of summer's approach in the warm breeze, the abundance of flowers that had burst in a colorful display and the twittering of the baby birds waiting impatiently for feeding time.

All of nature's beauty was lost to him, his chaotic thoughts making him a prisoner of his mind.

He was concerned for his sister. Sydney and he had discussed the matter late into the night. He had wanted to speak to her about her return and the future she came from, but when they had reasoned that there was a good chance that Gwen was under the influence of a witch it was all that had mattered. He wanted to make certain to protect his sister and he did not know how to protect her against a witch.

What troubled him and Sydney the most was that this witch had interfered in their relationship, but why? What was the purpose? What did this witch want? And who was he?

Sydney had mentioned that the witch who cast the spell of infestation had little experience. The spell was easily dispelled. A spell cast by a strong witch was not dispelled so easily.

Duncan had slept little after that, his concern for his sister's well-being strong on his mind. He woke near dawn when Sydney attempted to ease herself from his bed. He reached out for her and she snuggled back in his arms.

They made love softly and lovingly, and reluctantly he let her go and reluctantly she left with dawn's first light. He had wanted her to stay by his side, but he understood that for now it was best for her own safety if she did not remain.

Gwen was not present for the morning meal and he thought to discuss the matter of another witch's presence with Thomas, but then thought better of it. Thomas would be safer if he remained ignorant of any matters concerning witchcraft.

His friend had informed him that gossip was rampant about sending notice to the church about witchcraft being practiced in the clan. Duncan did not wish to place Thomas in needless jeopardy.

He was also concerned for Sydney's friends. It would only be a matter of time before they became suspect. Strangers did not always fare well when evil doings were suspected. And being they were true witches, they would certainly be in danger. He would need to make certain they were cautious while here.

The most troubling and constant thought in his head was how long Sydney would be able to remain here before she was seriously in danger. The unknown witch's target appeared to be Sydney, which meant that spells would continue and the clan would grow more fearful, placing her in ever more danger.

How long before it would be necessary for her to leave?

This time, however, she would not return to him.

He stopped suddenly, the thought tormenting him. He wanted to cry out his rage as he did in battle, but he kept silent.

He sat on a nearby stump and glanced up at the bright blue sky. "I know not how to cast spells, but I do know I believe strongly in my love for Sydney and her love for me. I want her safe and I want to share my life with her. If there is a way for us to be together, without bringing harm to any, then I ask for it to be so."

"Good spell." Sebastian stepped from around a tree to join Duncan. He sat down on a fallen tree weathered by time but still solid.

"I feel at a loss with what to do," Duncan explained. "And I see how strongly Sydney's beliefs are and how they brought her back to me."

"I understand. I was at a loss myself when I met Ali. She simply burst into my office, placed a finger to my heart and cast a spell. I thought she was crazy—beautiful, but crazy—and after that my life was never the same. I must add though that I wouldn't have it any other way. Life with Ali is a challenge—a challenge I love and could not live without."

"I feel the same about Sydney, though I know not what to do."

"I wasn't sure myself, though living in the twenty-first century made it easier than living in this century. Witches are not persecuted in the future, though they are not accepted as they should be."

"They continue to suffer?" Duncan asked with concern.

"No, they practice their beliefs openly, though there are those who continue to object and mostly because they do not understand the Craft."

Duncan smiled. "So ignorance continues to exist in the future."

Sebastian laughed. "Guess we haven't evolved as much as we thought we have."

"You mentioned that you are a novice witch."

"It was my choice." He thought a moment. "Sought of my choice. You see, Ali was certain I would love her and she cast a love spell to seal our love. The problem was she didn't count on my sensible side interfering, so it took some time to accept that she was a witch, understand the spell didn't force me to love her only that it was necessary for me to admit my love for her. Once all that was out of the way, none too easily I must admit, I joined Ali in a spell under the full moon and sealed it by—" He grinned. "You get the picture don't you?"

Duncan smiled and nodded.

"Dagon had told me what I was to do concerning joining Ali in the spell, though he failed to tell me—on purpose of course because we didn't exactly get along when we first met—that the spell would also grant me the powers of a witch."

"When did you learn of your new abilities?"

"On my wedding night. Ali told me, I of course didn't believe her and then I tried a spell and damned if it didn't work. Keep in mind though that I am still a novice compared to the others and I frequently make mistakes, which made me think about the present problem you're having. That frog incident is definitely the work of a novice. Any skilled witch would have performed a more convincing feat and an inept witch would have made the ordeal worse."

"Sydney and I reached the same conclusion." Duncan went on to tell him several of the issues he and Sydney had discussed, including the part about the witch having interfered in their lives thirteen years ago.

"Damn, somebody certainly doesn't want Sydney with you. Any ideas who that might be?"

"Nay, I have thought endlessly upon it and cannot find an answer. Those in the clan are here by birthright and there have been no strangers about, at least none that I am aware of."

"Don't worry," Sebastian said, hoping to reassure him.

"Tempest and Michael are powerful witches, I'm sure they'll be able to help."

"I hope so and I hope soon, for if not it will not be safe for Sydney or any of you to remain here."

"Sydney won't leave you."

Duncan was adamant. "She will have no choice. I will keep her from harm even if it means sending her away."

Sebastian shook his head. "She won't go and you won't be able to make her go."

"She is a wise woman, she will go when necessary."

"Nope, not without you." Sebastian was just as adamant. "She's spent too many, way too many, years without you. She will not return to the future without you, and I doubt there is anyone who would convince her otherwise."

"I can go to the future?" Duncan asked, surprised.

"I assumed you would be returning with her. Sydney and Ali are very close and then there is our daughter and Dagon and Sarina's son." He shook his head again. "They are definitely going to need her guidance, not to mention we would all miss her terribly. I guess I thought she was simply coming to retrieve you and she would be home before we knew it."

"She returned here intending to bring me back to the future?"

"I can't say for sure. She was given the chance to return as a gift from Tempest and Michael for all she had done for them and us. She didn't hesitate; she stepped through the portal and vanished and—" Sebastian stopped suddenly and glared at Duncan. "You still haven't discussed this with Sydney have you?"

Duncan raked his hair in frustration. "As I told Michael, we have attempted to talk many times, but something always interfered. It is as if something constantly prevents us from discussing the matter."

"I shouldn't say any more, this is for you and Sydney to discuss."

"Nay, Sebastian, I need to know. Think how you felt

when you suddenly discovered witches existed. I was raised on such tales and beliefs and old ways, so it is not completely impossible for me to believe. But people falling from the sky and traveling back from the future? It does get difficult not to think it all foolish, even if one sees it with one's own eyes. I continue to ask myself if I really saw all of you fall from the sky. Was it real? Did I imagine it all?"

"Believe me, I understand completely. And just when I thought nothing would surprise me, damned if something didn't pop up that did."

Duncan waved at the insect that flew past his face, barely missing it.

"Easy, that's Beatrice," Sebastian warned, quickly raising his arm and blocking Duncan's second swing.

Beatrice came to rest on Sebastian's shoulder. "You best introduce me so that he does not accidentally knock me out like Michael once did."

Duncan stared at the tiny, plump fairy perched on Sebastian's shoulder. "I am not seeing things, she is real?" He scratched his head. "I do not know what is real and what is not anymore, though there were many times when I had thought I had seen a fairy."

"I am real, and *you* have the abilities to see fairies," Beatrice said.

"Duncan meet Beatrice, a very dear friend to us all," Sebastian said, and held out his hand for her to rest upon. He then raised it up so that Duncan could get a better look at the plump fairy whose hands rested on her plump hips and whose one wing forever remained crooked.

Duncan was amazed and leaned in closer. "Pleased I am to make your acquaintance, and it was fairies I was seeing. I did not imagine it?"

"And pleased I am to meet you," Beatrice said, giving her tilted head wreath a shove. "And relieved I am to not have to hide myself whenever you are about. It becomes tiresome and annoying, besides, I miss too much. And nay, you did not imagine fairies—you have the gift of seeing the little people."

Duncan smiled. "I am pleased to hear that. Do you live here in these woods or did you travel through the portal with Sydney?"

"I traveled through the portal, and a rough landing it was." She rubbed her backside.

The two men laughed.

"My grandmother often talked about the fairies in the woods, but I thought it only tales to entertain the children. Even when I saw them with my own eyes I did not believe," Duncan said, amazed that he could truly see fairies.

"Your grandmother was a wise woman; she understood the old ways." Beatrice walked back and forth on Sebastian's hand.

"Much wiser than I realized, and I am beginning to respect the old ways more and more."

Beatrice pointed her tiny finger at Duncan. "Your grandmother's wisdom is part of you now, use it as wisely as she did and you will know much happiness. Begin now—Sydney intends to visit with Dora while Ali and Sarina feel it is best she stays away from the village at least for a day or so, until talk settles some. But she is being her stubborn self and refuses to listen to reason."

"What does Tempest say?" Sebastian asked.

"Tempest and Michael went off early. No one knows what they are about."

Duncan stood, his shoulders wide, his chin up and his look determined. "Sydney will do as I say."

Sebastian laughed.

Duncan grinned. "I see you know Sydney."

"Well enough to know that demands and threats won't work with her, though sound reason will. She does not leap before she looks, as my wife does."

"Yet you told me that she did not hesitate to enter the time portal when offered to her."

"Would you have if it had been offered to you?"

Duncan thought on Sebastian's question as they walked in silence to Sydney's cottage. He liked Sebastian. He spoke truthfully and offered good advice and he had courage. He was not afraid to embrace the unknown. He had crossed centuries to return to a time unfamiliar to him to help Sydney, and he very much admired and respected him for that.

What if a portal in time was open for him and he had been given a choice to travel to the future to reunite with Sydney? Would he have the courage to take such a journey?

He knew nothing about the future, the land, the people, or the customs. He did not even know where Sydney called home in the future. He knew Scotland and only Scotland. And what did she do in the future? What was her life like?

"I need time with Sydney," Duncan said when the cottage came into view.

"No problem, I'll have us all on our way in no time," Sebastian said.

"It is not that I do not wish to—"

Sebastian stopped him. "No need to explain. I understand and think it is better you both talk privately."

He clasped a strong hand on Sebastian's shoulder. "I admire you and your courage, and I thank you for being such a good friend to Sydney."

"It's hard not to like Sydney. She has a way about her that makes you feel comfortable discussing anything with her and she cares, really cares about people."

"Aye, that she does." Duncan removed his hand. "A matter you need to be careful of Sebastian is your speech. I am beginning to understand you, but others will think you foreign and being a friend of Sydney's—"

Sebastian finished for him. "They would think me a witch."

"I noticed that your wife can switch her tongue and sound passable enough to those around here. Michael does the same, while Sarina and Dagon appear to have no problem with our language, so I assume Scotland has been their home for some time. And Tempest?" Duncan shook his head. "I doubt there is a language unfamiliar to her."

"I will be careful to mend my speech," Sebastian said with the best Scottish brogue he could muster.

Duncan laughed. "Speak as little as possible in front of others and you will have no problem."

Their grins were wide when they reached the cottage though faded fast enough when they heard the arguing going on inside. They opened the front door slowly.

"It is better that you remain here at least for the remainder of the day," Ali insisted, standing in front of the door as if she intended to block her aunt's exit.

"I need to check on Dora and make certain she and the baby are fine." Sydney continued packing herbs and flasks in a basket on the table.

"If she required your assistance, I am certain her husband would have sent word," Sarina said patiently.

"Thomas is too busy being a proud father to think of anything else."

"Sarina is right. Thomas would have sent for you if necessary," Duncan said, entering the cottage and stepping around Ali.

Sarina and Ali glanced up at the man who filled the cottage with his large presence, and they smiled, both noticing the appreciative gleam in Sydney's eyes. The man did look magnificent. Long dark hair, handsome face, broad chest and muscled arms and a plaid kilt that showed off his firm, long legs.

Sebastian walked up to his wife, kissed her cheek and slipped his arm around her waist. "Ladies, I think we should go."

Ali was about to protest when her husband gave her slim waist a gentle squeeze.

"You're right," she said. "Duncan can handle this."

Sarina joined the couple as they headed out the door. "No one *handles* Sydney."

Ali glanced back over her shoulder at her aunt staring lovingly at Duncan. "Oh, I think Aunt Sydney likes the way Duncan handles her."

With that they shut the door behind them.

Twenty-eight

Duncan placed a gentle hand to her cheek. "This time now is for us. Tell me of the future. Where you live? What you do? Why you left it to return to me and—" He paused and kissed her firmly before asking, "Do you intend to return to the future?"

Sydney reluctantly drifted away from him to sit at the table, moving the basket she had filled to the floor.

Duncan took a seat to her right, reached out and took hold of her hand, his gentle touch a sign of reassurance that he would listen to anything she had to say.

She smiled and squeezed his hand, grateful for his understanding and his love. "I have wondered how you would react to the future. There has been tremendous progress and yet sometimes I feel we have regressed in areas. Unfortunately, the world continues to war over religious beliefs and greed."

"So the world has yet to learn from its own mistakes?"

"Very much so," she said, shaking her head sadly. "But

there have been wondrous advances in technology and medicine."

"Which was why you were able to help Margaret and Angus?"

"Yes, I brought a few modern medicines along with me just in case they were needed."

"I have been wanting to ask you, but I suppose I worried over your response, now you give me the answer without me having to ask. You used modern medicine to heal Gwen's burn. Was there something on your hand when you touched her?"

Sydney looked confused. "I did not heal Gwen's burn, though I would have helped her if she allowed me to tend it."

"But it was healed, she showed me her arm and told me you had touched it, causing it to heal. She insisted it was magic, but now I thought it simply modern medicine you used."

Sydney thought a moment, sensing Duncan's confusion along with her own. "Had you seen the burn before it had healed?"

"Nay, I did not." He shook his head. "There was never a burn was there? It is not like my sister to lie."

"Gwen is not herself, understand that, for only then can you help her."

He nodded. "I am so glad you returned to me, but you know you took a chance healing with medicine yet to exist."

"I had to," she said quietly. "How could I return and not make use of my knowledge?"

"I have not gained the knowledge that you have during our years apart, but I have matured and see life much differently than I once did."

"Life has a way of doing that to you. Many times I thought about us and the foolish decisions I made."

He would not allow her to take all the blame. "I made many foolish decisions of my own."

"Let us say we both made our share of mistakes. We cannot go back and undo what we have done; we can only go forward, our love stronger, our decisions wiser. Actually, it was my love for you that forced me to grow. I immersed myself in studies and my studies took me traveling. I have seen the world, and though it is a large place it is also small, for while there are distinct cultures, people truly are basically the same."

"My world is Scotland; I know little else, though the thought of learning about other cultures and seeing other places intrigues me. After all your travels did you return to Scotland to stay?"

"I have a home in Scotland." She did not think it was wise to tell him that her home sat on Tavish land. There would be time to explain that later. "I reside mostly in a place called America, in a state called Virginia. It is a beautiful home with much land that dates back to the 1600s. It is convenient for me, being the Wyrrd Foundation is based in America's capital city called Washington, D.C., only a short distance away."

Duncan shook his head, released her hand and sat back in his seat. "You speak of a time yet to come, of lands yet to be known and what is this Wyrrd Foundation?"

"It is a dream of mine come true and it carries my family name—Wyrrd." She smiled with pride. "I had wanted to establish a foundation based on the very heart of my beliefs. The foundation helps those in need. There are various divisions of the foundation, one that strictly deals with children, another the homeless, another education and so forth. It took many years of hard work but it has all been worth it. The foundation is worldwide and helps everyone, regardless of beliefs."

Duncan stared at Sydney for several silent minutes. "You take joy from this work."

"I receive joy from this work."

"It must be difficult being back here after having lived in such a remarkable time."

"This time in history has something the future does not." He smiled and thumped his chest. "Me."

She laughed and hurried out of her seat to plop down in his lap and throw her arms around his neck. "Aye, you." She kissed him and pressed her cheek to his. "No matter where I went or what I learned I never stopped thinking of you or missing you. You remained strong in my mind and heart."

He kissed her forehead and rested his head to hers. "You returned for me then?"

"Aye, for you. I had thought that I would never see you again and then I was given a chance to return—a second chance for us. Without thought to the consequences I took the chance."

"You had no plan in mind upon your return?"

"Only to find you."

He asked the question that haunted his thoughts. "Will you return to the future?"

She answered quickly. "Not without you."

He hugged her tightly as if fearful she would be snatched away from him. "We will make it this time, you and I, our love is too strong not to."

She rested her head on his shoulder. She was content here with him like this and wished it could remain so, but interference from an unknown source threatened their relationship and her very existence. Until that source could be determined and dealt with decisions were impossible to make.

A rap on the door followed by Tempest's melodious voice interrupted their solitude.

Sydney reluctantly removed herself from Duncan's embrace and went to open the door.

"We would not have interrupted if it was not important," Tempest said, entering along with Michael.

"You discovered something?" Sydney asked, hopeful

that the situation could be settled well and no difficult decisions would be necessary.

"Possibly," Michael said.

Sydney hurried them to the table to sit and reached for Duncan's hand as she took her seat.

"Do you know anything about the old woman who lives across the loch and who many villagers believe to be a witch?" Michael asked.

They all looked to Duncan.

"Elizabeth, though I have heard that she resides there no more."

"When did she arrive and depart?" Tempest asked.

Duncan gave the question a moment of thought. "If I remember right the old woman arrived several months before Sydney left and remained until—" He thought again. "Recently, she left only recently, though I cannot say for sure if she took her leave before Sydney's second arrival or afterward. I only know that she is gone."

"How do you know?" Michael asked.

"News spreads quickly in the village."

"So does gossip," Michael said.

"Are you saying that it is only gossip that she has left?"

"What I am wondering is has anybody been across the loch to find out for themselves?"

"I cannot say for sure, only what I have heard from others."

"Which means you are not certain if the old woman actually resides there or not," Michael said.

"True, I have not seen it with my own eyes," Duncan admitted. "Do you suspect she is involved in some way?"

Tempest answered. "There is something that draws Michael and I to travel across the loch. We are not certain of its origin, only that it exists."

"A powerful force?" Sydney asked

"Not overly powerful, but one that has substance and draws from the energy around it."

"A warlock," Sydney said with certainty, and Michael cringed.

Duncan noticed his reaction. "You have dealt with a warlock before?"

Michael was honest. "I was a warlock."

"You practiced the dark side of witchcraft?" Duncan sounded more curious than fearful.

"At one time I did," Michael admitted. "But that is all behind me now thanks to my wife." He reached out and took her hand. "Her strength and courage saved me and gave me another chance."

"Does your second chance have something to do with my second chance?" Duncan asked, wanting to know all he could about the circumstances surrounding Sydney's arrival back in time.

"I believe that one good turn deserves another."

"That sounds like the belief of a wise witch."

Michael smiled. "It only took me several hundred years to figure it out."

"But you did, and that is what matters," Duncan said. "It seems that this warlock we deal with has not found wisdom."

"None at all," Michael said. "We should pay him a visit and have a talk."

"I think it wiser if Sydney and I go," Tempest said.

Both men stared at her with looks that meant to freeze her in place.

Tempest stood with a smile. "Since you have no objections. Sydney, let us be on our way."

"Absolutely not," Michael said, jumping to his feet.

"Sydney goes nowhere without me," Duncan said as he stood and went to stand beside Sydney.

"We are capable of taking care of ourselves, gentlemen," Tempest said and held her hand out to Sydney.

Michael grabbed it quick enough. "Neither of you ladies is going anywhere without us."

"I must agree with Tempest," Sydney said, "and if you

both would be patient for a moment I will explain why."

Their combined silence told her they would listen, though their stern looks warned they would not be swayed.

She offered her explanation without thought to their stubbornness. "If the old woman is there your presence would threaten her and she would not cooperate. Two women, however, she would relate to and talk easily with."

"And if she is not there?" Duncan inquired.

"We will simply search the area and see what we can find," Sydney said.

"What if a man is there?" Michael asked.

"A warlock," Duncan added.

"I would confront him," Tempest said without an ounce of fear.

"Wrong answer," Michael said adamantly. "We go with you."

"I can take care of myself and Sydney," Tempest insisted.

"Maybe so, but I'm still going with you," Michael said.

"As am I," Duncan agreed and took hold of Sydney's hand.

A hard rap sounded at the door before it flew open.

"Sorry," Thomas apologized. "You better hurry back to the keep. Abby is insisting she saw a witch flying on a broom."

Duncan cast Sydney a quick glance.

"We have never flown brooms," she said in a whisper.

"Michael, you will go with them?" Duncan asked, giving Sydney's hand a squeeze before joining Thomas at the door.

"Perhaps it would be best if Michael joined you," Tempest said and offered sound reasoning before both men could object. "Someone may be creating a problem you will find difficult to handle. Michael can at least be there to offer advice."

"Damn, I hate when you make sense," Michael said.

She kissed his cheek. "Go, Duncan could use your help

more, Sydney and I will be fine." She gave him a gentle shove toward the door.

He went reluctantly. "Be careful."

Duncan turned to Sydney. "I cannot get you to change your mind and wait until I am able to join you?"

"Worry not, we will be fine," Sydney said. "Go and take care and assure everyone that witches do not ride brooms."

Thomas shook his head. "Abby insisted she saw a witch with blond hair riding a broom."

Michael, Tempest and Sydney exchanged glances and all three shook their heads.

When the three men were a few feet away from the cottage Michael turned to Duncan.

"Maybe I should go see how Ali is doing."

"I was thinking the same."

"I will catch up with you and let you know." Michael took off on a swift run. For a moment he was tempted to simply transport himself to the cottage with the snap of his fingers, but he wasn't certain if anyone looked on and he didn't want to create any more hysteria by disappearing in front of someone.

It didn't take him long to get to the cottage they all shared. He found the two couples walking in the nearby woods, the women collecting herbs and the men collecting berries, though they looked to be eating more than collecting.

"Have you all been here long?" Michael asked, his breath labored.

"About an hour," Dagon answered. "Is something wrong?"

Michael leaned against a large stone and calmed his breathing and his racing heart. "A woman in the village insists that she saw a blond witch riding a broom."

All of them looked at Ali.

"A broom?" Ali shook her head in disgust. "Please, my modes of transportation have never been that crude, not even in the crudest of times. And why at this time in history would I even think of performing such a stupid trick?" She grew angry. "Besides, it's an insult to our ways. Witches have never ridden brooms. Someone is attempting to make us look bad."

"She is right," Sarina said. "Someone is pointing a finger."

"What do Tempest and Sydney say about it?" Sebastian asked.

"They left the problem in Duncan's and my hands. They are going across the loch to see if the old woman many believe to be a witch still lives there or if there is anything there that will help aid in our investigation."

Ali shoved her basket into her husband's arms. "They leave without Sarina and me?"

Sarina gently handed her basket to her husband. "Yes, we should go with them. They may need assistance."

The two women hurried off before any of the men could object.

The three men stared after them.

"I wouldn't mind going to the village and seeing what's going on. I've had enough berry picking to last me a while," Sebastian said, placing the basket on the ground.

"Aren't you concerned with Ali's safety?" Michael asked.

Dagon laughed.

"He knows her so well," Sebastian said, hiding his own chuckle. "Anyone stupid enough to match wits with my wife deserves what the idiot gets. You should know that by now. Didn't she plop herself and Sarina down in the woodpile outside Tempest's cottage—in the snow—when they both were pregnant? And then proceeded to ask you questions and make certain Tempest was all right?"

Michael had to smile, recalling the time. "She has a way of doing what she pleases, and she certainly doesn't let anyone intimidate her."

Sebastian and Dagon laughed.

"You should have grown up with her as I did," Dagon

said, placing the basket he held to the side. "I was forever pulling her out of trouble."

Michael glanced in the distance where the women had disappeared into the woods. "You don't think she'll get them all into any trouble do you?"

Sebastian slapped Michael on the back. "There are no guarantees in life, pal."

"Especially when it comes to Ali," Dagon said. "Now let's go see if we can help Duncan."

Michael looked over his shoulder as the two men helped him along.

"Don't worry," Sebastian said. "Tempest has stronger powers than Ali and can repair any damage she does."

"Are you sure of that?"

"Of course," they both said in unison while crossing their fingers behind their backs.

Twenty-nine

"*Why don't we use our magic to dry ourselves off?*" *Ali asked,* the weight of her wet clothes burdensome.

Tempest and Sarina were busy dragging the rowboat onto shore, so Sydney answered the question Ali had inquired of Tempest, who had directed them to use no magic as the boat tipped over, sending the four of them splashing into the water.

"If we use our magic, which would be quite powerful among the four of us, then we might alert whoever practices magic here to our arrival."

"I should have realized that," Ali said, wringing more water from her skirt.

"You were too insistent about the monster in the water," Sarina said, between labored breaths from dragging the rowboat.

"Think me crazy if you want, but I saw something in the water."

Tempest wrung out her soaked black skirt. "Was it necessary to lean so far over the side of the boat?"

Ali went to work on her blouse, trying as best as she could to wring the water from it. "I didn't realize how far I leaned. The two huge eyes I saw had me captivated. I couldn't believe I was seeing a sea monster."

"This is not Loch Ness," Sarina said, the puddle of water around her growing larger as she continued to wring out her clothes. "And where was this monster when we all fell overboard?"

Ali sighed as if having to deal with a young child. "We frightened him away of course."

Tempest tried very hard to keep her laughter as quiet as possible, but Sydney did not help the matter. Her laughter erupted boisterously and Sarina soon joined in.

Ali's wet blond hair dripped in her face and her clothes clung to her shapely body, yet she stood with dignity and poise while the laughter continued around her. "I saw a monster."

"Just like the woman in the village saw a witch riding a broom," Sarina said between bouts of laughter.

"This is a land of mystics and magic," Ali reminded.

The laughter subsided.

"She is right," Tempest said. "Many tales and legends began here and spread far and wide producing similar tales in other cultures. It is an enchanting land full of enchantment."

A strange roar caused the four women to jump and huddle close. The sky grew gray much too suddenly, the sun disappearing behind the fast moving clouds, and a chilled wind swept across the land.

"Magic lives here," Tempest said, and with a snap of her fingers she dried off all of them from head to toe.

Sarina shivered. "Powerful magic? Magic strong enough to realize our presence?"

"No, it attempts to present a powerful image and yet falls far short." Tempest glanced about as if trying to make a determination of some kind.

"Something troubles you?" Sydney asked.

"There is confusion here. I sense someone who knows and someone who learns and then someone who knows much but does not realize it. They blend almost as one and yet are completely separate."

"Do you think they will welcome us?" Ali asked, looking about, her guard up, her senses alert.

"There is no one here," Sarina said, "only the energy is left behind, and as Tempest said it is difficult to distinguish one from the other."

"Then let us begin our investigation," Sydney said and started down a well-worn path.

"I tell you I saw a witch flying on a broom," Abby said, wringing her hands nervously. The short, round woman wrung her hands one more time then switched to shoving the loose strands of red hair that hung in her face back away, only to have them fall down again.

Her nervous gestures were causing others to grow agitated and Duncan feared he would once again have panic on his hands if he could not convince the small crowd that grew steadily in numbers that Abby did not see a witch flying on a broom.

Thomas spoke up, to Duncan's surprise. "I heard that witches only ride brooms at night."

"Aye, he is right. It is the dark of night they need to fly," said a man.

"And a full moon," offered another.

"Witches do not ride brooms in the sunlight," laughed a woman.

Abby looked near to tears. "Clouds rushed overhead, and along with them was the witch."

"What clouds? It is a beautiful day," Bethany said, extending her hands to the bright blue sky.

Clouds suddenly rushed in as if her raised hands had commanded them to come forward and she quickly dropped her hands to her sides, her eyes wide at the gray rushing clouds that filled the sky.

"Look out for the witch," Abby warned, though refused to raise her eyes to the heavens.

Everyone around glanced up as if they expected to see a witch on a broom.

"This is nonsense," Duncan said loudly and with an authority that had all eyes turn to him. "There are no flying witches on brooms. It is nothing but a tale that holds no truth. It is fabricated by fear and fear spreads it."

"Something evil lurks over this village," Abby said, shivering with her own made fear.

"A good rainstorm lurks over this village," Duncan said. "Now be gone with all of you and stop this nonsense. There is nothing to fear."

"I say we send for the clergy to make certain we are safe. There has been talk of sending a message to the abbey near Loch Catherine, but it has only been talk. We need to send that message now," Abby said, looking from one to another gathered around her. "The church will make certain we are safe from evil and then there will be no need to worry."

"There is no need to involve the church," Duncan said with a strength that caused several people to step away from him. "We take care of our own with no need or interference from the church."

"This is different," Abby insisted. "We do not know how to fight evil. We need those who know how."

"There is no evil." Duncan clenched his fists in anger, but kept them at his sides. Losing his temper would not combat their fears. Calm, rational words were his only weapons in this skirmish.

"They be witches too," a young man called out, pointing at Michael, Dagon and Sebastian as they entered the village.

Duncan rolled his eyes and clenched his fists tighter,

otherwise he would punch the young lad who spoke such
nonsense. "They are friends."

"Friends of the witch," Abby said.

The three men had decided that Dagon's tongue was
much more familiar to them so he would do the talking in
front of crowds; besides, the man was handsome enough to
charm any irate woman and his regal stance caused men to
take a step back.

Dagon stepped forward, and there was not a woman
there who did not smile at him, witch or not.

"We mean harm to none and only wish to assist you in
your search for the truth."

"The truth is there is a witch among us and she is a
friend of yours," Abby said, her words rushing from her
mouth, though she spoke them with a generous smile, Dagon's good looks affecting her as they affected most
women.

Dagon walked up to the woman, her face flushing and
her hands nervously fussing with her hair. "Sydney is a
friend of mine, a good friend. She is generous, caring and
kind to all."

"Especially wolves," called out a man.

Dagon looked at the man. "A wolf's instincts are keen—
they must be to survive the wilderness—therefore, a wolf
senses danger and keeps himself from falling prey to it.
The black wolf in the woods senses Sydney's kindness and
therefore befriended her. There is no magic involved, only
simple kindness."

Silence fell over the crowd for a moment.

Abby then spoke up. "Still, strange things have happened since Sydney's return."

"Have they?" Dagon asked, looking directly at Abby and
then from one person to another. "Or have things happened
all along and no thought was given to them, for things
happen in life, sometimes unexplainable things."

"A witch's doings," Abby said insistently.

"Why?" Dagon asked. "Is it because you always look to

blame, to find fault with someone or something? If an animal dies though he has been cared for, is it evil doings or did he fall ill and show no signs, giving his owner no time to tend him? If a crop fails, is a witch to blame or does one look and see that there was not enough rainfall to nourish the crops properly? Or enough sunny days?"

Dagon purposely stopped speaking to give them pause to think. They remained silent; a few men rubbed their chins, one or two scratched their heads and some nodded their heads slowly.

"What of the frogs?" asked one man.

"Nests that were disturbed," Dagon said.

"Angus's broken shoulder, Sydney mended it with her touch," Abby said, pointing to the young man, who grew uncomfortable when all eyes turned to look at him.

"It was not broken if it was mended that quickly." Dagon looked at Angus. "It continued to pain you?"

"Aye, as Sydney told me it would." He stood tall, his shoulders going back, his chest out. He called on his courage and it did not desert him. "Sydney said something about a bone slipping lose in my shoulder and she moved it back in place."

"How did she know that if she is not a witch?" Abby asked.

Duncan spoke up. "She studied the new ways and learned."

Abby grew annoyed that sensible answers were being given for all that was asked, so she asked one that could not be answered. "What about the witch on the broom?"

"Too much ale," called out a man, and the crowd laughed.

"I know what I saw," Abby said adamantly. "And I saw a witch flying on a broom in the sky." She crossed her arms over her ample chest and cast a challenging look at Dagon.

"You staunchly believe you saw a witch on a broom?"

"Aye, I do and nothing will change my mind about it."

Abby kept her arms firmly locked to her chest.

A sudden gust of wind swirled around the crowd, sending dust from the dry dirt into their eyes.

Someone yelled out, "A witch on a broom."

Everyone looked up and together they watched as a broom was caught up in a swirl of debris, along with a large black bird that looked to be riding the broom. As the wind died the bird took charge of his flight and took off. The broom came hurdling down to the ground, sending the crowd scurrying. It landed not far from Abby's feet.

The crowd gathered back around and began laughing and pointing at the lifeless broom.

"That was some witch on a broom," laughed one.

"Saw it with my own eyes and I still cannot believe it," chuckled another.

Abby stared with wide eyes at the broom lying at her feet. "The witch had blond hair."

A large man dismissed her claim with a wave of his beefy hand. "The sun probably caught your eye."

"There were clouds," Abby said.

"Straw," someone shouted, picking up the bits of straw that had been caught up by the wind and had swirled overhead.

Abby turned speechless, staring at the straw on the ground.

"Go back to your baking Abby and stay away from the ale," a man called out as the crowd began to disperse.

The laughter sounded good to Duncan's ears. The clan seemed content, as did he with the reasonable explanations. Now he needed to know how much of what Dagon said was reason and how much was magic.

Duncan turned to Thomas. "I need to speak with my friends."

Thomas stood by his side in silence, not moving.

Duncan sighed. "I leave you out of this to protect you. You have Dora and your children to worry about."

"You are my friend, nay, you are as close as a brother,"

Thomas said. "I will help you anyway I can."

Duncan placed a hand on his shoulder. "I know, but this could prove dangerous for many and if you know nothing, then you can be accused of nothing."

"My lips have always remained locked when necessary."

"That they have, my friend. I could always count on you and I do so now. Trust my decision. Know it is made for you and your family's protection, and when the time is right, we will talk."

Thomas nodded. "I will trust you as always." He cast an eye at the three men standing nearby. "You can trust them?"

Duncan slapped his back and grinned. "I trust them, but not as much as you."

Thomas smiled, pleased by his answer. "I will wait for our talk and I will be close by if needed."

"I know, and I will call on you if need be."

"Good, I needed to know that has not changed between us." Thomas hurried off with his smile wide, waving to his wife, Dora, who stood a distance away with their newborn son in her arms.

Duncan walked up to the three men and looked at Dagon. "Now tell *me* the truth."

Thirty

The men decided it would be safer to walk off into the woods to talk, and besides, they wanted to head back to the cottage in hopes that the women had returned.

"Much of what I spoke was the truth," Dagon said. "If people would take time to be aware, think things through and take appropriate action then many of their disappointments and fears would be dispelled."

"Sensible," Sebastian said, "but sensibility takes having some sense in the first place and all too often people have no sense about anything."

"It's easier when the answer is provided for you—then you don't have to do any of the work yourself," Michael said.

"So if one person screams witch it is easier for everyone to believe it is so," Duncan said.

Dagon nodded. "Of course, it is easier to blame one person for the ills of others for then it takes the responsibility off them or settles the problem fast and with little effort. A person does not want to believe that his animal grew ill and he never noticed any signs of illness. He thinks himself a poor owner not to have seen to his animal's care."

"And if someone convinces them of a more sensible solution they easily accept that," Duncan said.

"Easy answers is what they search for," Michael said.

"A witch is an easy answer." Duncan shook his head. "But what of the broom in the sky? Did you create that gust of wind?"

"I did," Dagon admitted, "but not the clouds. They moved in on their own."

"Clouds do that," Duncan said, "though I sense they were sent."

"Warlocks like to play with the weather," Michael said. "They often call down lightning and thunder. It puts fear in people, and warlocks thrive on fear."

"What do you think of the witch flying on a broom?" Duncan asked. "Did Abby see such a thing or did she just think she did?"

"That's a good question and one we need to find an answer to," Michael said, rubbing his hands. "But right now I am hungry and I think we should head back to the cottage and eat."

"I'm all for that," Sebastian agreed. "I could go for a cheeseburger and fries."

Dagon laughed. "Believe it or not so could I."

Sebastian grinned. "No fancy meal?"

"I'll add some lettuce and tomato."

The two men laughed.

"What is a cheeseburger and fries? Lettuce and tomato?" Duncan asked curiously.

Michael patted him on the back. "You are about to experience the wonders of the twenty-first century."

The women came upon a small cottage nestled in seclusion a short distance from the loch. At first glance one would think it abandoned, but on closer inspection one realized it was inhabited. Freshly chopped wood sat stacked by the door, herbs grew in two straight rows in front of the cottage and around the one side more herbs grew in a circle that began small in the center and spread wider as it spiraled out.

Tempest shook her head. "There is a contradiction here."

"Yes, there is," Sarina said, staring at the rune script carved in the front door.

"*Those who dare enter,*" Tempest read.

"A garden that appears to welcome and a door that warns about entering." Ali shook her head. "A definite contradiction."

"Two witches," Sydney said, "or one witch and one warlock."

Tempest approached the door. "The rune script is meant to instill fear and the field of energy around the house feeds off that fear. Definitely a warlock's cast."

"But the herb garden," Ali said, "has the hand of a witch to it."

Sarina glanced over her shoulder and turned to go where her senses directed. The other women followed down a path that looked once worn, though now was budding with summer's first growth.

They all stopped when they came upon a mound of dirt and a cross, made from a tree branch and inscribed with runes. Freshly picked flowers lay on top of the mound near the bottom of the cross.

"The inscription is so simple, yet says much," Sydney said with a tear in her eye. "*Friend.*"

"The old woman Elizabeth," Sarina said.

Ali cast a silent prayer for the departed woman before saying, "Someone befriended the old woman, and I would say it is the one who tends her garden."

"The old woman taught this person much," Sarina said, after her own prayer for the departed.

"But someone interfered," Tempest said, "hence the confusion I keep sensing."

"Let's see what the cottage tells us," Sydney suggested.

Tempest stepped past them. "You must wrap yourselves in a strong bubble of protection. We do not want any of our energies detected by the field the warlock keeps firm around the cottage."

The women nodded and took the precautions that Tempest suggested. They then returned to the cottage and Tempest cautiously opened the door.

They entered one after the other, each one's eyes catching something of interest and moving off to investigate.

Sydney went to the table covered with branches, herbs and berries. Sarina walked over to the bubbling cauldron that hung over the open flames in the fireplace. Ali's eyes caught sight of the stones that were stacked strangely on the chest near the bed. Tempest was drawn to the objects arranged on a black cloth on the high chest next to the door.

"Someone prepares to make a wreath," Sydney said, looking but not touching the items on the table.

Sarina sniffed at the bubbling contents. "A calming brew bubbles here."

Ali pointed to the stone structure. "Someone uses stones to enhance their powers."

"And someone practices the dark arts," Tempest said and held up a knife, the blade dark as the night.

"We should go," Sarina said suddenly. "Now, right now."

No one argued. Sarina could see things most could not, and the women hurried off, leaving everything as they had found it.

"Tempest," Sarina said, and before she could say any more, her sister waved her hand and in a flash transported them to the other side of the loch.

Ali stumbled slightly when she landed. "Wow, that was some ride." She turned to Sarina and reached out to ease her swaying. "You sensed danger?"

"Someone was about to return and it was not the someone who tended the garden." Sarina sighed, finally feeling
steady.

"Where is Tempest?" Sydney asked with concern, turning her head to look around her.

Sarina looked frantically about, calling out to her sister.

Ali shook her head. "I bet she remained behind."

"Michael is not going to like this," Sarina said. "And I
do not like it myself."

Sydney attempted to calm them both. "Tempest is more
than capable of taking care of herself."

"True," Sarina admitted. "But it worries me when she
faces things alone, you can never tell what might happen."

Beatrice flitted in front of Sydney's face. "All is calm
in the village. Dagon handled it well, calming even the
most disgruntled complainer."

Sarina smiled with pride.

Beatrice gave a quick glance around them. "Where is
Tempest?"

Before anyone could answer Finn cautiously approached
the trio, going directly to Sydney's side. He cast his dark
eyes up at her then lifted his head and howled at the heavens.

Michael shivered when he heard the wolf's lone howl and
stopped walking. "Let's go to Sydney's cottage and see if
the women have returned yet."

"I had the same thought," Duncan said.

Sebastian was more direct. "Something is not right."

The men hurried their pace, changing directions and
heading for Sydney's cottage.

The women walked out of the woods as the men arrived
at Sydney's cottage, Finn remaining close to Sydney's side.
The wolf's protective stance was the first thing that caught
the men's eyes.

"What's going on?" Michael demanded, looking around for Tempest. "Damn, she stayed on the island alone, didn't she?"

He directed his question to Sarina. Dagon, having sensed his wife's concern, hurried over to her to slip a comforting arm around her.

"I told her we all needed to leave the island immediately and with a wave of her hand she—"

"Transported all of you back here," Michael finished with a shake of his head. "She never considers that she could be placing herself in danger."

Duncan walked over to Sydney as she spoke. "Tempest is more than capable of taking care of herself."

Sebastian joined his wife, Ali reaching out to take his hand.

"But Michael is her husband and worried like any loving husband would."

"Thank you, Ali," Michael said. "Someone finally understands the difficulty of being married to the Ancient One."

"Is there anything we can do?" Duncan offered, his arm going around Sydney, relieved that she was safe beside him and that Finn was there offering his protection.

Michael paced back and forth, attempting to rid his frustration. "I would go after her, but I can almost guarantee that she sealed the island off after sending the women back."

"Do you feel she is in any harm?" Duncan asked.

"Not really, Sydney is right when she says that Tempest can take care of herself. It just doesn't make it any easier for me to stand here and wait, wonder and worry."

"I could get past the seal," Beatrice said, flying over to Michael to flit a few inches from his face.

"You can?" he asked hopefully.

"Aye, fairies know their way around such things."

"But past a seal that was cast by the Ancient One?" Dagon asked, sounding doubtful.

Beatrice grinned with confidence. "She sealed the island, not the water that surrounds it."

Sebastian laughed. "The seal stops on land; you sneak beneath the seal where it meets the water."

"You understand quickly, that is why you will do well in the Craft," Beatrice said.

"Can you go now and see that she is all right, or if she requires help, or if I should not worry, or—damn—just let me know she's all right," Michael said, frustrated.

"I will be back soon," Beatrice said, and off she flew, so fast that none of them saw where she took flight.

Tempest walked the woods cautiously, sensing the person's approach. She did not wish to be detected; she wanted simply to learn what she could about the mysterious person who was creating so many problems for Sydney.

She felt his presence grow stronger and stronger until a dark figure stepped from the woods into the clearing around the cottage. He was taller than the average man, his brown hair long and drawn back, his clothes various shades of black, brown and dark green. His brown eyes were intent, his skin pale and his features sharp, drawing the eye, though not in a pleasant way. He looked to be a man who a person would avoid rather than befriend.

He wore a pouch on his leather belt and a dark stone wrapped in a leather tie around his neck. He bent down near the patch of herbs in front of the cottage and drew his knife from the sheath on his belt. He quickly severed several leaves from various plants, stood and went inside.

Tempest cringed at his thoughtless actions. A witch would never treat a plant so poorly. He would touch the plant gently, trim the leaves off carefully and give thanks.

Tempest suddenly stilled and slowly raised her hand palm up in front of her chest.

Beatrice flitted to a rest in the middle of her palm. "You

sensed me and—" She shoved her head wreath back. "You purposely left a small opening for me to enter. I saw it as I approached the island."

"I knew Michael would worry and you would feel challenged to pass the seal."

"You are wise."

Tempest smiled. "Wisdom comes with age, and I have lived long."

"So should I return and tell Michael all is well?"

Tempest had no chance to answer. The door of the cottage flew open and the man ran out, his eyes frantically scanning the area around the house.

"Does he sense me?" Beatrice asked, upset. "Have I placed you in danger?"

Tempest shook her head and spoke so only the tiny fairy could hear her. "No, I purposely touched his ceremony blade when I was in the cottage. Now he knows someone was there, and he worries that he did not detect the presence when he first arrived."

"Which means he knows that someone more powerful than he is close by."

"And if he is wise—"

"Which he probably is not," Beatrice said with a glance toward the man.

"He would cease any further spells until he discovers more about the witch who has silently challenged him."

The tall, thin man crossed his arms over his chest and paced in front of the cottage.

"He knows not what to do," Tempest said. "He has never matched wits with a more powerful witch than he. He preys on the weak and fearful."

"He is a warlock?"

"Yes, a warlock who has much yet to learn."

"Which means there is still time for him to mend his evil ways."

Tempest stared at the man in thought. "There is more here, but I have yet to understand it all."

"Do you wish time alone?"

"Aye, tell my husband I will return shortly and that I am in no danger."

Beatrice nodded and took off in flight.

Tempest remained where she was and watched.

Michael was still pacing outside Sydney's cottage when Beatrice returned. He stopped when his eyes caught her approach. He held out his hand for her just as Tempest always did.

Beatrice flitted to a rest in his palm. "Tempest is fine and will return shortly. She says for you not to worry."

"Has she discovered anything?" Ali asked anxiously.

"A warlock," Beatrice answered, "though not a powerful one, more a beginner."

Duncan felt a sense of relief and spoke up. "At least now we know who causes the problems."

"A place to start," Michael said with a nod.

Tempest materialized right beside her husband, causing his nod to change to a shake and the others to smile.

"Damn, Tempest," he said and grabbed her firmly around the waist. "What am I going to do with you?"

She laughed softly and whispered in his ear.

He grinned at her suggestion and rubbed his cheek to hers. "Damn, but I love you."

"Someone approaches," Sarina warned, and then after a few moments of thought she smiled. "A friend."

Thomas soon appeared, walking out of the woods shaking his head. "Gwen forever sends me on errands. I feel as though I have two wives."

Sydney hoped that whatever Gwen wanted from her brother it would not keep him long. She yearned to spend time alone with him. She had hoped they could spend a quiet evening together and that he could remain the night, that she could wake in the morning wrapped in his arms.

And she sensed he wished the same, for his hand held hers tightly as if he had no intentions of letting go or going anywhere.

Thomas looked at the women and then to Duncan.

Duncan realized he had never properly introduced the women and that Thomas had not met all of them. "Thomas, this is Sebastian's wife, Ali; Dagon's wife, Sarina; Michael's wife, Tempest. They are all good friends of Sydney's."

Sydney knew he omitted the fact that Ali was her niece to protect Ali; being Sydney's friends was cause enough to suspect them of being witches. If it were known Ali was her niece everyone would surely believe she was also a witch, and Ali would be in even more danger.

"Good to meet you all," Thomas said, though he seemed a bit hesitant.

"What does my sister want now?" Duncan finally asked.

"Gwen *insists* that Sydney and *all her friends* join the clan for the evening meal."

Thirty-one

Sydney sat at the table in her cottage, cupping her teacup.
Frown lines wrinkled her usually smooth brow and her eyes
gazed steadily at the steaming tea, telling Duncan that her
thoughts troubled her.

Sebastian had suggested that it might be to his and
everyone's advantage if he was given a quick lesson in the
customs of the time so that he would be familiar with the
goings-on of tonight's gathering.

Tempest and Sarina agreed to prepare the other three for
the evening, being they were familiar with the time period,
and the couples went off, having only a few hours to spare.

Thomas was on his way back to the keep to tell Gwen
that Sydney and her friends would be pleased to accept her
invitation, and Duncan had followed Sydney into her cottage and watched how she had gone about preparing tea
and sitting at the table without a word to him.

He walked around to stand behind her then began to
massage her neck and shoulders. Her muscles were tight
and she cringed when he applied a firmer pressure to her

taut shoulder muscles. He massaged in silence, allowing her the time to think and the time to relax.

It did not take long; soon her body showed signs of easing and she sighed, a sure sign that his fingers had proven successful.

"I have missed your magical hands."

"You will miss them no more," he said, affirming the fact that he did not intend for them to part again. "Now tell me what troubles you."

Sydney tilted her head so that he could work on a muscle that consistently proved stubborn, but then her stubbornness probably caused its consistency. "I am not certain. I feel something is amiss but—" She shook her head. "I cannot quite grasp it. It is almost as if I see but I do not see. Does that make sense?"

"Aye, it is like having all the pieces to a puzzle in front of you, but you are unable to arrange them in the appropriate order."

"Precisely, I see them all but I am uncertain of where they fit."

"Give it time and you will discover," he encouraged. "At least we now know we have a warlock to deal with, and knowing that Tempest and Michael's powers far surpass his makes me more comfortable with the situation. It is difficult enough to think that my defenses are defenseless against him. I have always prided myself in my ability to protect those I love. The thought that this man has powers I cannot defend against angers me."

Sydney placed her hand over his where it rested on her shoulder. "Use what you know wisely and you would have no trouble defending yourself against the warlock."

He dug his fingers into the stubborn muscle once again. Her hand dropped away and she moaned with a mixture of pain and pleasure. The taut muscle was finally breaking down and while it was a bit painful the relief that followed was pure pleasure.

"Now all I need is a hot bath to soothe the remaining

soreness away." She sighed and allowed her body to relax in a slump.

"The stream is too cold yet to bathe in."

"The bathtub will do," she said without thinking.

"Bathtub?" His fingers stilled for a moment then worked their way up her neck.

Sydney decided it was time he learned about a few modern conveniences, besides she ached for a hot bath. A sudden smile lit her face and she laughed softly as she tilted her head back to peer up at him.

"I think you may favor the bathtub." Her smile grew along with her thoughts. With a little magic she could expand the tub to accommodate them both and make it a Jacuzzi style tub.

"It is a device you brought from the future with you?" He was curious and anxious to experience Sydney's world.

"I found there were a few modern conveniences I did not wish to do without, so I updated the cottage to handle what I felt were necessities."

"Show them to me." He sounded like a young lad about to embark on a grand adventure.

"First a few precautions." She stood and cast a protective spell around the cottage and sent a silent message to Finn to alert her to any intruders or unexpected visitors. Beatrice she did not have to concern herself with since the little fairy had joined with Tempest and Sarina to help instruct the others for this evening.

At the moment and for the next couple of hours at least Duncan and she were all alone.

She took his hand. "Come with me."

He grasped her hand and held tight, half expecting to take flight, but even flight would not have stolen his breath as did the sight that unfolded before his eyes as they stepped from what seemed like one world into another.

"A bathroom," she announced and released his hand so that he could explore.

He remained by her side, staring at the strange, large

room and suddenly Sydney saw it through his eyes and
realized the wonder of what he was seeing for the first time.

"Let me show you and explain," she said, anxious for
him to become familiar with her world.

She had replicated her bathroom in her Scotland home. It
was the one she favored the most. She had given the room an
old-world look; the color of the tub, sink and toilet was a soft
beige and the fixtures burnished gold. The floor was mosaic
done in browns, reds and gold, while the wall was a soft
mustard color with a gentle brown wipe applied over it to
make it appear old and faded. Branches with gold and red
leaves were painted as a border around the top of the wall
and burnished metal candle sconces hung beside framed old
maps and paintings whose frames looked worn with time and
blended perfectly with the old-world appeal.

She had a large window in the bathroom in her time but
here she had had to omit it, so instead she had created the
same scene through a painting. It was a large Palladian-
style window that filled the width of the wall and length of
the bathtub. At night she would light several candles and
place them around the corners of the tub then raise the blind
and enjoy the beauty of the Scottish countryside while she
relaxed in the tub.

A scattering of small colorful rugs, towels piled in baskets, baskets filled with lotions and creams, gold dishes
holding flower-shaped soaps and vases filled with fresh
flowers finished the room.

She explained how many of the items in the room were
from her travels, and any she felt were unfamiliar to him
she explained or demonstrated their use. She detailed the
workings of the sink, the toilet and the tub, which she left
filling with water.

Duncan was astonished with the toilet and flushed it several times, watching the water vanish down the hole. "It is
amazing. Now I understand Sebastian's comment about a
toilet."

"It is a necessity once you grow accustomed to it," Sydney said with a laugh. She began to light the many candles that filled the room then dimmed the electric lights.

Duncan instantly asked her what she had done and insisted she explain further, and she briefly described electricity to him.

He simply stared at her. "What other wonders exist?" he asked, as if he needed to know all of it.

Sydney however had other ideas. She had stopped the water when it filled the tub enough and then turned on the jets to the Jacuzzi. She walked over to Duncan and began to unwrap his plaid.

"There is time for such talk later. Now it is time for you and me to relax." She kissed him softly on the cheek and whispered, "Time to kiss." She finished removing his plaid and slipped her hands beneath his shirt, exploring every inch of his chest with her fingers. "Time to touch."

His breath caught and he grew hard in an instant.

She smiled and teased him with a deep kiss. "You and I are going to relax in the tub, but first—" She bent down to remove his sandals, and as she came back up she stopped and with a contented sigh took him into her mouth.

"Damn," was all Duncan could manage to say. He had missed this closeness between them. This time they could be free to love as they wished, to know each other so intimately and to satisfy each other with caring hearts.

He groaned from the pleasure she brought him and it was not long before the need to touch her and taste her grew intolerable, and he reached down and scooped her up.

He undressed her in minutes, lifted her naked body against his and walked to a wall to brace her body against it then entered her with an urgency that pleased them both.

Neither one of them wanted it to end quickly; they wanted to linger in the passion of their mating bodies and drink of the emotions that raced through them and thrill in the sensations that set their souls on fire.

Her legs remained tightly wrapped around his strong body and her arms held firm around his neck. She moaned loudly as the small burst of pleasure taunted her senses.

He could not get enough of her, never could he get enough of her. He once thought that their passion would fade with time, but it had not; it had grown stronger. He wanted her more and more with each passing day. He ached to bury himself inside her, to lose all sense of reality and know only the joy of their joining.

And when he was in the middle of such tormenting pleasure he realized that he looked forward to the next time and the next and the next when he would be with her again.

His movements took on a demand and Sydney met every thrust with her own eagerness. Their mouths met in equal enthusiasm. Soon they came to the brink of pleasure, and with several wild thrusts they toppled over the edge together.

Sydney collapsed against him, her breathing hard, and though he breathed just as hard he remained steady on his feet and held her firm in his embrace.

"Now for the pleasure of the tub," she said when her breathing calmed.

He glanced over at the bubbling water and smiled. He then placed his hands beneath her backside and hefted her up a bit before carrying her over to the tub.

She sighed, still feeling him snug inside her, and rested her head on his shoulder.

"I do not want to let you go," he said when he stopped next to the tub.

"We can do this again."

"And again and again and again? Promise me this?"

He was asking more of her, and she understood. He wanted a promise that they would never part. Her quick answer brought a smile to his face.

"Promise." She kissed his cheek. "Now let's get in the tub."

He released her. "You first."

She understood his reluctance. This was new and strange to him. She climbed in the tub, sank down into the heated water and sighed with absolute pleasure. She then held her hand out to him.

He took it and followed her lead. His sigh surpassed hers once he stretched out and the water covered his chest.

They rested against the sloping back of the tub, their eyes closed and the bubbling water soothing away any and all discomforts.

After a few moments he reached out to take her in his arms. "I think I like the future. Tell me more."

There was so much to tell him—where did she begin?

He settled the problem for her. "How do people travel in your time? Somehow I do not think horses and carts are in use."

She laughed. "Horses are used more for pleasure riding and for racing." She went on to detail automobiles, buses, trains, ships and airplanes. She decided against telling him of space travel, since he warned he had been overwhelmed enough.

He was speechless when she finished, and she feared she had told him too much.

"A world so full of marvels must be difficult to leave behind."

Again his worry surfaced that she would return to the future and she asked, "Are you not curious to see it for yourself?"

"The thought has crossed my mind," he admitted freely. "It would be an adventure to see such wonders, but then I am reminded of my duty here. This is my home; I have family here and—" He shook his head, uncertain how to answer.

"I understand," she said, a tingle of fear weaving through her. She would not indulge it. She had a second chance and she would do all she could for them to remain together. She would fight for their love and she would stay strong in her love for him. She would not allow fear to dent her strength or cause her to doubt.

"I am glad you do, for I do not." He closed his eyes as if wishing to close out the world.

Sydney allowed him silence, a chance to think, to understand and accept all he had experienced this day. It was not easy to accept what he had seen and what she had told him. He was suddenly a man out of place and time; nothing was what it seemed and nothing would ever be the same.

The hot water bubbled and the steam rose around them, and they lingered in the peaceful silence, each lost in their own thoughts and their concerns.

Duncan broke the silence. "I love you, Sydney."

She turned and nestled against his wet chest. "And I love you."

"My grandmother once told me that love determined one's fate."

"She was a wise woman."

"I am beginning to realize that she not only spoke of a love between a man and a woman, but love for all."

"All is the important factor here."

"Love makes you feel—" He paused, searching for words.

"You have it right," she encouraged. "Love makes you feel and that is what is important. Have you not felt more and understood more since you have loved me?"

"Aye, so much more," he admitted.

"Life blossoms when love is felt and it matters not if it is the love between a man and a woman, or a mother and a child, or father and a child or between friends. Love simply is—mortals fail to realize that."

"My grandmother did not."

"Then she was a wise witch."

"I remember her telling my father of things that would come to pass before they did."

"Did he listen to to her?"

"Always," Duncan said. "He respected her opinion, her thoughts and suggestions. My grandmother never forced her beliefs on anyone, she simply—"

"Lived them," Sydney finished.

"Aye, she lived them every day of her life and she lived a long life. I remember the day she died. She shed no tear and warned others to shed none. She insisted she was returning home and would reunite with those she loved. She told Gwen and me to fill our lives with love and we would always know happiness."

"I wish I had known your grandmother, she possessed such a deep knowledge."

"She was a witch, was she not?" he asked, though he knew the answer.

"She believed in the old ways."

"Witch's ways."

Sydney rested a hand on his cheek. "Does it upset you to think your grandmother a witch?"

He thought on her question for a moment. "Nay, it does not."

"You accept her being a witch?"

He smiled and hugged her tightly to him. "Aye, that I do."

"Why?"

"For then it means that I am a witch too!"

Thirty-two

The raucous laughter that filled the great hall died slowly when Duncan entered with Sydney on his arm, followed by Sebastian and Ali, Dagon and Sarina, and Tempest and Michael.

Duncan proceeded to the dais, where Gwen hastily rose to hurry around the long table to greet her guests. Whispers and mumbles followed the group and the word *witch* spilled accusingly from several lips. The group chose to ignore the snide mumbles and smiled pleasantly.

Dora and Thomas waved Sydney over to their table but Duncan held firm to her arm.

"You sit at the dais beside me tonight."

She thought to object but one hard look from Duncan told her not to bother, he would have his way no matter what anyone thought. She waved back to Dora and pointed to the dais.

Dora smiled, obviously pleased, though Sydney was certain she would be one of the few who were accepting of Duncan's decision.

"I am so glad you and your friends could join us this evening, Sydney." Gwen stepped forward and gave her a hug.

Her actions surprised Sydney, though she did not show it. Gwen had once been friendly with her. They shared much together, including their love for Duncan, and perhaps that is what brought them close. But she had been anything but friendly since her return, and while Sydney could understand her caution toward her unexpected return, she did not understand the hidden hostility she had sensed in Gwen.

Her appearance was also different. She wore her plaid, though her blouse was blue instead of her usual white. Her blond hair was twisted up in fanciful knots and tied with colorful ties.

"I am pleased by your invitation."

"Introduce me to your friends," Gwen said and hooked her arm around Sydney's, easing her away from Duncan.

Before the introductions could be made Duncan asked, "There is room for them all at the dais?"

"I made certain," Gwen said with a smile that caught Sydney's eye.

It was more a cunning than happy smile, and Sydney sensed that something was not right. She smiled herself as she made the introductions and intended to keep a careful watch on Gwen and the night ahead.

Sydney was proud of her family and friends, watching them take their seats on the dais. Sebastian, Dagon and Michael looked splendid in their plaids and they wore them with pride. Ali, Sarina and Tempest chose suitable skirts and blouses appropriate to the time period and relative to the common woman of any clan.

Of course Ali's blond hair was done up in a mass of curls and ringlets that caught the eye, though the modern hairpins Sydney was certain she used to secure the creation were hidden well. Sarina and Tempest chose simply to leave their hair hanging naturally down over their shoulders, Sarina having long dark hair that fell almost to her waist and Tempest having long reddish-blond hair that waved beautifully down her back and around her face.

Sydney chose to braid her own long dark hair, though she did it in a French braid, a style unfamiliar to that period, but one she favored. She had kept her dress simple, a dark blue peasant style skirt and blouse and of course her hematite stone necklace engraved with a protective rune symbol.

They all looked as if they fit in the year 1564, but eating a meal of that time was another matter.

They all had agreed that no magic at all could be used while at the keep unless of course it was an extreme necessity, an emergency of sorts. An emergency did not mean flavoring the food with magic to suit your tastes.

It was Duncan who had the hardest time trying to keep himself from laughing when he caught the look of utter bewilderment on Sebastian's face after one bite of rabbit stew.

Laughter was hard for them all to contain when they heard Sebastian say to Ali, "I will never make fun of your cooking again."

Trays upon trays of rabbit stew, mutton, fish and more were brought out one after the other and everyone ate with gusto. Ale flowed, talk filled the air and contentment could be felt. No one at the moment was concerned with witches.

Why then did Sydney continue to feel on edge?

A platter of mutton was placed on the long table, along with fish and fowl.

"The cook makes a delicious mutton," Gwen said, looking down the table to the guests. "You must try it."

Sarina stood quickly and reached for the platter. "Let me make sure everyone has a piece. It smells de—" Suddenly she tripped, sending the platter and mutton flying. The platter crashed off the edge of the dais and the mutton landed near the fireplace where the dogs patiently waited for scraps. They were on the large piece of meat in an instant.

Dagon hurried to help his wife stand.

"Do not eat any more food," she whispered.

He gave no outward sign that he heard her, though she knew otherwise.

Sarina turned her attention on Gwen, stepping around her husband. "I am so sorry, I feel awful about the wasted meat."

Gwen smiled, looking not at all upset. "We have more, do not concern yourself."

Dagon retrieved the pewter platter, handing it to a passing servant. He then returned to the table and before taking his seat stopped to speak with Sebastian and Ali and Michael and Tempest. His smile belied his whispered words of warning.

"Sydney," Dagon called out, his smile wide. "Join us a moment and settle a dispute."

Sydney understood that something was amiss. Sarina may have been clumsy at one time and through no fault of her own, but now with her powers fully restored and her keen sense of seeing beyond, Sydney realized that she had tripped on purpose.

"What say you about this—" Dagon's strong voice lowered as she approached and he continued to smile as he spoke to her of his wife's warning.

Sydney's light laughter drew no attention. Everyone seemed to be making merry and they were no different. She retained her jovial appearance as she talked softly with Dagon and the others.

"What does she suspect?"

"I am not sure," Dagon said, "though if she warned about the food it must be tainted somehow."

"On purpose?" Sydney asked, her smile brilliant.

"That is something we will need to determine."

Duncan joined them, feeling very much a part of them even though he had known them a short time. "Can I help with anything?"

Dagon placed a hand on his shoulder and looked to be

sharing a humorous moment with him. "There is a problem."

Duncan maintained his grin and nodded.

"The food—"

"Sydney, hurry, please," Dora yelled.

Sydney turned and watched as Dora's daughter Alice fell to the floor, moaning and grabbing her stomach. She quickly made her way over to the ailing girl.

With everyone's attention focused on the young lass, Sarina hurried to Duncan's side. "More will fall ill."

No sooner than she told him another person crumpled to the floor, holding his stomach and moaning in pain; another followed, then another.

Abby was the first to accuse. "It is the witches' doings."

Thomas looked to Sydney in question and Dora chastised him.

"Sydney has been nothing but kind to us."

Thomas looked contrite, though he asked, "My daughter will be all right?"

Sydney nodded. "The meat is tainted. I will give her a brew that will clean out her stomach. She will not feel well for a day or two but she will be fine."

"Who tainted the meat?" Thomas asked angrily.

"Then you realize it was done on purpose," Sydney said.

"You were all invited here, and I thought that odd since it is known that Gwen has not been happy with your return. Something smelled rotten to me about the invitation."

"The meat," Dora said, placing her daughter's head in her lap. "You will be fine, Sydney will see to it."

"What can I do?" Thomas asked.

An ill man attempted to cry out his concern, but fell to the floor repeatedly moaning—*witch*.

"Help to keep things calm," Sydney said and motioned to Tempest, Sarina and Ali.

They hurried over to her.

"Do you know if only the mutton was affected?" Sydney asked Sarina.

"I cannot be certain."

Sydney stepped close to Tempest. "We cannot undo what has been done and make all of the ailing well, for then we would surely be accused of practicing witchcraft. But I think it would be wise if we can stop the spread of it. Can you prevent others from falling ill?"

"I will see what can be done." She walked away, joining her husband and speaking privately with him.

Sydney spoke in a whisper to Ali and Sarina. "In the bathroom in my cottage are the necessary items we need. Can you transport yourselves there and back quickly and retrieve them?"

Both of them nodded, and Ali spoke.

"With this chaos I do not think anyone will notice what we do, but we will seek the dark night anyway."

They hurried out of the keep.

Sebastian and Dagon offered their assistance.

"What can we do?" Sebastian asked.

"See to the tainted meat. Tempest will clean up most, but there must be some evidence of rotten meat so that all believe the illness had nothing to do with witchcraft."

Sydney looked to Tempest and she nodded, letting her know that it had been settled—she would see that no one else fell ill. Michael stood beside his wife, waiting to assist her, though his look of anger puzzled Sydney. Whatever was wrong it was not with his wife. What had Michael learned that so disturbed him?

She had no time to give it thought. She would speak with Michael later; right now there were too many who needed attention. She turned, and before setting to work she noticed Gwen and Duncan talking and neither looked happy.

"Lower your voice," Duncan ordered his sister. "There is enough hysteria without you adding to it."

She was not pleased with his stern manner but she did as he instructed. "I invite them into our home in an attempt for the clan to see that they are not to be feared, and what do they do?" Gwen looked out over the chaotic scene; men, women and children lay on the floor, moaning in pain. She turned back to her brother. "They cause many to be ill."

Duncan shook his head. "Our guests did nothing. The food is bad; it has happened before."

"How do we know it is the food and not a spell?"

"What reason would they possibly have to cause the clan to fall ill?"

She lowered her voice. "To possess us with evil."

Duncan was near to losing his temper. "That is nonsense and you know it."

Thomas's strong voice suddenly echoed out, "It is the meat; it is bad. Look, the dogs are ill."

All eyes followed his pointing finger and it was as he said—the dogs were cleansing their stomachs of the foul meat.

A woman who held her husband's head in her lap and wiped his perspiring brow with a wet cloth spoke up. "Aye, but it was the one with the long dark hair that gave it to them. She made certain that she and her friends ate no mutton. And where is she now?"

"I am here," Sarina said, having entered the keep with Ali a few moments before the woman began her accusations.

"You are not ill," the old woman accused again. "Neither are your friends."

"You knew the meat was no good," Abby said, stepping around several people on the floor and marching toward Sarina.

Ali stepped forward, her hands going firmly to rest on her hips. "Watch what you say. I am tired of being falsely accused because of your ignorance."

Abby remained where she was but spoke up, feeling confident with the strength of the clan around her. "I saw you riding a broom in the sky."

A sudden hush drifted over the hall and barely a breath

was heard, even the crackle of the fire in the hearth stilled upon hearing the bold accusation.

Duncan stepped forward. "We settled that Abby."

"You settled it along with those who laugh at the idea, but I saw what I saw," she insisted. "And I have been fearful that more evil will be brought down on us—and it has been."

"Bad meat caused the illness."

"Witches' spells caused the bad meat," Abby said, sounding on the verge of hysteria. "And she—" Abby pointed to Ali. "Is a witch who rides a broom."

Sydney realized it was time for them all to leave and allow tempers to cool down before things turned much worse, but first medicine needed to be administered to those willing to take it. And knowing the cure would make the ill feel worse before they felt better did not help matters. She hoped Duncan could at least keep things under control until she could tend those who wished her help.

She motioned to Sarina to bring her basket of herbs, the modern medicine concealed beneath the many fragrant leaves.

Sarina looked to Ali, not wanting to desert her, and her return glance told her not to worry, that she could easily defend herself. She hurried off to help Sydney.

Gwen stepped forward. "This is nonsense Abby."

Abby grew more adamant. " 'Tis not, 'tis the truth."

Ali remained silent though firm in her stance. She had learned that to verbally battle a false accusation did little good. The more adamant you became in your defense the more people thought you guilty.

She noticed that Tempest and Michael stood in the shadows of the great hall. She knew they purposely remained out of view in case their powers were needed. It would do no good to have any attention called to them.

Sebastian and Dagon were only returning to the hall, having seen to the tainted meat as Sydney had instructed.

As soon as Sebastian saw that his wife was in the spotlight of accusation he stepped forward.

Dagon stopped him with a hand to his arm. "Now is not a good time. You will do her more harm than good with your foreign tongue. Ali can handle this herself."

Sebastian reluctantly remained where he was, though he sent his wife a look that let her know he was there if she needed him.

Ali reassured her husband with a soft smile that she was fine.

Gwen caught everyone's attention when she announced. "Oh for heaven's sake, Abby, Ali is not a witch and cannot make a broom fly."

Abby looked around at the strangers to the clan and then back at Gwen. "There is witchcraft afoot, and Duncan should do something to protect the clan. He should send for a church official and have him rid us of their evil."

"I will send for no bishop," Duncan said firmly.

"There is no proof of witchcraft," Gwen said. "It would be senseless to disturb church officials without proof."

Abby pointed at Ali. "She rode a broom, that is proof."

"*You* only saw her ride a broom," Gwen said. "That is not proof enough."

Abby wagged her finger at Ali. "You did it, I know you did. You are a witch, a witch who rides a broom."

"Stop it," Duncan demanded. "Stop speaking nonsense."

"She did, she did; I saw her!" Abby was hysterical, wanting to prove herself correct.

Abby's hysteria became contagious and some began to speak up out of fear.

"What if she is right?"

"We need protection."

"Send for the cleric."

"He will rid us of evil."

"Protect us, Duncan."

"Aye, protect us against the witches."

"Enough," Duncan shouted so loudly that his voice echoed off the walls. "I will hear no more."

The voices quieted and just when Duncan made ready to speak, the well-worn broom that rested against the hearth took flight and sent everyone into utter panic.

Thirty-three

Sebastian went straight for his wife and Dagon to his. They rushed them out of the hall while screams and shouts sang like a horrified chorus.

Tempest sent the flying broom crashing to the floor and placed a spell on all objects in the hall so that they would not take flight. Then she and Michael hurried to Sydney's side, urging her to leave.

Dora agreed with them, insisting she would see that those who wished the healing brew would get it.

"You need to look out for yourself," Dora said and shooed her off with a wave of her hand then turned to tend her daughter, whose moans had subsided.

Tempest and Michael had a hard time convincing her to leave and insisted that they would not leave without her.

Sydney found it difficult to leave those who suffered when she knew she could be of help to them, making a decision near impossible.

It was Duncan who decided for her.

In the middle of the chaos he went to her, yanked her

up off the floor and shoved her at Michael. "See that she is kept safe."

Sydney felt his fear for her and his need to protect her whatever way he could. "I will come to you later."

"Nay, you will stay away from the keep."

"But—"

"Go," he ordered roughly.

Michael practically dragged Sydney out of the hall, though he took a mere moment to say to Duncan, "We are here for you if needed."

"Sense and reason must deal with this now, not magic," Duncan said and went to a nearby table to pound his fist down on it repeatedly, causing quiet to slowly descend on the hall.

Sydney did not hear his words. Michael had her out of the hall before complete quiet reigned, and the three were soon hurrying off into the woods. Once there and under the cover of darkness, Tempest transported them to Sydney's cottage with the wave of her hand.

Duncan faced the quiet crowd with a stern expression, his words harsh. "This is madness and it has nothing to do with evil."

A man spoke up though his voice trembled. "The broom flew on its own?"

"We need the safety of the church to deal with this," Abby said, she and her friend huddling together out of fear.

Gwen stepped up beside her brother. "Duncan has always taken care of this clan and will continue to do so."

"His love for the witch blinds him."

"She has him under her spell."

Duncan would hear no more. He knew what he must do and he did it reluctantly for he also knew what it meant for Sydney and the others.

"I will send a message to the church in the morning and ask for a church official to be sent here. You will all be safe. I promise you this."

Sighs of relief were heard, while many smiled and

reached out to begin to help those lying ill on the floor and those cowering in corners and under tables out of fear.

"It is necessary," Gwen said, placing a comforting hand on her brother's arm.

"I fear it will only make matters worse and the innocent will suffer."

"Nay, Duncan, those who do wrong will be punished."

"Who does wrong, Gwen?" he asked. "Do you know for sure?" Ever since the warlock was discovered he feared his sister's involvement with him—and was it of her own doing, or was it dark magic?

She shook her head and looked at him strangely. "Sydney will be in trouble. She and her friends must not remain here. They must leave."

The truth of his sister's words weighed heavy on his heart, but he spoke as he felt. "I love Sydney."

"If you love her you must let her go."

"You speak to me the same words you spoke to her."

Gwen looked startled. "I do what is best for you both."

"Do you Gwen?"

"Do you honestly think Sydney has cast no spell on you since she has been here? Can you honestly believe what you feel is real and from your heart?"

"Aye, without a doubt I believe in my love for Sydney and her love for me, and I will allow no one, absolutely no one, to rob me of my beliefs. Our love is strong and it is true."

"Then what will you do, for she surely cannot remain here? Will you desert the clan and go with her?"

Duncan stared hard and long at his sister, and after a few moments she backed away from him, her eyes wide.

"You have thought about leaving with Sydney."

"I have lived without her for thirteen years—"

Gwen interrupted. "They have not been bad years. You have smiled and laughed and lived."

He shook his head slowly. "I have not lived, I have

merely survived. I know not why I possess such an endless
love for her—"

Gwen interrupted again. "She has cast a spell on you."

"Nay, Gwen," he said, annoyed. "My love for Sydney
is my own doing. She needs to use no spell on me. I have
loved her from when first I laid eyes upon her and I will
always love her, no matter time or place, my love will
always remain true."

"I do not understand."

"Because you have never loved someone." He was frustrated, wanting her to understand how he felt, and he prayed
for the knowledge to help his sister understand. "Think,
Gwen, you love the clan, how would you feel if you were
removed from here, never to return?"

She looked horrified. "I could not do that, this is my
home. I love it here, the people, the land—my home."

"I feel that way about Sydney."

She grabbed her brother's arm tightly. "You would place
your love for her above the clan?"

Would he?

What if he was given the chance to return to the future
with Sydney? Would he take it? The questions had haunted
him ever since he had discovered that Sydney had returned
from far in the future to him. She had taken a chance to
return, a chance at never seeing those she loved again.

And what of the clan?

Did he owe them his life?

"Duncan, answer me." Gwen shook his arm, shocked
that he had hesitated. "Do you not see the wrong of your
ways? She bewitches you."

"She loves me."

"As does the clan. Who is more important?"

Duncan shook her hand off him. "You will not like my
answer."

Gwen stepped back with a jolt as if he had slapped her
in the face. She stared at him, horrified by his words. "I do
not believe you can be so blind."

"Many are blind, Gwen, and do not know it. Are you as blind as me?"

She shook her head. "Your eyes should be as open as mine. Now I go to help those in my clan as you should rightfully do." She turned away from him and went to assist the ill clan members.

Duncan could not turn his back on his clan, and he joined his sister to do what he could for his family, for the clan was his family. And he had been taught never to turn your back on your own. So why now did he even give it thought—to leave the only family he had ever known for the love of a woman?

It was late at night when the hall was finally cleared of chaos and the ill clan members tucked safely in their homes, suffering no more thanks to Sydney's healing brew.

At first, few wanted to take the brew, especially after they had witnessed how the drink made stomachs revolt. But then they also witnessed how afterward the person felt better, pain disappeared and only a minor discomfort remained. Once that was realized, the brew was generously downed.

Duncan sat in the empty hall, alone with his thoughts. Gwen had exhausted herself helping all she could and had retired as soon as she was certain all had been tended to and were safely in their cottages.

She had not bid him good-night or looked his way. It was the first time he had ever known his sister to do so.

He rubbed the back of his aching neck, his thoughts as chaotic as the great hall had been earlier. There were so many decisions to make and damned if they were not difficult ones. At the moment though he did not wish to think of decisions, he wished he were with Sydney.

He wanted to know for himself that she was all right. He wanted to hold her in his arms, feel the warmth of her soft skin, smell the sweet scent of her and forget that life for them was about to change.

"I thought you could use some company."

Duncan looked up from where he rested on a bench in front of the hearth to see Sebastian walk out of the shadows. "How did you get here?"

"Ali has been teaching me about transporting and I like to practice now and again, nothing difficult mind you, and no far distances, only nearby transporting. But do not worry, no one saw me."

"I have no doubt of that," Duncan said and pointed to the bench across from him, inviting Sebastian to join him. "Everyone wore themselves out earlier and are asleep from exhaustion."

"But not you?" Sebastian sat.

"I cannot sleep, my mind is too busy with all that must be done."

"Decisions, you don't want to make, right?"

"Aye." He nodded his head slowly and stared into the low flames. "Did you give up much to be with Ali?"

Sebastian had specially returned to the keep for this very reason. He had known Duncan would begin to question just as he had, and he wanted to be there to help him through the confusion. Ali had agreed that he should return to speak with Duncan, though she was concerned for his safety.

She was also concerned for her aunt's safety and that her second chance at love was given the opportunity to succeed. It was that thought that caused Sebastian not to hesitate to come and speak with Duncan. Sydney had been helpful and supportive to him when he had fallen in love with Ali and was acting the fool. She had given him wise advice and he had been grateful. Now it was his turn to repay her kindness.

Duncan looked at him. "You take time to answer."

"I was thinking that there was nothing for me to give up, but then on more careful thought I realized that I gave up my life as I had always known it. I accepted a different way of living, believing and even loving."

"With no regrets?"

"None. At first I thought I was crazy for even believing

that witches and magic existed. Ali taught me differently about both and I discovered witches were nothing like what I had been led to believe."

"Your clan is accepting of her?"

"I have limited family, but the family I do have loves her dearly," Sebastian said. "If they didn't love her it wouldn't matter to me. I would still love her."

"And your family; you would deny them?"

Sebastian shook his head. "No, I would make certain they understood how I felt about her, then the choice would be theirs, my choice already having been made. Ali is part of me; if my family cares for me then they will care for her."

"It is not always that simple, and what if your choice is wrong? What if your family feels they are protecting you from an ill-fated match?"

"When we fall in love, there are no guarantees. Love needs as much attention and nourishment as a small child, without either that child does not grow and flourish as he should. The same goes for true love. If you do not give your love attention and nourishment it will not flourish and grow. It will not become strong enough to face the many difficulties that life presents us, including family members who think they know what is best for you. Love will eventually weaken and lose all strength and simply fade away without you realizing it. Then you will wake one day and wonder what happened to it and never realize that you allowed love to die from lack of nourishment."

"What you are saying is that only I can determine if I love and if that love will last."

"Right," Sebastian said. "Love is an individual choice and if we listened carefully to ourselves instead of ignoring what we know to be true we would all find love, maybe not where we expected it or with who—"

"Like a witch from the future." Duncan smiled.

"You got it."

"I think I am beginning to understand your strange tongue though at times it is difficult."

"Come to the future and learn it for yourself."

"Therein lies the problem," Duncan said, shaking his head.

"For Sydney's safety she cannot remain here much longer, and you find it difficult to leave the clan you lead."

"You are wise."

"Not really," Sebastian said, "just sensible. The clan is your home, your family, Sydney your love. How do you make a choice?"

"I do not know, yet I know that one must be made soon. What do I do?"

"Look at the consequences," Sebastian advised. "Ask yourself what you could and could not live without. Would the clan suffer if you left? Would you suffer if Sydney left? What would be the consequences of both, and which one could you live with?"

"A suggestion that sounds easy."

"I have realized that nothing sensible is easy," Sebastian said with a laugh. "You would think it would be, but it is not. Our emotions take over and then we're done for; nothing gets decided because either guilt or love is tormenting us and then there's disappointment, not to mention being called selfish, because we make a choice that is best for ourselves while others feel it hurts them. So what then is the right choice for all?"

Duncan shrugged, having no answer, but looking for one.

"There isn't a right choice for all. Someone will find fault or condemn you for your decision, but if you weighed the consequences and take responsibility for your choice then it is the right choice for you regardless of what others say."

"You make sense, but—" He shook his head.

"You haven't weighed your consequences enough. Could you go on without Sydney in your life? Could you wake every day knowing you made the choice to never see her again, never—"

"Stop," Duncan said, holding up his hand. "The empty ache is too much to bear."

"What of the clan? Would you miss your sister, your friend Thomas and others?"

"Thomas has his wife and family. My sister has the whole clan and looks after it well, and—" He hesitated to say more.

"What don't you want to admit?"

Duncan rubbed the back of his neck, the persistent pain refusing to ease. "It has been some time since I have had an adventure. The clan has lived in relative peace for many years. We live a distance from important borders, making our land not worth the trouble of attacking, and the few times I joined other clans in battle I found little reward in it. The poor fight for the wealthy, though it is claimed the fight is for God and country."

"You are a wise man who needs an adventure."

"An adventure to the future?" He grinned and his neck began to ease.

"It is possible if—"

"I believe," Duncan finished.

"Anything is possible when you believe."

Duncan leaned in closer, his voice low. "Tell me more of the future and tell me how I would journey there if I so decided."

Thirty-four

❧

"*I do not want to lose him again.*" Sydney wiped the tears from her eyes before they could spill down her face. She had slept well last night due to Tempest casting a sleeping spell over her upon their return to her cottage. She had been so distraught that sensible thought and conversation had been impossible. Tempest had suggested a good night's sleep and they would all talk in the morning. Sydney had objected, though not for long. In mere minutes she found herself yawning and ready for bed. Her eyes closed as soon as her head rested on the pillow and that was the last she remembered until she woke this morning to find Tempest and Michael sitting at the table, the smell of fresh coffee and cinnamon buns tempting her out of bed.

Sydney barely had taken a sip of coffee when Ali and Sebastian materialized in the room, followed by Dagon and Sarina. They joined her, Tempest and Michael at the table.

Ali reached out and grabbed hold of her aunt's hand. "We're here to help and we'll do whatever we can."

Sydney nodded. "I know and I appreciate the support,

but I am not foolish. I know that our love will only be if it is meant to be."

"It is meant to be," Sarina said, and everyone looked at her. "I can tell you no more. I only know that you two were meant to be."

Dagon took his wife's hand and kissed the back. "Sarina is never wrong, so therefore I suggest we get busy doing what needs to be done to clear this mess up."

Relief flooded Sydney and she smiled. "I am so very glad you are all here with me."

"You didn't think we'd let you have this adventure on your own did you?" Sebastian asked with a wink.

Sydney patted his shoulder. "You do the Craft proud, Sebastian. I am glad to have you as my nephew."

"Thank you," he said with a smile, though it faded slowly.

"You have unpleasant news to deliver," Sydney said.

"Unfortunately, I do and I think we better discuss it."

They all waited silently.

Sebastian reluctantly delivered the dreaded news. "Duncan had no choice but to send for an official from the church."

Silence remained for several minutes.

"It was the only thing he could do to keep the clan calm," Sydney said, clearly understanding the consequences of his forced action. Her time there had suddenly become extremely limited. "I expected it."

Tempest thought the same as she did. "It also means that you cannot remain here much longer."

"She is right," Michael agreed. "Even if we are able to settle this matter before the official arrives you will still be suspect. The clan will tell what they know, probably embellish several of the incidents, and you will surely be accused of witchcraft."

Sydney understood that better than anyone, but there was Duncan to consider, and though she would not choose to place herself in harm's way, she was not ready to leave

Duncan. "I must try all I can to right this wrong and not lose Duncan."

Ali was quick to reassure her aunt. "We all will help and see this thing settled in your favor, after all, you did not travel hundreds of years from the future for nothing."

Michael took charge. "One place we're going to start is with the witch over on the island."

Sydney recalled him looking angry last night during the chaos. "Does this have something to do with last night? At one point you looked quite upset."

"Angry is more like it," he corrected. "And yes it does. Tempest feels the male witch she saw on the island caused the illness at the keep. She saw him cut a bunch of herbs from their stems—those herbs when combined would cause the symptoms experienced last night."

"But how did he get the mixture into the food?" Ali asked.

"He had to have had help," Sebastian suggested.

"Exactly," Michael said, moving uneasily in his seat. "We need to find out who is helping him and—"

"Something's troubling you," Dagon said.

"Very much," Michael admitted.

"You know the warlock that's causing the chaos, don't you?" Dagon asked, with understanding sensing that Michael was visibly concerned.

"Damn if he isn't one of mine." Michael shook his head.

"One who followed your ways?" Sydney asked.

"One I taught," Michael admitted reluctantly. "Tempest detailed him for me and I knew immediately it was James. He was anxious to learn, though he thought he knew more than others."

"Including you?" asked Dagon.

"Yes, and the sad part was that he could have been an asset to the Craft, having come from a long line of witches."

"The old woman who is buried on the island," Dagon said.

"His aunt I think," Michael said. "He talked once of a relative that lived high in the Highlands and was an exceptional healer. He intended to learn from her."

"She would not teach him when she realized he intended his knowledge for harm. No witch would." Sydney said.

"You're right," Tempest said, "but if you remember the simple cross at her grave read *friend*. The old woman was teaching someone, and that someone could be the one who is teaching him, not realizing his true intentions."

"One thing we know for certain," Michael said, "is that he wants power, a warlock's power. He gains that through fear, greed, discontent—"

"All that he is causing," Dagon said.

"The more fear and such he causes, the stronger he becomes," Sebastian said.

Michael nodded. "Exactly."

"How do we get rid of him?" Ali asked.

"I'll see to that," Michael said, "though first we must find out who helps him."

"I know," Sydney said. She had known since the visit to the island, but had not spoken of her suspicions to anyone, wanting to make certain. The more she had thought on it the more it had made sense, and she was ready to admit that now to them—and to herself. "It makes so much sense now and helps me to understand what happened thirteen years ago." She shook her head, not wanting to believe but knowing she could not ignore the obvious. It had been right in front of her all this time and she had foolishly not seen it.

No one said a word; they waited patiently for her to continue.

She had been a young witch when Duncan and she had first met and knew little of what she knew now, and then of course love has a way of blinding you to the obvious. She should not be harsh on herself, but if she had been more aware none of this would have had to come to pass.

But then perhaps it did?

Perhaps they all were meant to learn something from the experience.

Sydney sighed softly. "I should have known this from the start and I should have been there to help her. The Craft is a part of her, an inherited part, and someone saw this and encouraged it—a *friend*."

"You are speaking of Gwen," Sarina said. "She is the one who crafted the grave marker for the old woman."

"And the wreath that lay on the table in the cottage. It was identical to mine," Sydney said, remembering how all the familiar material had caught her eye and made her think.

"Gwen?" Ali asked, surprised. "She speaks against witches."

"Not always," Sydney said. "There was a time she was a good friend to me and curious, asking me endless questions about healing and spells. Then she changed."

"The warlock's influence," Michael confirmed. "He wants to control the clan."

"Through Gwen," Tempest said. "She was eager to learn more—"

"And the warlock fed her eagerness," Michael finished.

"Sydney is a threat then," Sebastian said. "The warlock must have had plans for Gwen, Duncan and the clan, and Sydney threatens those plans."

Michael laughed. "A definite threat. She's more knowledgeable, more powerful, and once Sydney discovered that he was using Gwen for his own benefit he knew his time here would be finished and wasted. What would he have gained?"

"So he gets rid of my aunt," Ali said, annoyed, "by making everyone believe she is an evil witch and forcing Duncan to send for church officials. They arrive, my aunt is sacrificed, leaving him to—"

"Grow in power," Michael said.

"Does Gwen realize what he is doing to her?" Ali asked.

"No," Michael said adamantly. "He uses spells—"

"But a spell cannot work if it is meant to harm," Sebastian interrupted.

"You're right, but he causes her no harm, instead he charms her with words and praise and feeds her—"

"Ego," Sebastian said, shaking his head. "And she doesn't see what he truly intends."

"Then he makes suggestions about her brother, the clan and what should be and if she objects he convinces her otherwise until she thinks the idea was hers to begin with."

Sebastian looked angry. "Damn, he's a good manipulator."

"Dark magic relies on manipulation and weakness."

"That is what I don't understand," Sydney said, confused. "Gwen has always been strong, not the type to be manipulated."

"Desires, wants, ego make manipulation easy," Michael explained.

"Which is why you were never successful in manipulating Tempest," Dagon reminded with smile.

"You're right. She kept her desires, wants and ego in prospective, therefore giving me not an ounce of power, no matter how hard I tried."

"Which made her even more appealing, I would guess," Sebastian said.

"Definitely," Michael agreed. "The idea that she had the power to understand and control those emotions was extremely tempting, especially to a warlock who hungered for more power."

Tempest reached for her husband's hand. "It worked out for us. It was meant to." She looked to Sydney. "Sarina says it is meant for you and Duncan to be together, and I agree with Dagon, my sister has never been wrong in what she sees. But that does not mean we can sit by and do nothing. We must help move things along. We must free Gwen of the warlock's power and see that she is instructed properly." She paused, removing her hand from her husband's grasp, and reached out to Sydney. "The rest is up to you and Duncan."

Sydney nodded slowly.

"What do we do first?" Ali asked, eager to help her aunt.

Michael answered. "I go to the island—"

"With me," Tempest said, taking her husband's hand once again.

He shook his head. "To see to the warlock."

"How do we know he remains on the island?" Dagōn asked.

"Beatrice keeps a watch on him," Michael said.

"I go speak to Duncan," Sydney said. "Though I think he already realizes what I know."

"What do we do?" Ali asked.

Tempest looked at each one of them. "Prepare to return home."

Thirty-five

Duncan sat alone in his solar, staring at the empty hearth. Summer was upon them and the fires were only needed on occasion. Sydney had arrived with spring, and in the short time she had been there so much had happened and so much more was about to happen.

His decision last night to send for a church official had sealed her fate. She would have to leave and soon. A messenger took the letter to the church this morning and promised he would not return without a cleric. They had but a week or so until his return, not much time.

All was set in motion, but the outcome was yet to be determined.

With Sydney unable to remain here in his time he had only one choice left to him.

Go with her.

But did he dare make such a choice? He had a clan to lead, responsibility to see to, friends and family. Gwen sacrificed much for him and the clan. How could he walk away from her? Now, when she would need someone to help her understand?

But then how could he spend his life without Sydney?

He shook his head and rubbed his aching neck, confused by the decisions and upset that they were necessary.

A rap on the door brought him out of his thoughts.

Thomas called out to him and Duncan bid him to enter.

Thomas took the chair opposite Duncan. "I have sat in this chair often beside you. We have had many a debate, argument and simple discussion here. We have shared much as friends, including many good birthday celebrations."

"Like brothers we have shared."

"Aye, I have felt the same."

Duncan could tell he had something on his mind and that it would take him some time to get to it, which was his way. Thomas could forge ahead into battle without thought and handle himself like a true warrior, but words often failed him. He simply could not express himself with the confidence he took into battle.

Duncan saved them both time and Thomas anxiousness. "What troubles you, Thomas?"

The large man shifted nervously in his seat. "I am not good with words, but I feel I must say something to you."

"Have your say," Duncan encouraged.

"I know your decision to send for a church official places Sydney in grave danger. I know it will be best for her to go away and—" He paused as if he searched for the courage to continue. "I think you should go away with her."

Duncan sat forward in his chair.

Thomas held up his hand. "Let me finish. I have seen the way you have missed Sydney. How you went about your day and attempted to live your life, but you never did. Part of you left with Sydney that first time and life was never the same for you again. I realized how much you love her, and while I do not want you to go, as your friend I know you will not be happy here without her."

Duncan attempted to argue. "The clan—"

"Will survive, your sister will see to it."

"I cannot believe you tell me this?"

Thomas shrugged. "I cannot believe I tell you this either, but you are my best friend and I wish to see you happy. You will not be happy without Sydney. You will go on, but you will never live—you will merely exist."

Duncan had no intentions of telling Thomas about the future. He wanted him ignorant of the truth in case he was questioned by a church official. He would then know nothing more than the others. He wanted him and his family protected, and he would make certain of it.

"I appreciate your honesty, Thomas."

"But you know not what to do?"

"My heart and duty to the clan war and I am uncertain of the victor."

Thomas stood. "I would not want to live without my Dora. If she were made to leave the clan for any reason, I would go with her and not think twice about it."

"You do not lead the clan."

"Neither do you," Thomas said, placing a firm hand on his shoulder. "Think about it, and then give the leadership of the clan to the one who desires it the most—your sister."

Duncan stared at him as he walked away, closing the door quietly behind him.

Thomas was right; Gwen loved the clan and did all she could to see it thrive and flourish. Would the clan really survive if he made such a choice?

He shook his head. How could he think of walking away from his duties as leader of the clan for the love of a woman?

Suddenly that woman materialized in his solar, and without thought he stood and they both embraced each other as if for the last time and the thought frightened him.

"We need to talk," she said.

He wanted to hold her, kiss her, and love her perhaps

for the last time. His mouth took hers and his kiss spoke much stronger than words.

Tears slipped slowly down Sydney's cheeks. "I cannot lose you again. I cannot." Her head rested on his shoulder and she could not stop the tears from falling or her heart from breaking.

"You cannot stay here."

Sydney attempted to explain to him about the warlock and how Michael and Tempest were, as she spoke, ridding the clan and especially Gwen of his presence.

He listened though he shook his head. "That does not mean you can remain here. I sent for—"

She pulled away from him. "I know who you sent for and I do not care. I will not be forced to leave you again."

"Forced again?"

Sydney wiped at her falling tears and hoped that her explanation might change his mind. "The warlock interfered with our relationship the last time and he does so again."

"The warlock? How so?"

"I had wanted to wait to tell you this. I wanted to speak with Gwen first and help her understand."

"Help me understand what?"

Duncan and Sydney turned to face Gwen, who had quietly opened the door and entered.

Now Sydney had no choice and perhaps it was better this way—she silently cast a spell of hope for them all before answering.

"I know you have been learning the Craft."

"She attempts to blame me for her own evil doings," Gwen accused with an angry tongue.

Sydney was determined to make her understand how she had been used through no fault of her own. "The old woman taught you well."

Gwen's tone turned defensive. "Elizabeth was my friend and wise in the ways of herbs and healing, and aye, she taught me her knowledge."

Sydney remained patient and her tone soft. "And the old ways—the ways of your grandmother and her grandmother—your heritage."

"They were not witches." Gwen sounded insulted.

"They understood the Craft and practiced it. It was up to them how well they developed their skills and to what extent they applied those skills."

Duncan interrupted, for he had no idea that Gwen had been learning to heal from the old woman. "You learned Elizabeth's ways and never spoke of this to me?"

"There was no need. I merely wished to learn about healing so that I could be of better service to the clan," Gwen said. "And besides, Elizabeth passed on, she teaches me no more."

"But another does," Sydney said.

"Her nephew." Gwen once again turned defensive. "James, and he is a good friend."

Sydney spoke the truth, keeping accusation from her voice. "He is a warlock and the cause of the clan's problems and he manipulates you to do his work."

"You lie just like you lie to my brother," Gwen accused, her voice near to a shout.

Duncan said nothing, for things made so much sense now and all he wanted was to help his sister understand and free herself from the warlock.

Gwen flung another accusation at Sydney. "You cast a love spell on my brother."

Sydney spoke honestly. "I have never cast a spell on your brother."

"You have cast no spell since your return?" Gwen demanded. "No spell that pertains to my brother?"

Sydney did not answer directly.

"See, she hesitates," Gwen said, pointing an accusing finger at Sydney.

"I cast a spell upon my arrival," Sydney said, "though I do not think you will understand the significance of the spell, especially now since you steep yourself in the dark side of the Craft."

"Do not blame me for your evil doings," Gwen said, her anger growing.

"Do you not realize that your anger gives James strength?"

"You attempt to change the subject, knowing that if Duncan hears the spell he will finally realize the truth."

"Perhaps I would," Duncan said and looked to Sydney. "Tell me the spell."

Sydney recited it without hesitation. *"Powers of light; powers of time; bring to me he who once was mine; have him remember me; and remember the magic that used to be; unite our hearts once again; so that our souls may fully mend; when our joining is as one; know the magic has begun."*

Duncan stared at her for several silent moments.

"See, she places a spell over you."

Duncan walked over to Sydney and gently touched her face. "Nay, Gwen, she simply gave us another chance to love. She asked only that I come to her, remember her and remember how we once loved. Our hearts could not unite if our love was not strong nor could our souls mend, and when we finally admitted that we were one, a whole, never to be parted—only then could love's magic begin."

Tears pooled in Sydney's eyes. "You understand."

"It is simple, how could I not understand?"

Gwen was startled by his response. "That is nonsense."

Duncan slipped his arm around Sydney and held her close to his side. "Nay, Gwen, it is love."

"She blinds you to the truth."

Duncan looked to his sister. "You have been blinded to the truth by—"

"I have not. I do what—"

Ali suddenly appeared in the middle of the room. "James cannot be found."

"Of course," Gwen said with confidence. "Evil has no power over good."

"She doesn't get it yet, does she?" Ali said, annoyed. "And we have no time to explain it to her. Michael thinks that James is up to something and it probably means trouble for us all."

Duncan reluctantly released Sydney and went to his sister. "Do you not see what this man has done to you?"

"He has done nothing," Gwen insisted. "I do not love him, he is but a friend who teaches me skills I wish to learn."

"Like hurting those you love?" Ali asked bluntly.

"I have hurt no one."

"You hurt your brother, Sydney, your clan, but mostly you have hurt yourself. You have allowed another to take control of you. He causes chaos for your clan and you help him. You cannot see what he does is wrong because of your own wants, though they are not selfish wants. You want what is good for all, though you fail to realize that what you want someone else may not want."

"You speak foolishly," Gwen said and shook a finger at her brother. "And you listen to their foolishness."

Ali walked over to Gwen. "What would you say if I could prove James was not who you thought him to be?"

"You cannot prove what is not so!"

"Afraid I may be right?" Ali challenged. "If he is as good as you say and we are evil what would he have to fear?"

"She is right, Gwen," Duncan said. "If I see for myself that James helps and does not hinder then I will send Sydney and her friends away."

"Truthfully?" Gwen asked with a shred of hope.

"I give you my word." Duncan did not wish to hurt his sister and the hope in her voice tore at his heart.

"Then I will bring him here."

Beatrice flew through the partially open door. "No need

to, he is already here. A clearing in the woods, he and
Michael face each other."

Gwen smiled at her brother, though she cast a strange
eye on Beatrice. "Now you will finally see the truth."

Ali shook her head. "Hold on, I can get us there faster."
And before Gwen could protest, Ali swirled them up in a
whirlwind and transported them to the clearing.

Ali joined Sarina and Tempest where they stood off to
the side. Sebastian and Dagon stood behind Michael prepared to help him if necessary. Gwen immediately took up
a guarded stance beside James and Duncan and Sydney
stood off by themselves, their hands tightly locked.

The moon was full though clouds filtered the moonlight,
casting a muted glow on the odd circle of people on the
ground. A gentle mist kissed the ground, wrapping around
feet and drifting up legs.

Sydney shivered and Duncan squeezed her hand. Out of
the darkness walked Finn to stand protectively at her side.

Beatrice took a firm and protective perch on Duncan's
shoulder.

This was the defining moment that would seal their fate,
and Sydney felt herself turn cold.

"It is all right," Duncan assured her, his warm hand firm
in hers. "We will make it, you and I—our love will allow
for nothing else."

She could not respond, the lump in her throat blocked
all speech, and she fought the fear of losing him for she
knew any fear would only give James power. She cleared
her thoughts and kept constant in her mind that they would
be as one for always.

"I cannot believe you have turned against your own,"
James said. "And look at you." He sounded disgusted.
"You dress as them and not in the garments of darkness."

"You know this man, James?" Gwen asked, pointing to
Michael.

James addressed Gwen calmly. "We must remain strong
in our beliefs if we are to conquer evil."

"My beliefs are strong," she said.

"And remember you want what is best for the clan and your brother and that woman is not good for him," James reminded. "Keep those thoughts strong."

"I told you he manipulates you," Ali said from the sidelines.

Gwen turned an angry glare on her. "He does not."

Ali stuck one hand on her hip and pointed a wagging finger at Gwen. "Listen and learn, honey. That man has manipulated you since the beginning. He uses you to get what he wants."

"What he wants is good for me and all concerned," Gwen said, as if she challenged.

"He wants control over you, your brother and the entire clan and when he bleeds all dry he will leave and never look back."

"Pay her no mind," James ordered.

"Why? Because I know you for the phony that you are?" Ali challenged.

James flung a bolt of energy at Ali and she deflected it with ease.

"You defend like a child," Ali said with a laugh.

James turned red with anger and with his hands fisted at his sides he made the ground rumble slightly.

With one wave of his hand, Michael ceased the rumble. "This is nonsense. These are skills a witch learns at a young age and learns that they are not to be used to impress or for trickery. Your time here is finished, James. You are to leave and never return and you are to release Gwen."

Gwen continued to defend James. "He has cast no spell over me."

Michael corrected her. "He keeps you bound to him through manipulation. He feeds your desires—"

"I desire nothing," she snapped.

"You desire that your brother rule the clan as you see fit," Michael said.

"She sees correctly," James said, enforcing his control.

Michael went right back at him. "You have blinded her to the truth. There was a time she favored Sydney and Duncan together. She understood their love and understood what her clan needed."

Gwen shook her head as if trying to clear the confusion.

"Stay strong," James urged.

Michael simply asked, "What does your brother need? Your clan?"

"She—" Gwen looked to Sydney to accuse and her glance fell on her hand clasped tightly in Duncan's firm grip.

"They love each other. Is that so wrong?" Michael asked.

James marched over to Gwen and grabbed her by the arm. "She is no good for him. We have discussed this and you understand."

"What are your intentions for the clan?" Michael asked, walking slowly in a circle around him. "What were your intentions when you had Gwen add a bit of flavoring to the food last night?"

James lifted his chin. "I will provide Gwen with the knowledge she requires to see the clan thrive."

Gwen answered the other part of Michael's question. "He warned me that Sydney would try to poison the clan and hoped his herb mixture would work against it, but Sydney's powers are too strong."

"And the animals killed in the woods and blamed on the wolf?" Michael asked.

Again Gwen answered. "He used the entails to read the future and alert us to any problems."

"Yet he allowed another to take blame for his act," Michael said, hoping Gwen's thoughts would clear and she would see James for what he truly was—a warlock who fed on deception and manipulation.

"He did it to secure the safety of the clan," Gwen said, though her voice faltered as if she suddenly questioned her response.

Ali stepped in. "What did Elizabeth teach you? Was it to harm none and work as one with nature? Has James followed these teachings?"

Gwen shook her head. "He told me he could continue to teach me after Elizabeth died."

"Think on what he has taught you," Michael urged. "Did Elizabeth advise you that Sydney was wrong for Duncan?"

Gwen was quick to reply. "Nay, she told me often that Sydney was meant for him and that they would be together for a very—" She stopped and looked to her brother and Sydney. "A very long time, more time than I knew existed."

Sydney reluctantly released Duncan's hand and walked over to Gwen. "I have always admired your strength and courage and I often thought that you would make a strong clan leader. You possess the knowledge and skills of the women who came before you, and they in their own unique ways led the clan. You need no one to advise you, especially someone who wishes to take and not give in return. In your strong passion to aid the clan you fell prey to a warlock." She took hold of Gwen's arm. "Remember all of Elizabeth's teachings, and you will know what is right. Simply tell James you *need* nothing from him and he loses his strength, his purpose for remaining here, and you gain your freedom."

"Why should I believe you?" Gwen asked, though with hesitation.

"Why should you not?" Sydney smiled softly. "What have you to lose?"

"Do not listen to her, she tempts you to her way," James ordered firmly.

Sydney ignored him. "If he is good and just in his teachings and beliefs then he has nothing to fear. Didn't Elizabeth teach you that? If you are true to yourself then you will know and see the truth for yourself."

James became agitated. "Do not listen to her."

"We were once like sisters; *remember*, Gwen, that is all I ask."

Ali, Sarina, and Tempest walked over to Gwen to lend their support.

"We are here to help," Ali said and laid a hand on her shoulder.

"Tell him you need nothing from him," Sarina said, "and see for yourself the results."

"You need do no more," Tempest said.

"They put spells on you, do not listen, step away from them, come over here to me," James urged frantically. "Come here, to me, Gwen, at once, do you hear?"

"Do not order my sister to do anything." Duncan's deep voice rumbled with anger.

Gwen looked to her brother and smiled. "You have always protected me."

"I always will," he assured her.

"Nay," Gwen said with a slow shake of her head. "It is time for me to do what is right, to do what Elizabeth taught me and urged me to do. She had told me that one day I would rule the clan with your blessings. I worried that it was because you would take ill and I tried so very hard to learn all I could about the healing ways so that when that time came I could save you. I was so foolish and in my own way selfish."

"Nay," Sydney urged. "You love your brother and wanted what was best for him. James preyed on that love and used it against you. You did nothing wrong. You did everything out of love—the true way of the Craft."

Gwen hugged Sydney. "Can you ever forgive me for being so foolish?"

Sydney grew teary-eyed. "If you can forgive me for wanting to take your brother away?"

Gwen smiled. "His time is with you. He will be happy, and that is what I have always wanted for him." She gave Sydney another hug then turned to James and in a strong loud voice said, "I need you no more."

James grew red with fury. "You cannot discard me. You need me, do you understand? We have plans for the future of the clan. You can do nothing without me. You have no powers. You are useless."

Gwen looked stunned, as if she was seeing James for the first time. "I do not need you. I have never needed you." She shook her head. "I foolishly listened to you instead of listening to myself. Your aunt had taught me that from the start. Listen to your heart, mind your thoughts and seek understanding and then you will live wisely and make wise choices."

James spat his words out. "My aunt was a fool whose power could have surpassed all others; instead she lived by the foolish creed of witches."

"Harm none," the women chorused.

"Go, James, you are not wanted here," Michael ordered.

James laughed. "I will depart, but not before I leave you all a gift." He raised his hands to the dark night sky; the mist suddenly grew heavy and clouds rushed across the moon. In a thunderous voice he recited, *"Powers of darkness; powers of might; send the wind to torment the night; make it hard; make it fast; make it through the night last; when it fades and all is done; make certain there is minus one!"* He pointed a finger at Duncan and laughed.

The mist rose fast and hard along with the wind, and Tempest stepped forward to counter the spell.

Sydney ran toward Duncan, but the heavy mist swirled up fast and made it impossible for her to see him.

James's voice rose high. "This is one spell you taught me well, teacher."

Suddenly a scuffle pursued, fists flew and the women shouted for their husbands. Several chaotic minutes passed before Tempest finally got the mist and wind under control.

When all had cleared Duncan was no place to be seen.

Thirty-six

"Where is Duncan?" Sydney asked Tempest anxiously.

"I do not know." She looked about. Michael had subdued James with mortal blows and looked quite content. Sarina and Dagon stood beside each other, as did Ali and Sebastian. Gwen looked with worried eyes for her brother and Sydney stood where Duncan had been standing.

"You countered the spell, did you not?" Gwen asked.

"I never finished it," Tempest said, "but I am certain I can find Duncan and return him."

"That might be a problem," Sebastian said, stepping forward, his wife's eyes turning wide.

"Oh no, Sebastian, what did you do?" Sydney asked, feeling completely distraught.

"I sent Duncan to safety," he admitted.

"And where is that?" Tempest asked.

"That's the problem," Sebastian said with a shake of his head. "I'm not sure."

"Tell me the spell quick," Tempest said.

"Another problem," Sebastian said reluctantly. "I recited

it so fast that I can't remember the whole spell. It went something like—*send him where he must go*—then it goes blank. There was so much chaos and not being able to see through the fog didn't help and I thought time was of the essence since I had clear sight of him."

Ali marched up to her husband and gave him a firm poke in the chest. "Remember."

Tempest remained calm. "He could not have gone far. We will find him."

Sarina rushed over to her sister's side. "A church official is a short distance away. The messenger found him on return route to the church and after telling him of the clan's problems, the cleric insisted on returning with him immediately."

Upon hearing the news Gwen rushed to Sydney. "You must go, all of you. It is not safe here for you. Now I know what my dream signifies. I had spoken of it to Duncan. I thought it concerned you but it was meant for me, I must tend to the mess I helped create."

"I cannot leave you alone. You need guidance and help in dealing with the church official." Sydney was adamant and then there was Duncan. If she left would she ever find him?

"I will be fine. I am strong and much wiser now, thanks to you and your friends. I realize my skills need work and I will see that I work hard. Do not worry. Go and be well," Gwen urged and gave her a hug. "And when you reunite with my brother, tell him I love him and wish him well. I know now how happy he will be with you. And tell him not to worry about the clan. I will lead it well." A tear trickled down her cheek.

Sydney hugged her tightly. "How can I leave you when now is when you need help the most?"

"You have no choice," Gwen insisted. "Go and find my brother."

Horses and carts could be heard not far in the distance.

Sydney turned to Tempest. "If we return to the future, will we be able to locate Duncan?"

"I cannot say for sure. Sebastian in his zeal to help could have sent him anywhere in time."

The men's shouts and horses' snorts grew louder.

"We must go now," Michael urged. "There is no time for discussion."

Tempest waved her hand and her husband joined in and together their powers opened a portal in time. Tempest waved them all through.

Sarina and Dagon jumped in together.

Ali and Sebastian went next, though Sebastian stopped beside Sydney first.

"All will turn out well." He hugged her and then walked to the portal with his wife. He stopped briefly to speak with Tempest before he and Ali entered the portal.

Sydney looked to Gwen.

"Remember, give my love to my brother and tell him I understand now. I understand about love and I am so very glad he has found it with you."

Beatrice plopped on Sydney's shoulder and grabbed hold of her blouse. "Let's go. It is finished here."

Sydney gave a quick glance to see if Finn was in sight, but he wasn't, and she was upset that she would not get to say good-bye. She entered the portal with a heavy heart.

Tempest looked to Gwen. "Duncan will not be returning here."

"I know," she said.

"You will do well."

"I know that too." Tears fell down her cheek.

"I have sent a message to a friend who will come and teach you the ways," Tempest said with a smile.

"Thank you, now go and know you go with my appreciation and love."

Tempest and Michael stepped into the portal and it disappeared.

Sydney woke on the ground under a night sky. There was a chill in the air and she could smell the heather. It was autumn in Scotland.

She lay there several silent minutes. She had returned alone and though she held hope close to her heart that Tempest could locate Duncan, she also feared he would never be found. She admonished herself for allowing herself to fear, for then surely all hope would be lost.

"That was some ride," Beatrice said, flitting over to her.

She got up and brushed herself off. "We should find the others and see if they are all right." She wanted to find Tempest in particular. There was no time to waste; they must get started immediately on locating Duncan.

"I will see if I can locate them," Beatrice offered and flew off.

A fine mist covered the ground and gave her reason to pause. She thought how the mist had swallowed up Duncan and stolen him away. She glanced around and realized she was in a small grove not far from her manor house in Scotland. She had kept watch on Duncan's clan throughout the years and when the land finally went up for sale well in the future she had bought it and restored it to its glory. Duncan would be proud of it.

A tear threatened her eye. How she wished he could see this land he had loved so much. How she wished he had returned with her.

"How I wish," she whispered.

"It is about time you arrived."

Sydney froze, unable to move a muscle.

Was she dreaming?

Was that Duncan's voice?

She turned slowly and watched a shadowy figure emerge from the woods and mist; two bright green eyes followed beside it.

"Duncan! Finn!"

She ran to him and flung herself into his outstretched arms.

His mouth insistently sought hers and she returned his eagerness with her own, remaining locked in a kiss that expressed both their sentiments. They intended never to part again.

Short of breath from the passionate kiss, she bent down quick to give Finn a hug then asked, "How did you get here?"

"Sebastian," he said. "We talked one night about the possibility of me returning to the future with you and I asked him about it. He told me that he didn't think it was that difficult, especially since Michael had advised that most witches were capable of time travel. Sebastian then explained that he thought of time travel like a computer. You send information to a particular place to be retrieved when needed. I had no idea what he was talking about, but he promised to show me how a computer works. He did not however advise me of how hard the landing would be and that a black wolf would travel through time with me, but both of us managed to survive. And we remained right where we landed, Sebastian having assured me that you would not be far behind."

Sydney laughed. "I cannot believe he accomplished such a remarkable feat of magic."

"He told me that to be on the safe side somewhere along the way he would advise Tempest of his plan so that she could retrieve me if he had miscalculated anything."

"That was why he stopped and spoke with her before he entered the time portal."

"I trusted Sebastian explicitly. He is a man of his word."

"Sebastian is wonderful and I will forever be grateful to him for bringing us together."

Duncan hugged her and then took her hands in his. "Sebastian also told me that there was a spell I was to recite with you under a full moon—that was what he was uncertain of—that he could return me on the night of a full moon." Duncan pointed to the sky. "He succeeded, and now we must cast the spell that will forever unite us and grant me the powers of a witch."

"Are you certain, Duncan?"

He laughed. "Why do you think I traveled hundreds of years into the future? I love you, Sydney, now and always. Thomas made me realize how strong my love is for you and even Gwen saw the truth of our love in the end."

She kissed him and rubbed her cheek to his. "I love you so very much, and your sister sends her love and tells you that she now understands about love and that she will lead the clan well."

He smiled. "That makes me happy, for I believe she will."

"She will," Sydney agreed, certain Gwen now had the strength she needed.

"Sebastian also mentioned something about sealing the spell once it is cast, though he refused to tell me how to seal it. He told me my instincts would advise me what to do."

Sydney grinned. "And do they."

Duncan laughed. "I have no doubt at all how to seal the spell."

"Good, then let us cast it well and seal it with our love."

They stripped their clothes off, oblivious to the night chill. Duncan stood behind her, his body pressed to hers, sharing his warmth, their hands extended to the heavens, and they recited the spell together.

"Mother of the earth and sky; hear me ask; hear me cry; your son and daughter wish to seal a love so great; please open up your portal gates; grant us an everlasting love; only you can send from the heavens above; and when our lips and bodies meet; let our love for eternity keep."

Sydney turned around in his arms, wrapped her arms around his neck and they slowly descended to the carpet of leaves, both eager to share a magical life together and to always remember the magic.